# NOTHING LASTS FOREVER

*Battle Born MC- Reno*

*Book Two*

*BY*

## Scarlett Black

Nothing Last Forever
Copyright © 2018 By Scarlett Black
All rights reserved.

This book is a work of fiction. Names, characters, groups, businesses, and incidents either are the product of the author's imagination or are used fictitiously. Any resemblance to actual places or persons, living or dead, is entirely coincidental.

**Cover Art by Opium House Creatives**

WARNING: This book contains sexual situations and VERY adult themes. Recommended for 18 and above.

# NOTHING LASTS FOREVER

Axl's world is skidding out of control, threatening to rip the MC he's pledged to, and the woman he loves, away from him. Reeling from unexpected life shattering changes, he pushed away all those that care about him and is now speeding headlong down a path of self-destruction.

Dana barely recognizes the cruel man that Axl has become. Her own insecurities surface and have her convinced she's already lost him. After all, if the past has taught her anything, it's that everything she loves, she loses.

But when Axl's fast living results in an accidental death, he must turn to the club and Dana for help before he finds himself in cuffs. Can love save the struggling VP from himself?

*Or will the mistakes he's made land him behind bars?*

# PROLOGUE

## Axl

The bass hits the speakers and the stage lights dim, except for a spotlight in the corner of the stage. The fans scream, "GNR! GNR! GNR!"

Axl Rose and the rest of the band strut out with a guitar raised high. Drumsticks flip up high in the lights and then they're caught behind the drummer's back. Stage lights of all colors beam around in all directions. The band takes position as *Sweet Child O' Mine* starts rocking the crowd.

It is 2006, at a Guns N' Roses concert at the MGM Grand Casino. Me and the boys pass a joint around the group. Smiling, I eagerly take my first drag for the night as deep as a I can. The smoke hits my lungs hard. I hack and choke it back up. Blade laughs and grabs the joint from me to take his own drag.

"Easy on the grass, dickhead, we have the whole night." He shakes his head at me and hands me a cold beer. The foam hits my hot, dry throat, it is so good.

Song after song plays through the speakers as we laugh, smoke and drink. My mind is so fuzzy that faces and bodies blend in the crowd. Living it up to my youth, I am experiencing everything that I can.

Since we are pledging in as brothers in the Battle Born MC tomorrow, there are no guarantees in this life after that, only for right now. That's exactly what I do, I live for right here and right now, nothing lasts forever.

Some stupid drunk asshole behind me plows into my back, spilling my beer on my GNR shirt and pissing me the fuck off. Handing it off to Tank, I turn to shove that motherfucker back. Stumbling a few steps forward, he turns back around to face me. "Sorry." He says it, but not really giving one fuck that he slammed into me as he smiles like the dickhead that he is. Dickhead turns back around to his date, throwing an arm around the hot blonde bitch that he's with.

"Take this little punk ass bitch down, and then take his bitch." Tank is shoving at my shoulder to get to it, then crosses his arms, waiting for me to deliver.

Spider, Blade and Tank surround me. The anger and vengeance pump like a shot of adrenaline through me. Grabbing the smiling asshole's shirt, I whip him around to face me, then throw my fist high and wide into his nose. Blood splatters with a crunch from the force of it. His right hand comes flying from down low up for my face.

Ducking to the right, I dodge the uppercut, and swing my weight forward, hitting him in the stomach

3

with a jab. The force of it arches him toward me, and my left fist smashes his cheekbone. That's followed by a right and another left. The punk is left lying on the ground.

The security guards come running toward us to haul both of our asses out. Blade catches one of the them, palming him some cash. The passed-out dickhead is taken out of the pit.

I walk over to the scared blonde that's nervously looking around for an escape. Grinning her way, I show her my party boy face as I take her hand in mine to apologize.

"Sorry, princess," I say while stroking my thumb over her knuckles. "That prick you came here with was an asshole. Come party with us, and I promise I'll be good."

I spot that she has a disposable camera in her hand. I pull her close to me. "Come on, beautiful, take a pic with me? That way you'll always remember this night and then you can trust me, because you'll have my picture on your camera."

Encouraging her further, I snatch it from her hand and pull her body close to mine. She giggles nervously with our backs to that stage. I slide behind her and place my hand on her stomach while my other hand holds out the camera. I rest my chin on her shoulder and we both smile when I push the button to snap the picture.

She turns around, so I grab her by her shirt to pull her to me and lay a smacking big kiss on her juicy pink lips while snapping another picture of us. Her hands go straight to my chest for balance, and then she relaxes herself into the kiss.

I start walking backward, and Blondie follows me over to the guys. I pocket her camera as I introduce her and take my beer back from Tank. I wash down that hot kiss with a cold drink.

Blondie eyes me over the white plastic cup that someone must've given her, then grabs the bottle from my hand. She shoots the rest down and pulls me toward her for another kiss.

The smell of grass pulls me away from her lips. Tank hands out the joint to us, and Blondie grabs it, then takes a short drag from it, coughing it back up almost immediately. I laugh at how cute she is. Between the two of us, we manage to finish it off. Her beautiful hair catches the light, drawing me to her body.

More chicks from the crowd join our little party up front by the stage. Blade and Tank each have a handful of bitches entertaining them. The songs play on through the late-night hours. Hot bodies continue to grind and touch. Sweat, weed and alcohol permeate the air.

More grass goes around, and the boys and I are lit. We are so high off weed and hormones. Blonde Girl and I rub all over each other when she grabs my dick and pushes her tits against my chest. She yells over the noise into my ear, "Let's go to the bathroom!"

She pulls on my hand and starts walking forward. My feet and dick anxiously follow her. I watch her ass that's covered in a denim skirt and her long, lean, tan legs in a haze.

Excitement laces itself around my intoxicated mind. The primitive need to touch her tits and pussy takes over. We make it to the bathroom where I shut the stall door and spin Blondie around. She trades me places and ends up with her back against the door.

My hands find the bottom of her GNR tank and pull it up over her tits, palming them and loving how soft they are. Sucking one nipple, then the other, my hands find her toned thighs, and I push her skirt up.

I pull my mouth from her breast, releasing the nipple with a pop to gaze over her almost naked body. I run my fingers over the pink thong she's wearing, then move it to the side. I start pumping my fingers in and out of her tight pussy.

Blondie moves forward and starts kissing and nipping at my ear. I grab the condom from my back pocket while she keeps kissing my neck up to my lips. My fingers rub her clit and fuck her pussy.

She undoes my pants, pushing them, along with my boxers, down far enough to get my stiff dick out, before rolling the condom on.

Lifting one of her legs over my hip, and then the other, I push her against the door with my body, and sink my dick into her very tight pussy. She howls out in pain, only to be drowned out by *November Rain* as it blares around us.

Not taking the time to think too much of it, I use her body to pound out my release. As soon as I come into the condom, her feet hit the floor and she is straightening herself up. She pecks my lips and is gone before the song is over.

Best fuckin' concert ever.

# CHAPTER 1

*This story goes back to the night the girls get stoned...*

## Axl

Coming out of Church, I think over what Blade and I relayed to the other chapters, the information that our club gathered on Skid and that other asshole, Johnny.

Having answers to deliver gives us pride, but also leaves us feeling tense and angry over unresolved issues.

That is until I turn the corner and find the bar full of smoke. Not terribly uncommon, except for the fact that Dana is sitting with the girls with a lit joint between her fingers, and big smiles stretched across all their faces.

Blade reaches the bar before Tank and I even have a chance to get there. Watching Dana take a hit off the joint is hot as fuck, but it also pisses me off that she did this at the club without me here. Any of these assholes could approach her.

I take the joint from her hand and give her a stern look. I don't know how to handle this shit right now. So, I take a couple of long drags of my own while chatter goes on around me. I breathe the stress out with a long cloud of smoke.

I snap out of it when Dana starts clapping while talking to Kat. "Did you see that? That right there," she points between Blade and Vegas, "That is how you greet your woman right there."

I start choking and coughing out my next drag at her words. Did she just confess she wants passion without her realizing what she just did? Her outspoken thoughts throw me off guard but excite me at the same time.

Pushing my chest against her back, I tell her all too happily, "Princess, I have all your needs right here."

I step back to look down at my dick and catch her eyes staring at it too when I look back to her flushed face.

"But, it isn't happening tonight. The first time I take your lips," I run my thumb across her bottom one and bring her eyes back to mine, "I will take your body. Just be warned, Dana, when you do kiss me, you will be mine. I would rather take you sober, but don't mistake, I'll take you any way I can. You. Are. Mine. You getting yourself drunk and high to keep me from you and my bed won't work. You're still sleeping with me. And in my bed."

Gently, I keep her chin still with my fingers while holding her gaze with my lustful one.

Dana's tantalized eyes are locked with mine in a silent war of control over herself. And not moving an inch out of my hold.

"Fuck, Blade, he just killed it with that one. That even made me feel a little shaken up." I hear Vegas, but I don't lose sight of Dana's light blue eyes. So rarely will she look at me in the eyes.

I run the tips of my fingers across her forehead and down around her ear, tucking her golden blonde hair back.

"You dickheads are really putting me in a tight spot here." Tank pouts like a little bitch, causing Dana's face to move in his direction. My hand loses the touch and connection I desperately crave with her.

"Easy, lady killer, you don't have to confess your undying love for me. Keep it casual, big guy," Kat lets the fucker off the hook.

Feeling frustrated, exhausted and in need of sleep, I grip Dana's shoulder. "Let's get to bed, princess, I'm beat." I nod my head in the direction of the rooms.

Dana's body hesitates, but her eyes tell me she knows where she's sleeping. I, for one, am excited to see those long, lean legs wrapped around me. I mean, wrapped in my sheets. No, I definitely mean both me *and* the sheets.

Finally giving into the inevitable, she stands at my side and tells the group good night. I fist bump my brothers, and Tank gives me a nod of approval and a wink like the kid he is sometimes. Dumbass.

I lead Dana with my hand touching her lower back, and she leans into me just slightly the further down the hall toward my room we get. I open the door for her and she walks past me.

She steps over to where I placed the bag I gathered from her house earlier. Sitting down next to the bed in a chair, I smile as I watch her looking for her pajamas. I'm very happy with myself that I didn't pack any. Can't say that I'm sorry about it.

Her head whips in my direction and she eyeballs me with her icy blue eyes. "I know that you went through ALL my clothes, Axl. Where the hell are my pajamas, you asshole!"

I stand and close the distance between us, pulling her taut body against mine. One of my hands lands on her hip and the other behind her head. I speak softly into her ear, "Princess, you will wear my shirts to bed from now on or nothing at all. I give you choices, Dana."

Letting her go, I reach into my small dresser and hand her an original concert t-shirt from back in Las Vegas, one of the many, but also one of my favorite memories from when I went to a Guns N' Roses concert.

She looks at the shirt a little shocked, or confused, but grabs it and takes it, along with her bag, to the bathroom.

Stripping out of my clothes down to my boxer briefs, I listen to her move all her shit around on the counters. The sound of it is gifting me with a sense of peace.

Blade did give me the option of staying at her house with her. I said no knowing that she would be forced to sleep in the same bed as me if we stayed here. I'm a dick like that.

A few minutes later, she steps out from the bathroom wearing only my t-shirt. The light cascades around her, making her long blonde hair and toned legs shine.

Fuck, I want, no, *need* to see the rest of her gorgeous body, but I hold myself back. Barely.

"Where did you get this t-shirt from?" she asks as her fingers nervously toy with the hem. I watch her thigh muscles move as she steps closer to the bed. Her questioning gaze finds mine as she slides her body next to mine under the covers.

Rolling over onto my right side, I prop my head up on my hand. "I got that shirt at a concert we all went to a while back in '98, in Vegas. It was a hell of a crazy night that night. I remember only a few things. We smoked a hell of a lot of bud. We drank our weight in beer." I run my hand over hers under the covers.

"I've been to a few of their concerts too. We could go together, if they ever put on a show in Las Vegas again." She lets a long sigh out. Rolling to her left side, facing me, she smiles when she asks, "Tell me about that concert, was it your first?" Running my fingers from her calf up to her knee, I pull her body closer to mine, resting her leg on my hip.

Laughing a little, I say back, "Well, let's see, I was sixteen then, and my dad took me, Blade and Tank for my birthday. That was the first time we blazed with our dads. Half of the club was there that night. He bought me a shirt, I can't wear it anymore, fucking thing is so small. I wanted to be Axl Rose, the lead singer, so bad, I wore a red bandana on my head, too. I was a skinny ass, little punk kid. My dad started calling me Axl, the brothers caught on, and that's how I got my road name."

Dana's eyes sparkle back at me in amusement. "You're very close with your dad, aren't you?" She tries to stifle a yawn back as she brings her hand up to cover her mouth

"Yes, my dad is pretty badass. We can talk more tomorrow. My princess needs her beauty sleep." I kiss the corner of her mouth and rest my left hand on her waist.

Dana snuggles into me and relaxes her hands on my chest. Within minutes, she is lightly snoring. My body shakes a little when I try to quiet my laughter at my little snoring, stoned, drunk princess.

I'm lying on my back, fighting to stay asleep, but the sun's rays hit my face through the window and wake me from a deep, comfortable unconsciousness. My hand naturally glides across the cool sheets looking for Dana's hot body. My body's craving hers for comfort. All I find, though, is cool empty sheets.

Popping an eye open, I'm frustrated when I can't see her anywhere and realize that she's left the room without me. I toss the covers back and locate my jeans from the night before, shoving my legs through, then stomping down the hallway in search of her.

I round the corner from the main room and find Tank and Blade by the kitchen door. Blade's arms are crossed over his chest and he's standing in the hallway blocking the way in. Tank places a finger to his mouth to shush me. Curiosity over what they're watching has me walking closer.

In the kitchen, I see the girls standing around, dressed in nothing but all our t-shirts, except for Vegas who's already in her workout clothes. Blade's face is impassive as always. If you didn't know him, he would look like he couldn't care less. But the tiny wrinkles around his eyes say otherwise. He loves that crazy bitch, Vegas.

"Is this bitch still high?" Kat says to Dana who's blowing on her black coffee.

Dana answers, "Nope, I think she's hungover, but still high on Blade, though. I asked her how the rest of her night was, and she got this faraway look in her eyes. She was daydreaming, and I didn't want to shake her out of it." Dana flips her hand, disregarding the scene before us like she's used to Vegas daydreaming frequently.

"Must've been one hell of a fuck then," Kat reasons, with Dana nodding along.

Grinning like a vixen, Vegas responds, "Oh, it was, I think Blade knows G-Easy turns me on. He played *Lady Killer*, song gets me so hot. It was like we were in our own porn. The world a faraway place. Clothes came off, touching ourselves, then each other. Fucking till the sun came up. Every orgasm he owns. Never felt anything so strong. His intensity wraps around my thoughts and heart and I bow to whatever that man gives me."

Dana moves her head and gets a peek at us spying on them. "Dana, what's that face for?" Vegas' annoyed look is written across her face.

"You kind of got lost in your lovers' monologue to realize who's standing behind you," Dana tells her, jabbing her pointed finger in our direction.

"OH!" Vegas' slightly pinked face turns to see us guys smiling ear to ear. "Hey, you guys hungry?"

"Not as hungry as you are. Word of advice though," Tank shoves his way around Blade. He grabs a piece of bacon and starts chewing on it, continuing, "Keep that story to yourself, because, if I was a bitch, after hearing all that, I'd try to jump your man's bones the first chance I got."

Tuning out most of the girls' chatter, I grab my own coffee and food, then go to sit down next to Dana. I caught on that they are all going out, which means that one of us has to go with them. If they are going to the gym to work out, then I'm definitely volunteering so that I can watch her.

"I'm coming today," I abruptly interrupt to inform them.

Dana turns her head to stare at the side of my head. "To do what? Watch us work out?"

"No, I'm going to watch *you* work out." I turn toward her to make sure she pays attention. "And to make sure you all don't get blazed to and from anywhere else." That shit will not happen again. Not on my watch.

Dana rolls her eyes at me. "Doesn't matter, Axl, you're not my man, and you can't stop me!" Standing, she bolts and leaves the table, heading toward the door.

"Doesn't matter?" Goddamn chicks, so frustrating. "The next time your friends hand you pot, just say no! Better yet, I'll kick Pawn's ass for giving it to you."

I stand up from the table and bellow, "Did you hear that, Pawn!" I move to follow Dana's retreating back down the hallway.

She doesn't say anything to me, but is kind enough to slam the door to my room in my face. I charge into the room right behind her, just in time for her to slam the fucking bathroom door into my face too. "Fucking woman!" I slap the door with my hand, then turn to leave, pissed the fuck off, before I say something that I'll regret later.

I slam the door behind me and make my way back out in search of Pawn. I find him still passed out in his room, with one of the naked sluts draped over his back. I kick the side of the mattress with my boot and bellow off the top of my lungs, "Pawn, you motherfucker!" He startles awake.

"Do not give Dana weed without asking me first, motherfucker!" I kick his bed again seeing his dumbass grin. The rage is consuming me, and I turn around to leave, slamming that motherfucker's door too.

In a hurry, I stomp down to my room to get ready to get this fucking torturous day over. Dana's still in the bathroom, so I throw a t-shirt on and walk out.

After I wait outside for thirty minutes, these bitches fuckin' finally make it here. Vegas walks to the driver's side of her Tahoe, keys in hand. Snarling, I pluck them from her, get into the driver's seat and lock the front door.

I do not want to be fucked with and they take the hint, all three of them taking the back seat. Occasionally, Dana's eyes catch mine in the rearview mirror. She's throwing blue daggers at me all the way

17

to the gym until I park the car, and, in return, I throw my own back all the way inside the building.

I'm frustrated and pissed off on so many different levels. And I don't even know fucking why!

I'm probably in a bad mood from Dana's sass, and I really wanted to be in a good mood to watch her working out, which just pisses me off that much more. I know I'm brooding, but this just sucks. I don't know what this is I'm feeling, or care to fix it, I'm just pissed the fuck off.

I lace my sneakers up, because the stupid fucks at this gym make you pay to come into the class. I tried telling them at the desk that I was only going in for security reasons. They didn't get it, so fucking stupid. That made me call Pawn to bring me gym clothes and sneakers. Which has been the only thing that's made me happy so far today, making him get his ass out of bed. I'm standing back when I pick up on the conversation Jenn and Kat are having.

"What the hell did you bitches do last night without me!" Jenn shrieks at her friends. "You smell like weed and a hangover still. Look at me in the eyes, Dana." Jenn holds onto Dana's shoulders. "Did they pop your blaze cherry and I wasn't there? I'm so freaking pissed I wasn't there." Jenn drops her hands to look over at Kat who's standing up straight, eying her right back.

"Who the fuck is this?"

"Vegas and I popped your girl's cherry. She was so sweet too," Kat mocks her. "Oh fuck, Axl looks a little

18

mad right now." She points her long black nail toward me and James.

That twisted bitch, Kat, would be right, and she thinks she can talk about my woman like that?

Jenn starts laughing. "I'm Jenn, and you're sticking around because I can use you now that these two are getting all domesticated. And Axl is giving you some hateful looks. I need someone like you on my team. I can't wait for you guys to spill what happened last night."

Having enough of listening to these sassy bitches, my voice drops low to threaten them, "That's my cherry pie, and you girls won't be popping anymore of her cherries. The rest are all mine!"

If those two weren't enough, now Vegas thinks three sassy bitches are better. "Axl, I've popped so many of her cherries over the years... She's been mine way before she became yours. I've tasted her Cherry Chapstick..."

"Have not, no, no, you have not!" Growling low, I stare her down.

My cherry pie walks over to me and starts caressing my arm. "We were in high school, wearing our white nighties..." She drags her nails down my arm, causing my skin to shiver and my heated gaze to find hers as she goes on. "Watching a movie... I said, 'I wonder what it'd be like to kiss a girl.' We turned into each other..."

Not enjoying her little game, or whatever the fuck she thinks she's doing here, I pick Dana up around her ass and her legs wrap around my waist. I pin her body to the wall and feel her hands going to my hair. My lips claim her lips and body. I brutally take her, forcefully nipping her soft flesh. Before setting her back down, I give her one last bruising peck.

Charging over to where Vegas stands, I stake my claim on Dana over her, "Mine," while thumping my chest with a fist.

"Dude, we've never kissed, and we never will," her hands go up in defense. "She's my sister, you freak! You need to work on your bullshit game. It's hella weak. Go take a cold shower before I puke!"

"Don't need a cold one." I take Dana's hand and drag her behind me into the locker room.

# Dana

I've only ever really seen the happy and joking side of Axl. This other intense side of him has my heart pumping in my ears. It makes me see him now in a whole new light than I had before. So much more of the dangerous man that he has been hiding. Axl's six-foot two inches height towers over my five-foot six frame. My steps falter as he's dragging me into the locker room.

A few girls in the locker room giggle on their way out as they're running late to join the class. Stammering my words, I gasp, "Ax-x-l, stop!" I pull raged breaths into my lungs while trying to catch up on this out of control situation.

He abruptly stops on the spot at my protest. I wasn't prepared for that change in pace and my chest and face collide with his strong arm. Axl doesn't let go of my hand and presses his other hand against the lockers, dropping his head forward. He takes in a few deep breaths before turning to face me.

"Dana," he starts, then pauses, pulling in a few more haggard breaths. "I don't know what it is." He stops, looking just as confused as I feel. He runs both calloused hands up my arms, stopping under my chin and holding me there. He looks into my eyes as his thumbs stroke my cheekbones back and forth.

"Don't push me, okay?" Axl's softened voice rasps over my face. "I can't explain what it is that I'm feeling, and I can't get a handle on it. It's as if I know you, but, how can I? You're mine though, I can feel it through every part of me. But, then again, you aren't either, are you?" Axl rests his forehead on mine.

My hands slide up his olive skin and run over his muscles and the veins in his arms. Gripping his wrists, I say softly, "I want to take my time with you, and get to know what this feeling is. I feel it too, and it scares me. This need to feel your hands all over my body, it's as if you already know your way."

Axl's body stiffens at my words and his hands grab my hair at the back of my neck, lifting my head to meet his lips. When Axl's lips caress mine, it's so much different than before. He's worshiping me with his attention.

My hands find their way to the bottom of his shirt and I push it up and over his head. His excited green eyes track my movements, pulling him away from our kiss. My eyes devour his beautifully built chest. Not bulky, but ridges of lean muscles to show how well aged he is, a man.

His restrained grip on my shirt loosens and he starts to slowly lift it over my head, my ponytail whipping my back on the way back down. He moves further into my body, and I follow his lead, stepping back till I hit a wall. This dance we do feels so familiar, so much like a practiced dance we've done before. His hands glide over my sides to my breasts, then under my sports bra. He explores further down to my shorts and pushes them down my legs. Smooth, controlled hands hit my center, rubbing my clit.

My hands find his shorts and they begin running back and forth over the waistband. His lips find mine, slow and sensual, as his fingers slowly caress my cunt. I push his shorts the rest of the way down.

Axl laughs light heartedly. "We should take this back to your place, I want you naked for me." He bites my lip. "I want you all day and night." He kisses down my neck as I stroke him while his fingers glide in and out of me. "I want to feel your sweat dripping down on me." Axl's lips capture mine as we both reach higher and closer to our orgasm. A few more eager strokes and we're both coming, together.

"Mine, Dana, all of you is mine," he moans as his cum hits my stomach, and mine is coating his fingers.

Kissing his full lips, I whisper back, "Yes, Axl, all yours."

Releasing one another to clean ourselves up, we walk back out to class to see that we basically missed it, and there are only a few minutes left of it. Vegas and the girls are squatting their asses off. She still manages to smile over her shoulder when she spots us, missing the grand finale of the class.

Axl and I decide to go hang out in the small café inside the gym. We stare at each other from across the table, sipping on our smoothies. Not talking, just watching each other. Axl has a gorgeous smile painted on his face as he sips on the cherry mango smoothie he got. His boyish choice of a drink, along with his smile, has me grinning back like a fool. You would never know that he belongs to a motorcycle club unless he's wearing his cut. His features are sharp and masculine. His soft, dark hair has a tight buzz cut.

Breaking out of our trance, Axl asks, "You got work tonight, princess?"

"Yeah, I'm going to head home, grab some work clothes, and then head in."

"How about we go together? I've got a few clients coming in for tatts. I'll meet you at the bar, then I'll give you a ride to the clubhouse after work?"

"Axl, I'll be fine at home if you can drop me off and I'll take my own car to work and then home. I'm not staying with all your brothers every night till you guys figure your business out. No one is after me, and I'll be just fine. No way do I want to camp out in that small room full time!"

"We'll see, princess, we'll see." That's all Axl says as he's ignoring my small tantrum. He then stands up and goes to throw away what's left of his smoothie, leaving me to stare at his strong back as he walks away to wait for all of us back at the car.

# CHAPTER 2

## Dana

At The Black Rose there's a decent crowd out to celebrate the middle of the week. Since Vegas has started the planning of her brewery, we asked Kat to start working for us tonight. I hate to admit it as I'm watching her, but she has some skills I wasn't mentally prepared for. She flips the vodka bottle up with her right hand, and then catches it, pouring out a few ounces as her left hand is already pouring the soda into the glass, then tossing a lime into it.

Later, the girls and I are going to hound Tank for more information on this girl. Every so often, we catch glimpses of this dark creature she holds so close.

James runs in from the back office, his face looking scared and tense. "Kat, Vegas needs you in the office. Now." He then turns away from us, hollering out over the crowd, "Everybody out! Sorry, we have an emergency, the bar is shutting down for the night. Please leave quickly!"

Jenn shuts off the music and starts chasing behind Kat and me into the back office. My eyes sting with tears when I see Vegas' limp, cold and unmoving body lying on the desk. Blade's strong frame is folded over her, all protective, as if his hands and heart could bring her back from wherever she went. My hands find my mouth, desperately trying to mask my own despair.

Kat stands next to Vegas while she calls 911, then lays her phone down on the desk as she starts talking with the dispatch on speaker. She covers Vegas with a coat and checks her for a pulse and dilated pupils.

I feel desperately useless and helpless watching. The fear seizes my heart and mind and paralyzes me on the spot. I notice Tugger on his bed and he's not moving either. What the hell happened? Silent tears streak down my face as I take in the scene before me.

Fuego and Snake come busting through the back door, their anger floating like a cloak in their wake. They start cursing and yelling at seeing Vegas' unmoving form.

Blade ignores them, too focused on her to see anything or anyone else in the room.

"What the fuck happened? *Mija!*" Fuego yells, hitting his fist on the wall. Vegas' eyes start fluttering, and she moves her head slightly at all the commotion.

"Blade, what happened? She was fine after Johnny attacked her and we got her out of there!" Snake's fear is firmly gripping him, making his voice crack.

Jenn wraps her hand lightly around Fuego's arm, encouraging him to back away from Blade. Frustration booms all around the room as Snake bolts back out the office door.

Kneeling next to Tugger, her poor Tugg, I notice blood on his head. I sit on my ass next to him, watching the seconds tick by while petting his back. At a closer inspection, I see that he's bleeding on the side of his little head. Jenn's eyes find mine from across the room, and I see the same fear on her face.

James barges into the room and yells at no one in particular, "The EMT's are outside!"

Blade is up with a small Vegas curled protectively into his body, walking out the door with her. Terrified, I can hear my heart pounding in my ears.

James squats before me. "Dana, honey, it's going to be okay. We better get Tugger to the vet. Vegas will shoot our asses if we don't get him back to her, right?" James says, trying to snap me back to reality.

"We better make sure he's ok and get him back to her," I agree with a small nod. Jenn and I follow James to his truck and jump in for the ride. Not able to hold my questions in any longer, I turn toward him. "James, what the hell happened? You were out there with Vegas just minutes ago!"

James speeds down the freeway, not looking at me. "I was, then I got a call from Cuervo to cut the power,

I didn't know." He slams his fist against the steering wheel. "I should have made her come back with me. FUCK!"

Seconds go by as James breathes in and out, doing his best to calm down a bit before continuing with his take on tonight's events. "Johnny and Tanya cornered her in the garage, he tried fucking strangling her, and Tugg tried to stop him." He pauses, choking back his words. "Johnny slammed the butt of his gun across Tugg's head." James' hands white knuckle the steering wheel as he turns into the parking lot of the vet's office.

Quickly, the three of us rush into the emergency vet clinic, an older man already waiting to assist James and Tugger to a back room. I hold my breath while Jenn and I wait for him to come back with an update. After a few minutes, we move outside, not wanting to stare at the curious faces of the staff anymore.

Finally, James comes back out. Jenn steps into his arms and starts crying into his chest. My heart is breaking a little more, feeling all alone, and I turn away from them to face the mountains. I pray to God to bring Vegas her Tugg back. She'll be so pissed if anything happened to him.

I hear James and Jenn walking away behind me, and, moving on autopilot, we find ourselves back in the truck, then to the hospital waiting room to get an update on Vegas. Blade comes walking in, and he's looking relieved, thank God.

"She's going to be okay, she'll go home tomorrow. No one says shit about Tugg till we know for sure if he's going to wake up," Blade warns us before letting us back into her room.

James looks Blade straight in the eyes and says, "Blade, I fucked up, man, I shouldn't have left her there alone."

"Your fault, huh? I let her walk back there by herself, so don't unload your guilt here, I've got enough of my own." Blade's eyes flash with anger and regret, he then turns to leave us there, not caring if we're following or not.

I rush behind him, wanting to see for myself that Vegas is okay.

# Axl

This whole garage is a fucking mess, body parts everywhere. Solo and Pawn, the prospects, are going to have their work cut out for them cleaning this up. Blood is splattered on the walls and coating the concrete floor.

Fuego has Johnny's hands tied together above his head, suspending him from the ceiling with chains. His body sways back and forth with each blow of the fists delivered by Snake. One of his eyes has popped out from his shattered eye socket. The uncontained rage from Fuego and Snake, as they take turns hitting him, is breaking his bones one by one. The wood beams creak up above from Johnny's limp body weight swaying back and forth.

"Enough!" Fuego shouts. "This *puta* dies by fire. Load him up, he's going out to the mine."

The men untie his body and it crashes into a heap of useless shit on the floor. They drag him by the arms to the rock crawler truck, his feet leaving a trail of blood and dirt behind. There is no doubt that Fuego and Snake will make a bon fire out of his remains up in the mountains. So far into the desert, not another soul could trace the stench or the flames lighting up the starry night sky.

A woman's scream erupts from the opposite side of the old garage. Tanya's cry of agony has her head flying back from the punch that Ice administered to her nose. Her tears mix into the blood and dirt that's matted on her pale skin. Blood is pouring from her shattered nose and uneven breaths are racking through her chest from the pain. Her terrorized, naked body shakes from the fear and the adrenaline, which is the only thing keeping her alive at this point. Her trembling hands are tied above her head and her body is lying on top of an old table.

Ice, the Elko Prez, rips his teeth away from her large, fake tit. He spits out blood, and, fuck, was that a nipple? Getting into her face, he growls, "Tell me, bitch," his hand wraps around and squeezes her slender neck with ease, "the story, and stop lying to me, or don't. I can fuckin' torture and rape you all night." His soulless face leans in next to her ear, licking and biting her lobe.

Sobbing, Tanya shakes her head back and forth. Her face turns into a deep shade of red. Ice continues, "You had someone working with you and Johnny, someone above him, and at least one more with you. How did you get so many kids?" Ice questions while wiping the blood from his face with his arm. Frustration paints his face along with a smear of bright red blood. Her pleas of surrender entice the devil within to come out stronger.

Grabbing her ankles, he tosses her, forcefully twisting her body onto her stomach. Her knees make a cracking noise on the side of the table as her lower half gets thrown over. Her ass is in the air and bare feet hit the concrete. It's so cold in here, and her body uncontrollably shivers. Except her arms can't move with the weight of her body over table and the tension of the rope keeps her frail body in its grips.

Ice moves behind her. "Remember those nights I fucked you in the ass?" He runs his fingers with a lover's touch up the inside of her thigh, over the round curve of her ass. "I really loved sticking my dick in there."

Caressing her asshole with his thumb coated in her blood, he groans loud into the room. He's entranced by her impending death, by her tortured, yet still breathing body, falling deeply in love with his creation.

"How about one more time? Huh, baby? You wanna give Ice your ass?" he taunts her, pulling his stiff dick out and covering it with a condom.

Tanya pleads on a tortured whisper, "Ice, I'm sorry, I didn't have a choice!"

"The fuck you didn't, you stupid ass cunt." Ice grips her hair at the back of her head, fisting a handful of it and smashing her once pretty face into the table. Blood spatters from her already shattered nose. Ice groans, grabs her hips and shoves his dick up her ass. He rapes her, unrelenting and uncaring to her pain and screams that are asking for his forgiveness.

Blubbering through the pain, she resigns herself to her fate as Ice pounds into her. He's like an animal, catching and devouring his pray. Thin lines of blood drip down the insides of her legs, exciting Ice until he roars behind her like the beast that he is.

It all gets eerily quiet when she stutters, "Johnny sold the diamonds for ca-a-ash when the old Prez, Demon, and Bear died. I g-g-ot a cut for the kids. Johnny still needed transportation, that's when Skid was brought in." She sobs more, realizing that she's at the end of her bad choices. She played with a bunch of animals and lost.

Ice takes no mercy on her, allowing a line of men to take what they want from her. He has nothing left in his dead heart, nothing to lose. Never go against a man that has no fear of death or consequences, unless you can say the same.

He moves to pull her head up to look into her eyes, shaking it till they open. The bruising and swelling have taken over, so there isn't much that she can see. "Who was Johnny selling the diamonds to?" Ice seethes into her face.

"I don't know, j-j-just that he had a drop at the casino. I never met who he paid." Tanya is so quiet now that her voice is barely a whisper of a wish for death to take her soon. Ice finally takes pity on her and pulls his knife from his waist band. In a practiced move, smoothly, with a deep pressing, slow motion, he cuts her throat. Tanya's head hits the wooden table and dead cold eyes stare into mine.

Sitting here at the hospital, I watch as everyone talks with Vegas. My body grows tired from the day, from all the information I need to tell Blade and the brothers about. This fucked up mess is far from over.

Blade finally steps back from the hospital bed, allowing Dana and the girls their time with Vegas. Nodding my head in the direction of the hallway, I push my body up from the chair, and he follows me out.

Vegas catches the movement in the corner of her eye and turns her head our way to squint at us in suspicion. Bitch is always watching, even when she's beat to shit. I flip her off on my way past the bed and out to the hallway. Blade sees me giving her the finger and slaps me on the back of the head. "Better not be flipping off the Prez's woman, dipshit."

Rubbing at my head where he hit me, I grin at him. "She doesn't want me to treat her like she's hurt, and that was courteous as fuck of me." I smile more at Blade's irritability.

Locating a closed off corner down the hallway, Blade and I face each other. Both of us are looking haggard from the long day. Reluctantly, I catch Blade up on what Tanya confessed.

"Johnny didn't said much. He was in over his head in a game he didn't know how to control. He couldn't stand on his own feet by the end of his beating. Even though you have every right to kill him, I don't think any of us could have stopped Fuego and Snake from doing it. Those fuckers beat him with a rage none of us had ever seen. Even Cuervo, man, went at him with metal rods, busting and crunching bones. By the time they dragged his useless body out of there, he was a pile of shit. Nothing left to him, he was praying for death."

Hearing footsteps from down the hall, I stop talking, looking and waiting to see who it is. Tank rounds the corner. He spots us right away and stops in his tracks to come over to us.

"Snake just called and said Johnny confessed before they lit him up. He has a large gambling debt at the Nugget Casino. Apparently, the dead asshole owes a couple million to the boss. Must be tied to this whole fuckin mess with the kids and the diamonds."

Whistling long and low at that number, both Tank and I turn to our President for some direction.

Blade rubs his hand across the two-day old stubble on his chin, all deep in thought. "Put out a text for Church late tomorrow, but, before that, get in touch with Spider. Find out if he's got any new information before then. Axl, are you taking Dana back to stay at the club?"

"Fuck no! First off, I don't trust those chicks or dicks around her. I'm going to be staying with her at her house. All this moving of shit around is high maintenance though, man. I moved her shit yesterday, now I've got to move it all back again." I huff out that last part.

"Jesus, Axl, just buy more shit tomorrow and leave her old shit at the clubhouse for later. Chicks hoard enough for a morning or a day to get by. I had Solo buy Vegas all new shit and to keep it in stock for her too."

All of a sudden, he pauses and looks at me. "Why am I telling you this for? Fucking pussy ass shit, and you're a dumb fuck if you can't figure this out on your own." He grumbles to himself as he walks away from me and Tank.

"Fuck me, Blade, I don't know if you're smart or just a romantic motherfucker?" I laugh at my brother.

Blade eyes me over his shoulder. "Smart, you dick, I have my woman where I want her 24-7. Fucking smart." He turns back around, making it his mission to get back to Vegas.

Following him back into the room, I hear Jenn promising Vegas a night out when she's feeling better. That only causes Blade and I to cringe at the thought of following this crazy ass crew around when they're drunk.

Stepping up close to Dana, I tug her by her waist and into my side. "Blade's tired, babe, we need to head out." I kiss her temple and let her go.

She nods, "Vegas, I'll bring you some food tomorrow after I check in on our Tugg." She says it sounding so hopeful. "Text me later what you want to eat."

"I want tacos. Definitely a big plate of tacos!" Vegas shouts out at the thought of food.

"Alrighty then, I see your appetite is okay, tacos it is. See you girls tomorrow." Dana waves while talking and backing out of the room. Me? I hurry to catch up with her and grab her hand in mine. Then, I take us home.

Dana pulls the comforter back on her bed, snuggling herself in. I take in the clean smell of her room that's wafting up to me from the movement of the blanket. I love her fresh, clean smell. All natural. Most chicks like to wear perfume, but Dana just loves to be natural, more herself. I love it and find it sexy and comforting.

She holds the blanket up for me, so I slide in next to her with my boxer briefs on. She rolls to her right, giving me her back, and I look down at her ass that's clad in a black lace G-string. She's killing me!

Not wanting to be a horny dick, I decide to move in behind her to hold her back to my chest. I kiss her shoulder and she exhales the breath she was holding in.

"Axl, what happened tonight?" She tenses just a little in my arms.

"I won't be pissed that you asked, princess, but I can't tell you everything. I can tell you just that Johnny and Tanya won't be around to be a threat to anyone anymore. There's still some cleanup to do from the shit they brought to the club. We'll get it all handled though."

"What about the kids you found, where are they now?"

"The really young ones went into a group housing they have in California for foster kids. Tami, the oldest of the kids, she is staying with Kat. Kat's helping her get back on her feet since she's seventeen, about to be eighteen." I yawn my way through the words.

"I'm feeling so tired." Her yawn is following mine. "Thanks for staying with me tonight."

"I'm not leaving." She tenses a little again at my declaration. Hand to God, this woman couldn't get rid of me if she tried. "I'm here every night, Dana, take that shit in."

Taking my hand in hers, she places our joined hands together above her heart, scooting her body as close to mine as she can get it. She kisses my hand and snuggles in, ready to sleep.

# CHAPTER 3

## Dana

I'm holding Tugger in my lap, and it's giving me a deep sense of happiness inside of me. Today, I am taking him home.

The vet called right after Blade did this morning, stating that we could pick him up. The swelling on his head is down, and he only has a few stitches. I rub around little Tugg's c-collar, while he barks at it, trying to get it with his teeth. James, Jenn and I laugh at his frustration.

"Take that collar off him. He won't touch it if Blade is around. That dog loves him as much as he does Vegas," James says as he pulls into Blade and Vegas' small, gray with black trim house. He parks and walks around to take Tugg from my lap, so that I can jump down from his jacked up, lifted, blue truck. I grab the bags of Mexican takeout for Blade and Vegas before shutting my door.

The three of us walk up to the house, and I lightly knock, then wait. Blade's tired face answers the door. He opens it wider for the three of us to walk inside. As soon as he closes it after us, he takes Tugger from James and gives him a big hug. He then walks him down the hallway, back to their room, and we all follow. He sets him on the bed next to Vegas and she starts groaning in her sleep from Tugg licking at her face. Then again, until she rolls onto her back.

She jumps awake, startling Tugg with her scream, "Tugg!" He happily barks back at her, thinking that it's play time. She pulls him to her and starts peppering his face with kisses and tears. He keeps barking and licking on her face. Vegas calms him down by petting him and he settles in by lying across her lap. She chuckles, "My little man missed me too, huh, Tugg?"

Vegas is finally realizing that the rest of us are also here watching and says, "Hey, you guys staying to eat? I'm starving, hand me the food, woman!"

"You know it," Jen says, grabbing a bag from me and handing it to James and Blade. Her and I settle in on each side of Vegas, with our backs to the headboard and the takeout tacos on our laps.

Blade gives us a dissatisfied look, raising a brow at us. I raise both of mine back in return. Dude has control issues. He narrows his eyes at me, then decides to leave and nods at James to follow. "Beer?" Is all he says as they both leave to the front of the house.

"What's his deal anyway?" I look at Vegas for answers. I notice the bruising from yesterday is more purple and bluer today, especially around her eyes and neck.

"Blade is still shaken up over the whole thing from yesterday. He just needs some time to adjust and gather his thoughts. He's not ready to share me yet. Be a little patient, the man isn't going to tell you that."

Jenn looks sad. "How are you doing today though, babe?" she asks while taking a few bites from her *carne asada* tacos.

Vegas sighs, "Not too good right now. I didn't, or rather couldn't tell you guys until I talked to Blade first. But I lost a baby we had, I was pregnant." She stops to take a shuddering breath. "Makes me feel so broken to think about it, and that I didn't know what I had. Had I known, I would've never gone out there by myself. I didn't think being pregnant was even possible to happen right now." A few small tears drip from her eyes. Her head falls back against the headboard and she closes her eyes.

My voice and heart lodge in my throat to find out she was pregnant and lost her baby over what happened last night. Over being beaten by that asshole and that bitch.

Exhaling loudly, she wipes her tears away with her shaking hands. Quietly, she starts talking, giving us more of her thoughts than ever before. "I knew I always wanted babies. I just didn't realize how ready I was until last night." She tilts her head back down to face us again, allowing one lone tear to fall, hitting her shoulder.

Lending her a piece of me to hold her together, I say, "I'm not going to tell you it's not your fault, even though we all know it's not. You need to come to that conclusion on your own. You lost a baby, Vegas, you didn't know you had. Yes, you would have done it all differently. But you can't, so let's not entertain those thoughts. Let go of what could have been and start living on what can still be. You still have time, Vegas. Embrace what you're feeling and let it go. You have all your dreams still waiting for you. When you're ready, go for it, okay? Bring Vegas back, stronger, and take it on, make me some beautiful babies."

Vegas smiles at me. "You sure do love happy stories with cute babies in the end," she finishes, laughing at me.

"Babies are the bomb dot com, they are so cute. I just read this baby daddy book. He had a cute little baby and the mom died, that was sad. Then he meets the hot nanny, and, hello, baby number two by the end of the book."

I am a little obsessed with baby daddy books, it's obviously true. "We are going to wait, and one day you are going to have the cutest damn babies."

Jenn shakes her head at me, "I can't wait for little Axl and Dana babies. It's going to be so cute too." She holds her hands up under her chin, mocking me.

"Bitch," I scold her. "In the meantime, we'll have fun like we always do until shit gets better."

42

Vegas nods along, "Yeah, when I'm ready... I had a dream of the cutest little boy last night and he was rocking a tiny little hawk like his dad's." She heaves in a strengthening breath. "Fiery too, like Fuego. I was chasing after him." She silently cries a little more. "I could feel him, I can feel him still." The tears are pouring out along with her pain.

Jenn grabs Vegas' hand. "He's not gone forever, Vegas. You ever think maybe it just wasn't his time yet? Who says he's gone forever? That little guy is waiting for the right time, just like his momma, and telling her to get her shit together. I like this kid that rocks the hawk. I'm with Dana now, we need a fucking little punk in Cortez shoes running around here soon"

"Fuck, Jenn," Vegas laughs and shakes her head as she smiles through the tears. "I was so busy stressing over it all to think of it that way."

Jenn smiles back, "Life isn't simple or black and white, you know that. It's why we all got each other. Help each other through this crazy shit, you know?"

"I hear you, girl, I hear you," Vegas agrees.

I bump Vegas' shoulder with my mine, and she, in turn, bumps hers with Jenn's.

I gently say, "Vegas, you'll get back what you lost temporarily. In the meantime, we can have fun and cheer you up."

Jenn says with an evil gleam in her eyes, "Tank is our perfect target." She starts rubbing her hands together. "I'm going to think of some pranks to tie us over. You'll be laughing too hard to be sad." She pops up from her seat on the bed and walks into the bathroom. "You got a whole lot of family, and a whole lot more on the way," she states while shutting the bathroom door.

Vegas finally opens her takeout box and takes a bite, then another, moaning with each one. "I haven't eaten in hours. That's just not normal or right," she states, shoving more food into her face.

Opening my box, I inhale the awesome aromas and feel my mouth watering. Like Vegas, it's my first time eating too since the whole mess from yesterday. I'm feeling happy, but also sad for my friend. Vegas is a strong woman, but I know she needs a little time to process her feelings. Wouldn't any one of us?

"Hey, Vegas, you call me when you need me. It's always been us against the world, and always will be."

"Always, Dana, there isn't anyone I love more than you and Jenn. Just sitting here is all I need."

We sit in silence and munch on our lunch. Talk more about Kat and the bar. All of us are looking forward to the holidays and being together.

Just as we finish, her mom comes barging in, with tears in her eyes, and pulls Vegas into her embrace. She whispers promises of her love and strength. I give Cindy a quick hug and leave so they can have some privacy. James, Jenn and I head out to get ready for work.

It's a few hours later when I pull up at The Black Rose and see that there's a considerate number of cars and bikes in the parking lot. Smiling, I walk into the tattoo shop first.

Battle Born Tattoo is hopping with new business. The new girl they hired as a receptionist is a beautiful, young, twenty something, brown haired, brown eyed girl. She's always happy, and we all took it upon ourselves to call her Sunshine.

"Hey, Sunshine, is Axl busy?" Even though I can see he's cleaning his room, I still like to ask.

"No, his client just left. His next one isn't due here for another thirty." She smiles back at me while picking up the ringing phone.

As I walk toward his room, my stomach drops at the sight of him as I inch closer. His calm presence makes me feel comfortable, but at the same time so anxious.

He hears me nearing him and turns around, his eyes doing a full scan of my body. I'm so happy that I wore my tight jeans, loose sweater and ankle booties. This morning, he left me with a kiss before he went to the club. We've never done the morning after thing. Not that I've ever had or felt so off around a guy either.

"Hey, princess, you gonna hover outside my room? Or are you going to come in and say hi?" Axl leans his head to the side, enjoying my indecision.

"I, uh, brought you some tacos for lunch. I know it's late and they are cold by now, or, if you're not hungry, you can always give them away." Taking a few more steps inside, I stand at an arm's length away from him.

Axl takes a step forward and runs his hand up my forearm, hooking my elbow and pulling me into his hard body. His gaze is focused on mine as he takes the bag from my hand and sets it on the table next to us. My breathing deepens as his touch runs from my arms to around my back and waist. Embracing me into his hold, Axl kisses my lips, and my arms snake around his neck.

"Thanks, Dana," he says and kisses my forehead. "Perfect timing, I'm having a late lunch today. Why are you so worried?" He rubs his thumb between my eyes where I can feel a crease forming, then shows me his perfect white teeth in a bright smile.

"I honestly have not a damn clue what you and I are doing. Are we seeing each other, or what is this?"

"You planning on seeing someone else, Dana? I thought I made that pretty clear over the last few days. So, I don't know why you're worried..."

I try to pull back a little and he doesn't let me, so I continue, "I'm not used to all this. The changes... Doesn't feel real yet I guess. I'm not used to having someone around, my mom picked drugs over me and my papa picked the club. I've never had a steady family life or a guy to count on. It's all a little weird for me. I'm not seeing someone else. I'm not okay with being open to you seeing other girls either. Let's get that out there too while we're talking about this."

"Damn, woman, you really need me to lay it all out there. Would you feel better if I gave you all the words while our clothes were on?" Axl says while rubbing my back and pulling my body tighter against his.

"Yes." I can't help the smile as I beam up at him.

"Okay," he feigns as if he's thinking hard over it. "My princess only gets Axl, and Axl only gets his princess," he says kissing my lips again. "I only want you, Dana, just you and me. We are a long-term thing. I want to have it all with you, but let's see where we go. I'm definitely in your bed as much as I can." He gives me his best predatory smile. "But I'm starving for food right now, so sit with me for a few while I eat?"

Axl kisses my lips one more time before he turns to sit at the table next to us. Just as he has a taco halfway eaten, we hear Vegas slamming the door open as she and Blade walk in. Why are they here? Then, I hear her yelling at him, "I CAN. NOT. Believe you just asked me that!" She shrieks her disbelief and stomps down the hallway toward the back where she bangs the door closed in his face.

"For FUCK'S SAKE, Vegas! I'm not accusing you of purposely taking too many pills! I was checking on you that you didn't accidently take too many!" Blade yells through the door, then pushes it open and storms behind her as they continue their fighting now outside in the back parking lot. Where everyone can see and hear. Lovely.

Axl menacingly chuckles around another bite, so I ask, "How is this fight funny, Axl?"

"Ever since this whole thing went down, Vegas' hormones are all outta whack. She's fucking batshit crazy and giving Blade so much shit." He takes another bite and continues to talk with his mouth full of food, "I love the drama, shit, it's fucking entertaining to watch Blade squirming like a worm on Vegas' hook."

I have no words. Did he just call my best friend batshit crazy? I know I should be pissed at him for talking shit about her. On the other hand, his little nosy personality is kind of cute too.

I'm in so much trouble of my own here.

# CHAPTER 4

## Axl

Blade sits at the head of the table, waiting anxiously to start Church as the brothers file into the room. After Cowboy shuts the door behind him, he slams the gavel on the table. The haunted and angry look on his face quiets down the noise, blanketing the room in an anxious energy.

He looks around until he's ready to address the issues we have. "You all have heard that Tanya and Johnny are dead. Stryker is back down south in Las Vegas, while Fuego rushed back to California to handle some urgent business. Snake stayed back along with Vegas' mom, Cindy. Snake is staying with them when I can't. If he can't, Tank, you have Vegas' watch."

Tank answers, "Anything for my little ninja, Prez."

Blade pushes on, not really hearing anything other than Tank's confirmation. "With the fucked-up mess those two got our club involved in, we are left cleaning the shit up, so there is no blowback on us."

A chuckle from the back of the room interrupts Blade and has the brothers looking over to Hitch, as he says, "Vegas sure did fuck those two up the best she could. Too bad Tanya got her fine ass caught up in..." He chokes on his words as Blade abruptly stands and rushes over to stand right in front of him. His fist grabs a fistful of his cut and slams him against the wall.

He pulls a long-bladed knife from under his cut, behind his back, and holds it up across Hitch's face. Blade's body is vibrating with his demon coming forward. "You wanna talk over me, Hitch? You think the shit coming outta your fucking mouth is funny?"

He waits as Hitch denies with a shake of his head. "You also think it's fucking smart to bring that dead as fuck cunt into the same thought as Vegas? She not only played my woman, she disrespected and sold out our club, you motherfucker."

He drags the blade slowly across Hitch's face who, in turn, groans as he takes his earned punishment from the Prez. Blade drags his knife diagonally from under Hitch's eye, down across his cheek, and stops at his chin. "Get the fuck out of here, your stupid ass is on probation, motherfucker, till you can show me some goddamn respect, to me *and* the brothers. Go!" Blade shoves at Hitch as Cowboy opens and shuts the door behind him.

Blade sits back down next to me, placing his dirty knife on the table. He's looking for me to continue the meeting, to keep our Prez from cutting more brothers up.

"The information we got from the dead bitch is this. She was helping Johnny all along, even in Las Vegas. She was feeding him info when she had any and was able to share. Until she got a cut in on the action. She and Skid were working together. Johnny had a gambling debt when he went to Bear a while ago and used the club to pay off his debt. Bear and Skid fucked us over in many ways. Our main concern is getting in contact with the boss of the underground at the casino, Tony Riva. That twisted fucker is going to want payment for his debt. Since Bear and Skid were in on it, Tony will more than likely see it as our problem too now that Johnny is out of the picture."

Blade, who's still looking like the shell of a killer that's holding on by a thread, turns to address Tank. "Get us a meet for as soon as possible. Tonight. If the fucker doesn't respond, we are going after him. One way or another, I'm done. This shit ends soon." With that, Blade hits his gavel to the table.

Church is done, assholes.

The Battle Born brothers walk out from the clubhouse to their bikes. One by one, each man kickstarts the engine to their bike, the loud roar exciting the wolves that we wear on our patches and in our souls.

I tie on my red bandana and put on my leather gloves, ready to roll out.

The club is on a mission to fuck up anyone who dares to get in our way.

We head out down the dark freeway. Most people are at home at this time at night, leaving the road open to a bunch of wolves and thieves.

Our Prez rides out front, Tank and I follow behind him. Two by two, the club brothers back up our Prez and our club. Solo and Pawn, our number one prospects at our backs, down the freeway we roll, our momentum eating up the road.

Walking up to the back doors of the casino, we go in from the back alley. Blade looks up into the camera as the doors unlock and slightly pop open.

Blade, Tank and I are the only ones permitted into this club. A handful of brothers stay put with our bikes while another handful are watching the main floor of the casino where the tourists gamble on dime machines.

We walk into the real part of the casino, the part the tourist never sees, where the real deals and gambling go down. High stakes and fat stacks of cash sit on the tables. Bitches in only thongs and bras wait on tables. Others strip down for high profile gangsters and businessmen in private show rooms.

Security guards with AK's and plenty of clips stand guard by the boss himself. Tony Riva. His black hair is slicked back, and he's wearing a black shirt and suit and tie. Over the top motherfucker.

A couple of beautiful bitches sit at his sides, smiling at all the men who are gambling at the tables. The men in suits are smoking cigars while holding up their cards.

Tony's loud, boisterous laugh echoes around the room as he tosses his cards down and taps the blonde girl on her ass. She stands and walks away with one of the men, heading down together to one of the private rooms.

Blade nods over to Tony, catching his attention. Tony drops the face he uses to entertain his "guests" while taking their money. He stands and hands the cash over to a guard after which he walks over to us.

"Blade and the boys are here. I told Tank over the phone that we could meet later when I didn't have so many guests in town."

Tony gives off a nonchalant comment, but his jaw grinds at the movement, giving away at his true emotion. The fancy suit wearing gangster is pissed because we don't scream the high-class dollars his glitzy pussy lifestyle sells. "Since you came all the way here, let's move our meeting to the office." Tony walks in the direction of his office as the men gambling on the floor turn their attention back to their tables.

Barging through the door, Tony glares over at the three of us while his guards check us for guns but miss the knives in our boots. His eyes gleam like the sadistic fuck he can be to ask Blade, "Tell me, how's Vegas doing these days? From what I have been told, she gave as good as she got. I always loved that tough bitch, send her my regards, Blade, won't you?"

Blade's fake smile comes across his own face. "No reason to make any of this shit here today personal. The ex-club president and member are both gone for the shit they got wrapped up in with Johnny. We cleaned up their shit. I'm here as a courtesy to clean this bad blood up. We are done here." Blade turns to leave, but Tony halts his movements.

"Not fucking likely I'm going to leave a couple million hanging out there, Blade. Johnny had a deal that associated with your club. Word gets out I let a bunch of assholes slip out on payment, then I'm fucked. Also, there won't be a fucking man who will do business with you as soon as your name gets out for not paying the debt off that's now on the club. You know I'm right." The dick chuckles at the end.

Blade straightens and turns back to face Tony. "You must be high on your own supply if you think I'm going to be selling kids for cash. Don't give a fuck, start running your mouth about non-payment, and I'll pass around these pics of you shaking hands with the men you bought and sold the kids from. I think we were able to find you with a few young girls yourself.

You like them barely legal and no experience." Blade's face flashes a big fuck you in return.

Tony takes a moment to think over what Blade said, and comes back with, "No one said we had to deal in the skin trade, kids or otherwise. The raw diamonds were easier to transport and sell. We also have a fight club, Saturday nights. I assume you would have some men to knuckle it out, fists for dollars? Each fight pays fifty grand if you win, if you lose, you get nothing."

Blade's heated gaze meets mine, our signal for me to take over before his psycho tendencies take over. "We'll fight our way through our debt. We will not take a dive for a fight. If we lose a fight, then we make nothing. But we won't stack the odds for you either to make cash off one of us taking a beating. We'll be in touch after we get our contacts set up with the diamonds. And, Tony?"

Tony laughs at me and answers, "Yeah?"

"We only owe you half, motherfucker, half of what those two assholes got into. One million for the club, in diamonds, or fists for cash, you hear me?"

"In six months then, half the cash, then half the time. Or you owe me the other half within a year." The devil smirks at us.

Blade steps closer to Tony, causing the guards to raise their guns at us. Blade's blood thirsty eyes watch Tony not flinch. "You fuck with me and my shipments, or with the men fighting, I'm coming for you, Tony. Debt or fucking not, you're fucking dead. Don't think I didn't figure out you had Tanya selling out Bear too.

Scamming their loads right out from under them. I smell your stench close to any of my deals, you're fucking taking a ride with me to the mountains."

# Dana

"Hey, Tami, what's going on?" I ask, hoping today is better than it's been for her lately. Tami stops sweeping the floor to look up at me. She catches me off guard when I see her beautiful face and the makeup she has on that's making her hazel eyes pop.

"Wow, your eyes are so pretty. I love your eyeliner. Did you and Kat run to the makeup store at the mall today?" I'm genuinely interested in her day, in her new little spark.

She looks at the floor for a moment, then back up at me before saying, "Yeah, we went shopping, and I picked up this outfit too." She smiles before her attention is caught at the door where Solo is just walking through. He sees her before he finds her eyes just as Pawn runs into his back. Tami's face reddens, then she looks back down to the floor, finishing her task and wanting the attention away from her.

Kat calls from across the floor, "Hey, pups, over here." She whistles at them like they're little puppies. Pawn laughs and Solo glares her way. "Take this box that came for Vegas out to the brew house, and then your Prez wants you to report back to the clubhouse."

Solo picks up the box and looks at Tami one last time, when their eyes meet. He smiles and, nodding at her, says, "Catch you later." He takes the package and Pawn with him out the back door.

"That's my girl!" Kat yells out pumping a fist into the air. She walks over to Tami and gives her a high five. "You have those two-pound puppies drooling over you. But, I have to warn you, if you pick a brother to make a go with you, only get one." Kat holds up a finger lecturing her. "You're not the kind of girl they would share." Then, she holds her at arm's length and says, "Good for you! I'm so excited, I am making you into the hottest little woman those little man-tards have ever seen."

Tami's horrified face stares at Kat, not knowing what to say back. "Kat, I would never sleep with two guys at the same time. I am still, you know..."

"I know, babe, and just wait, when Solo pulls his head out from licking his own balls, and figures this out, he's going pack-man on you."

Tami's face bugs out. "He's going to eat me?"

Kat and I roll with laughter. "Oh, honey, I certainly hope he eats the shit out of your girlie parts. But I meant, 'pack man' as in a wolf that protects his family. He'll claim you. P.a.c.k. man, not p.a.c. man. Well, both actually." She laughs out at Tami's innocence.

Finishing up my bills on the desk, I realize that I haven't heard from Vegas all day. Instantly, I feel like crap for not checking in with her sooner, so I send her a text.

**Me: Yo, hot pants, are you home? I'm coming over.**

After about fifteen minutes, I get a text back.

**Vegas: I'm about to watch Judge Judy without you, bitch. Hurry your ass up.**
**Me: I'm going to do something to get you spanked by Blade. I'm leaving now. Pause that shit or you're dead to me!!!**

I race over to her house in my little Volkswagen GTI, aka Rabbit. It's normally a twenty-five-minute drive, but I make it in about fifteen. I skid into my parking spot, that's now Blade's. But it was mine first.

Rushing through the door, I find Vegas sitting on the couch with the remote in hand. She pushes play just as the door slams shut. Laughing at me, she says, "I should text you that more often when I need you STAT!"

"Judge Judy just knows her shit, and I love it when she tells people they are stupid and ugly. Makes my day!" I squish in on the couch as we start watching and eating snacks.

Two episodes later, I start yawning, and, turning to Vegas, I say, "Let's run to the store, grab some cokes and buy some frozen yogurt on the way?"

"Sure, let's go, I just need to grab Tank first," she tells me.

Dumbfounded, I ask, "He's here?"

"Yeah, he's sleeping in the guest room. The club is wrapping up the Johnny bullshit, so, until then, I have my own security guard, one who likes to take naps," Vegas says, rolling her eyes, and, even though I know she doesn't know, her comment makes me a little sad.

Is Axl only staying with me because he was told to?

Tank walks behind us, carrying all our groceries. His annoyance is obvious, and we keep walking around the store looking at more stuff that we don't really need, but just to see how far we can push him before he breaks.

"Vegas, I swear to fucking Christ! You said you needed two things! We've been walking around this goddamn store for fifty-eight minutes, and we're ten things later! I'm leaving, and both of you are coming with me!" Tank storms off, speed walking over to the check-out line where he drops his armfuls of groceries and supplies on the belt.

"Wow, he made it to almost sixty minutes, that's by far the longest," Vegas states. "The man's got stamina. And he bought a rope. Tank is a whole lotta freaky. When are we testing Axl?" Her voice is eager, but her smile falls when I just shrug my shoulders. "Dana, what's going on?" I see the concern in her eyes.

"Oh, shit, sorry, hold that thought!" She all but yells at me, grabbing my hand to run behind her just as we are about to reach the door.

Tank is walking toward the exit, holding two bags of groceries. As we reach him, a group of teenage girls walk up, eyeing the much older Tank up and down. Vegas whispers, "Get his pants." She hisses, holding the 's'.

She grabs his shirt at the bottom and pulls it up to his chest, lodging it under his arms, as I de-pant Tank. Since he wears sweatpants but no underwear, I get a full view of his tight fine ass.

Quickly, Tank drops the groceries to the ground to grab his pants just before these girls get to see his "little tank." Vegas and I run off as he yells after us, "I'm taking your two crazy asses home! Are you trying to get me arrested? Get your little punk asses back here and carry your own shit to the car."

His last threat makes us stop in our tracks, Converses screeching across the pavement as we turn to check if he's serious. He's stomping in our direction toward the car without our bags. We both make a wide path around as we pass Tank while he glares at us.

Laughing, we pick up the grocery bags only to see the teenagers watching us from the store window. Vegas gives the girls thumbs up and they wave back. Tank is waiting for us with his hands on his hips, and, true to his word, he watches us load the car while we smile at him.

Shutting the back of the hatch, we step closer to the back doors as Tank pulls on the locked driver's door.

Tank growls, "Dana, unlock the damn doors with your remote."

I dig my keys out to unlock the door. It clicks, and Tank grabs the handle just as I lock it again. "Don't fucking play with me, woman. I will spank the shit out of both of you, hog tie your spoiled little asses to the back seats and drop you off to the brothers that way. Try me." His cold stare is penetrating me.

I click the remote to unlock all the doors. I go to hand my keys over, dangling them from my fingers at an arm's length, to the beast that is Tank.

"Too far today, ladies, too far." He snatches the keys from me and slips his large body into the front seat.

Vegas and I stare wide eyed at each other at how pissed off he is. I mouth over the car, "What the fuck?"

Vegas' eyes bug out a little more and mouths back, "I know! Hog tied?!"

Finally, we snap out of it. We both reach for the handles just as Tank starts laughing at us like a possessed demon and locks us both out. Our hands snap back from us pulling on the handles. He laughs again and unlocks the doors. We try again, only to have him lock the doors, and our hands pop off the handles. Again.

I walk towards the back of the car and whisper to Vegas, "Let's walk over to the strip mall across the street. Grab some frozen yogurt?"

A large smile spreads across her face, "Let's do it." Determination laces our faces for payback.

Tank grimaces as we start walking away from the car. Getting out, he yells, "Alright, enough, let's go."

We just smile and keep walking away.

"Not fucking around with you two," he threatens.

Vegas and I keep walking and laughing as she says, "What is he going to do, rope us both?"

We simultaneously turn when realization hits that he is in fact darting in our direction with his rope in hand, and that he will rope or hog tie at least one of us. We both pick up our pace and haul ass, sprinting toward the store.

Tank gives up his pursuit on foot and runs back to the car, starting it and driving in our direction. By the time he catches up with us, we made it to the Big Freeze. Heaving inside the store, with our hands on our knees, we try to catch our breath. We look up and see Tank sitting on the hood of the Rabbit, glaring at us. We look at each other and laugh, shrug and grab some frozen yogurt.

Being the nice girls that we are, we really are, we take Tank some frozen yogurt, handing him strawberry with chunks of cheesecake on top. He hesitates before reluctantly taking the frozen treat from me. Vegas and I get into the car. We enjoy our treat on our way to the bar together to check in with the girls.

# CHAPTER 5

## Dana

Axl, Blade, Kat and Jenn laugh while Vegas and I tell the group what we did to Tank at the store today. Axl throws his head back, laughing and squeezing me tighter around the waist. Feeling a little off since Vegas' comment earlier, I step back just a bit. Axl's eyebrows raise up in question.

Vegas interrupts our moment, telling the group, "I have to say that Tank has, by far, been the hardest to crack and the most fun. Good God, today was classic, Tank! Love you, dude." Vegas tries to fist bump him, but he slaps her hand away. "You were my favorite, little ninja. Not anymore," he pouts.

"Aww, Tank, you're still my favorite bodyguard." She sweetly lays her charm on thick.

He shakes his head, but his hard exterior cracks just a bit as he tries to hold back a grin.

Vegas keeps going. "Come on, you know it was funny." She bumps his shoulder.

Tank gives in a little more, "It will be funnier tomorrow." His smile is stretching across his big head. And the room laughs again at his little concession.

Axl breaks up our little party. "It's time I get my badass, little prankster princess home. Catch you all later." Waving everyone good night, Axl and I head out to take me home.

# Axl

I'm worried and anxious to get Dana home so that we can talk about what has her acting differently and stepping away from me earlier. Getting right to it, because I'm too tired and worn out to be patient, I blurt out, "Why the hell did you step away from me for, Dana?"

Stunned at my approach, her attitude kicks in. "You don't have to stay here because you were told to, Axl," she spits her words at me.

Slapped, I feel slapped in the face.

65

"What the fuck do you mean, Dana? I wasn't told I had to do anything."

"Oh, so these nights and days you've been with me weren't for my protection, and Blade didn't order for you guys to keep watch over us?"

"Yes, Blade said you all needed a person on you, so what?"

"So, you admit that you are here only because of orders from your Prez!" Dana yells at me.

I yell back, "You have lost your shit, Dana!" I point my finger at her crumbling face. "I've been too sweet to you, too soft. I wanted to show you the man I could be for you. For you to sit here and tell me that I am only here because of a job? Dana, I didn't want us to be just a fuck. I wanted to be the man to take care of you!"

"This whole thing we are and have been doing confuses me, Axl! You say you want me, but what do you really do to have me? Nothing. I don't want a perfect man, Axl, I want a man. A real man that takes what he wants from me. All this toeing around us is driving me crazy!" Dana's face is reddening, and her chest is heaving from shouting her words at me.

I step closer and my hand reaches for her face to bring her mouth closer to mine. I slam my lips against hers. Nipping and biting them until she opens for me, I wrap my tongue around hers. My hands hold her head in place while her hands clench at the front of my black t-shirt. Teeth are clashing, each trying to devour the other. Taking my mouth from hers, I kiss down her throat, tilting her head back with my thumbs.

"Dana, no more pussying around with this. I'm taking you, all of your heart and body tonight. You want me to take it, I will."

My hand swiftly takes her tan sweater off, then I unbutton her jeans, sliding them down her slender hips, taking her underwear with them. I couldn't give a fuck, she's getting naked for me.

Dana hops on one foot then the other, kicking her sneakers off. I tug my own shirt off as she reaches for me, helping me to take my pants off. I reach around her back and unsnap her bra at the same time that my pants are pushed down, and her black bra hits the floor at my feet.

Dana's small hands wrap around my dick, pumping and stroking aggressively right before she slides to the floor and wraps her lips around me. She takes me deep and hard to the back of her throat and I groan out loud. My head falls back as I let her suck my cock, and suck it well she does.

I wrap my hand around her golden hair and pull her up. A gasp of pain escapes her mouth.

"You'll suck my dick later, princess," I tell her and smash her lips in a quick kiss. Reaching around her, I grab her ass and pick her up. Dana's hands lace behind my neck as her legs lock behind my back.

Taking two steps forward, her back hits the wall just as I push my dick through her silky, hot pussy.

Dana gasps again, pushing at me, "Where's your condom, asshole?"

I laugh at her little fists pounding at me. This bitch is really mad at me?

"Shut the fuck up, princess." I grab her chin. "I'm taking what's mine, you better be on birth control or you'll be having my baby. I don't give a fuck."

I smash my body against hers again and she stills as I kiss and nip at her neck, rocking forward into her. My mind and body buzz with lust as I pound out my energy into her body. A few more thrusts and then I pull out and kneel, throwing one of her legs over my shoulder. My tongue eagerly finds her cunt. Starting from the back, I claim her with my tongue. I find her clit and my tongue starts licking at an unrelenting pace.

Dana's body tenses before she comes on my face and tongue. I don't let her come all the way down before I'm back up onto my feet and into her body, pounding into her. I chase my own release to coat her pussy and claim her body. I use her for my pleasure, taking what she said was mine, and roar out my victory as I come long and hard into her.

My forehead is resting on her shoulder and her fingers run along the back of my head. She hums out her satisfaction, as our bodies relax together. Pulling out, I take her hand and lead us into the bathroom and into the shower. The hot water hits our bodies as I hold her to my chest never wanting to let go of this moment.

Today, Dana is finally mine.

"Why do you always believe I'm out the door, princess?" My voice softens as I reach for her face and lift her chin up to me. I find her sad and defeated eyes. Softly, I pull her lips to mine. Dana's face crumbles a little more as her gaze finds the sheets.

"Katie, my dad's wife, is not my real mother. My dad left my mom when I was around five."

Dana rolls onto her back, staring up into the darkness. My hand starts gliding across her stomach, stopping at her hip and giving her a light squeeze.

"My mom was constantly angry at my dad, for him always being gone and partying. Who knows what else he was doing. About the time I turned eight, they were both constantly gone. I was left home alone to take care of myself."

She releases a sigh before continuing. "It wasn't all bad. I had Vegas and her parents. Jenn and I had each other in this fucked up mess. For a while, Fuego and Cindy took Jenn and I in as their own. Jenn and I had our room together at their house."

Through the moonlight, I can see a small smile creep across her face. "The three of us are sisters. Did everything together, her parents always took us with them on vacation. Even though Snake hated us being there."

Dana stops, her eyes tracking back and forth as her mind replays the memories.

"Princess, what happened next with your mom and old man?"

Taking a breath, she continues, "Eventually, when I was in middle school, Mom died of a drug overdose. My dad, right about that time, started seeing Katie. He had his shit together shortly after that because of Katie." Dana's muscles tense at her last statement. "They have a son together, Gabe, my little brother. He's in his teens now. He sees the stars when he looks at my dad. And Katie is an awesome mom."

"I take it that your dad didn't do shit for you for a lot of years?"

"No, he didn't stop doing what he was doing long enough to see how messed up Mom was, or my life in general. Papa was a real wild man. He would stop by every now and then. Take me out for a movie or something like that. Mom was real smart about covering her shit up, so he didn't see it. He was heavily involved in his club, and, as long as it appeared like his cash was keeping me safe and fed, he didn't have a reason to invest much more of himself. After she died, and he was forced to take me, only then did he see how fucked up I really was. Katie made sure of it, they almost split over it. He tried to make it better with me. He tried to right the wrongs. I was an angry teen though, and he had his work cut out for him. It was Katie I responded to the most. She got me to settle down after high school, God knows Vegas and Jenn didn't help."

Dana's laugh is lighting her mood. Her stomach is tightening under my arm with the movement.

Turning her toward me, a smile plays across my face. "A wild child in high school, huh?"

Her hand lands on my cheek. "Oh yeah, rock and roll fed my fucked-up soul."

"Don't believe you," I tell her, egging her on for more.

"I snuck around a lot. Lost my virginity at a Guns N' Roses concert."

"Shut the fuck up! Jesus, I wish I was there."

Dana rolls further into me, spooning with me, her back to my front. I hold on to her, wishing I was the man at that concert. Of all the concerts I went to, I wish that was the one.

My mind wanders off, thinking what it would have been like. What if we *had* met all those years ago.

That's my last thought before I drift off to sleep. Dreaming of my little pained rebel.

# CHAPTER 6

## Dana

This last week has gone by smoothly except for Jenn. I have been feeling worried with how recluse she's been.

"Jenn, you want a coke?" I call out over the dance floor to my girl. For some reason, her set is a little more tired and lagging tonight than usual. Not that we have a big crowd, thank God for that.

Jenn chuckles back in response as she reaches the bar. "Yeah, give me a coke, straight up. Hand to God, you love those things a bit too much," Jenn says while plopping her ass onto the bar stool in front of me and Kat.

"Jenn, you love these just as much as me, bitch," I tell her as I pull a classic glass coke bottle out of the fridge that's reserved for all special drinks. Popping the cap off, I slide the soda over to her.

"What's got you beat, girl? You aren't hitting the tracks as hard tonight?"

Jenn twists her bottle around on the bar top, staring down at it, then picks it up to take a long drink before answering. "Shit has just been hard. You know, in our early twenties it didn't matter all the things we had happening to us. We were too busy being young and taking in the new-found freedoms of the world. Now that all that has slowed down, it's almost as if the world has caught up with me, forcing me to look at it or deal with it."

She sighs and looks down again at the bottle that's resting in her right hand. "Someday, I will tell you all about what's going on up here," she says and taps her head, then her heart, "and in here. But for now, I just gotta let it be."

"Fair enough. You know that Vegas and I are right here when you are ready, and you never have to fight your demons alone, right?" Jenn nods back non-committedly, turning her head to look through the crowd, and finding James. Concern is deep into his eyes as they hold on to hers.

Turning back to me, she says, "James helps, he really does try so hard for me. I can't let him in until I get my shit figured out, Dana. This shit inside of me is a mess. It wouldn't be fair to him."

She stops and looks again for James, who is working and watching the floor. "He can't see how messed up it is in here." Jenn points to her head, then closes her eyes, taking in a deep breath to calm the rage and pain reaping havoc through her. "The music, though, it is getting me through it. I will get there, I hope I can."

I take a minute to digest her words. She has me a little shaken with her impromptu confession. Not wanting to spook her, I don't pry any further.

"You got this, sister. Do you have any new mixes you've worked on lately?"

"Yeah, I do. I've got a new set ready for the Santa Crawl Event coming up," Jenn finally smiles in response.

"Should be a good night then, with the tattoo shop next door, our business has doubled over night. You remember Emilia, the old owner who passed, his wife, she's going to start working with us too, especially on the weekends. We are crammed pack on the weekends."

"No shit, I'm happy to hear that she's doing better and coming out on top of it all. God, it's been what, about four years since he passed?"

"I think so. No one has asked her, but she did say they'd been together their whole lives. Real love stuff, she didn't want to be here without him. But I think we changed the bar so much that it gave her hope to start over, and still remembering the past isn't as hard for her anymore either."

Jenn finishes her coke, sliding the empty glass bottle over to me, then she turns to leave, throwing over her shoulder, "Good, us wounded girls should stick together."

An hour goes by and drinks are passed along with laughs, and smiles are traded across the room. I can see now why Vegas needed this bar to start over. She needed to be the chameleon in the crowd. Stealing smiles and happiness from strangers to initiate the healing. Surviving. Aren't we all looking for our paths? Our own road to happiness and healing?

Looking over across the bar, I see Kat laughing with Tank, only to keep him at arm's length later.

Spider is sitting alone, as usual, evaluating the crowd, or is he appearing busy to keep others at bay?

Solo and Pawn are sitting together in a comfortable silence at another table, watching Tami clean tables and glaring back at the other boys as they watch her sway with the movement. That show has my heart melting a little bit more every day. When will either one of them go for her? Go for the woman they want?

"After Jenn had her bathroom break, her songs and mood picked up. Thank God, she was putting me to sleep," Kat says, getting me out of my thoughts.

"Something snapped her out of her funk," I agree.

James flags me over to the side of the bar. "What's up, dude?"

"Kat is right about Jenn snapping quickly out of her funk."

"What do you mean?" What are they seeing that I'm missing? Jenn's always had highs and lows.

"I don't know for sure what is going on. It's more than her normal hot and cold that she usually has. Her emotions are getting more extreme and unpredictable," James tries to keep his voice low as he's telling me all this.

"You keepin' tabs on her?" Snake asks out of nowhere.

James and I jump at the sound of his voice and turn around to look at him behind us. I laugh at his abrupt appearance, holding a hand over my chest and willing my heart rate to slow down. Snake smiles back at me, looking a little too interested in my hand. He's got a smirk on his face, and I tilt my head in reaction, trying to gauge were his sudden interest is coming from.

"Fuck, Snake, why do you always do that creepy shadow shit around people?" James asks, clearly annoyed with him.

"Not my fucking problem you were too busy girl chatting with Dana to hear me walk up behind you," Snake says with a dumb ass tone back to James. "What's going on with Jenn?"

"I was just telling Dana that Jenn is more out of her norm than usual. Not her normal attitude toward everything. And yeah, I've been watching her for a long time. Since she got back from California from her visit a year ago, she's been getting gradually worse."

"So, what are you doing about it? You want me to get Cu- Fuego on it?" Snake stutters a bit, concerned and annoyed that we haven't mentioned it sooner.

"Snake, you want me to call up every time these girls act up? That would be weekly, sometimes daily updates, asshole. Call Fuego if you want, but I got it handled," James states and moves back out to his spot on the floor.

"Snake, why are you so hard on James for?" I say while passing him a cold beer from the tap.

"It's not James I have a hard on for, Dana," Snakes says, lowering his voice and stepping in closer to me. He takes his glass and brings it to his lips to take a long drink.

I can't help staring at his throat as it moves while he chugs half the glass in one go. The man is fine, and, once upon a time, in my own personal fairytale, he was the knight in shiny armor. But not anymore.

"I'm not playing around with you, Snake."

"That may be true for now, but there was a time when you liked playing around." He leans in over my heated body to my ear. "Remember who your first kiss was," he whispers, and I see his eyes going to my lips. Then, they go back up to my own, giving me a determined look.

"And I know that you haven't ridden on the back of his bike *or* worn his patch."

# Axl

"Is Tank ready for this?" I question Blade.

"You better never ask that anywhere close to Tank, brother," Blade warns me.

The crowd grows louder and louder as Tank jumps up over the top rope of the ring.

"Tony has this place packed. That fucker is making some serious cash running this joint," I say while looking around to check it all out again.

Girls scream for Tank as he makes a show of taking his shirt off, whipping it out into the crowd of eager women.

"Fucking show off, he better have his head in the game. The guy he's going against has a legit good record."

"Wouldn't worry about his record, shit doesn't matter. Tank's been undefeated since we've known him," Spider says as he's looking over the crowd and spotting Tony. "Looks like Tony is here to keep tabs on us. What is this fight paying out?"

"Twenty thousand if he wins, thirty-five thousand if he knocks him out," Blade answers, then nods over to the cashier cage where Snake hands over a fistful of cash. He's not wearing his cut as he's placing a bet on us to earn the club some side cash. Tony won't see us taking from him.

"Tony never said we couldn't bet on ourselves, but we'll keep it our secret for as long as we can," Blade continues and we watch Snake take his ticket, then moving to the back of the room alone as if he doesn't know us.

As the other boxer takes the ring, one of the ring girls starts signaling the beginning of round one. She's a pretty, blond girl with fake, hard looking, large tits that are not moving when she walks around topless in her string bikini bottom and stripper heels. None of us look over at Barbie like she's intended us to. Fake huge tits are not my kink, neither is the plastic Barbie lookalike.

The house MC declares over the speakers, "As you know, these matches are not scored. It's last man standing or knocked out. The longer the match goes, the less the fighters are paid," he chuckles as the crowd roars in approval. "At the sound of the bell, round one will start. Each round lasts three minutes."

Tank and the other man are in a standoff, sizing each other up. They're almost equally built, but Tank's muscle mass is outweighing the other guy, and he's also few inches taller.

As they start circling each other, the bell rings and Tank's opponent bounces forward on his feet, already throwing out a few jabs. He's testing Tank's agility and speed. Tank plays his reaction slower than it actually is, allowing his opponent to land a few indirect hits. He then steps back and bounces on his feet, still assessing the other guy.

The boxer grows impatient, circling Tank, then moves in to throw a few body shots to his ribs, nailing him in his lower back, straight in his kidney.

"Fucker felt that, his body clenched up with that hit," I mutter to myself.

Blade just stares ahead, ignoring my comment, waiting for Tank to get to business. Tank sharply turns, facing the throws, then directs a jab with his left fist, and the guy's head snaps back. He keeps his hands up as Tank steps forward leading with his right fist.

They tap gloves couple of times after which Tank jabs his left then right fist, followed by a quick upper cut. The boxer stumbles back and bounces off the ropes. Finding his balance again, he comes back at Tank, jabbing left and right until he finally lands a good hit on Tank's chin.

"Fuck!" Blade roars with the crowd. "Time to get to work, Tank!"

Tank licks the blood from his lip and smiles toward the other man. Rolling his shoulders up and forward, he makes himself look bigger. He holds them higher in anticipation as the guy struts around the ring a little cocky.

The fighter then comes at Tank, with a left, then a right. Tank bobs with each hit. When the fighter steps into him with his left foot, Tank takes advantage of his body opening and delivers a blow to his gut. The boxer heaves forward. Tank slams his fist on top of his head and he falls to the ground with Tank on top of him.

The fighter tries to recover as Tank delivers blow after blow to his back and head. He rolls over onto his back to cover his face. Tank knees him in the ribs as the fighter's hands come down at his sides. Tank punishes the man's face with another punch.

The boxer tries to recover and get Tank in an arm lock by wrapping Tank's arms in his and using his legs to strengthen his hold, but Tank's massive frame picks the whole man up and off the floor, body slamming him back onto the ground.

The fighter's hands fall to his sides going limp. Tank grabs the man by the hair and busts his face open with blow after blow. Blood splatters Tank's face and pours from the man's nose and mouth before the bell is rung and Tank is declared the winner.

The MC steps in and holds Tank's arm up. "And the winner by knockout and defeating the previously un-defeated champion... Tank!"

Solo jumps up into the ring to hand Tank a towel as the crowd whistles in agreement. Tank cleans up before throwing his cut back on and jumping down from the ring with Solo in tow. Following our Prez, we make our way to Tank through the crowd.

As soon as we meet Tank on the floor, a few of Tony's guards signal us over to Tony, then lead us down a long hallway. The guards stop in front of a door where he knocks one time. It opens, and we walk in to meet up with Tony in a smaller room off to the side of the fighters' locker rooms, in this old warehouse where the underground matches are being held.

The lights are dim, and we spot only a small desk and chairs. Tony pulls out a marker book which he lays out on the table. He opens it to a page that's marked with our club name, deal details and amounts.

Blade, Spider, Tank, Solo and I stand at our Prez's back as he reads over the page. "And you want me to do what? Sign off on today's fight?"

Tony appraises Blade before answering. "Yes, I want a confirmation on the amount we agreed upon for each fight before you leave each match."

"I'm not signing my name for shit. You can take my word for it or not. Spider will keep track of our balance. We paid up our thirty-five thousand for today. Send Spider only a list of dates and times and when we need to be there. That will get this debt paid off and we never have to talk."

Blade rips the page from the book and hands it to me. He then forcefully pushes the book back across the desk.

"Never the businessman, Blade. Ever heard of making friends? We could make money working

together, but you continue to make that part difficult."
Tony's face has gone dark, in complete contradiction
with his taunting statement.

"Fuck your 'let's get along bullshit.' I've got shit to
do, just send Spider the information," Blade barks
back.

Glaring at each other over the desk, we back out of
the room mindful of Tony and his guards. We carefully
keep tabs on everyone as we make our way out. Most
people are focused on the current match as two other
guys go blow for blow.

As soon as we make it to the bikes, I ask, "Why the
hell is Tony writing this shit down for, Blade? If he
gets raided, he takes us all down with him, or he'll try
to use that information against us later."

"I agree, Axl, he has an ulterior motive, other than
just the club paying him back. That dirty cocksucker is
up to something. Even though we cleaned up Johnny's
mess, our asses still have to pay for what the old Prez
did before."

"Aye, Prez," I pat him on the back. "How about we
put the prospects on him, and we get you to Tahoe and
to your Ol' Lady?"

# CHAPTER 7

## Dana

I see Vegas in the mirror getting ready for her wedding night. She's ratting her dark hair to create a high bump on the back of her head.

The girls, Kat, Jen and Tami and I, we all couldn't wait for this day. Blade gave us a fistful of cash a week back to buy what we all needed to surprise her tonight.

We are a wedding party made of wet dreams, not necessarily the picture of happily ever after. Every one of us is in a pair of black leather pants, boots and black silk blouses, except for Vegas who is killing it in a miniskirt.

My phone vibrates on the bed and I pick it up to see missed calls and texts that came in from Axl. To the side, I hear Jenn humming low in appreciation, "This is definitely Vegas. Blade does you good, girl."

**Roger Rabbit: Answer your damn phone, woman!**

Then another two...

**Roger Rabbit: Get your asses down here, Blade is being an asshole.**
**Roger Rabbit: I'm giving you five more minutes, then I'm dragging Vegas down here. I don't give a fuck!**

Smiling at my phone, I text back to Axl, **Easy, tiger, we are headed down now.**

It's a total lie. I know it's bad, but it will buy me fifteen more minutes before he sends another text. Chuckling to myself, I walk over to Vegas as she steps into her tall black boots. Jenn steps in front of me, knocking me a bit off balance in the process. Damn, what the hell was that? My phone buzzes again with a notice.

**Roger Rabbit: Right the fuck now, not in 15**
**Roger Rabbit: I'm serious, woman. RIGHT. FUCKIN. NOW.**

Shoving my phone in my back pocket, I clap my hands together to grab these girls' attention.

"Let's get moving, Axl already texted me five times in the last twenty minutes. Blade wants you in the chapel. Now!" I smile at my best friend and let her lead the way out the door and through the casino.

Getting to the entrance of the chapel doors, I see Axl standing at the end of the aisle next to Blade.

Looking left, he finds me staring. He looks so hot in his cut, with black jeans and boots. We follow Vegas and her dad, Fuego, down the aisle as we stand off to her right side and the officiator starts talking. I catch a few words along the way as Axl won't let my eyes go. My heart flutters in my chest from his intense stare.

"Will you take William Johnson to be your lawfully wedded husband in all things, until death do you part?" The officiator asks Vegas and she responds, "I do," barely containing her happiness.

A tear threatens to leave the corner of my eyes. The emotions from Vegas, her happiness, and the intensity from Axl are all overwhelming me. Blinking back the traitorous bastards, I look back over to Blade and Vegas.

"Will you take Alessia DeRosa to be your lawfully wedded wife in all things, until death do you part?" The officiator asks Blade.

"I do, for this life and the next," Blade says.

The pull coming from Axl has me looking back toward him again. It seems all too soon to feel this connection between us, but it's also right at the same time.

"You may now kiss the bride."

And it's done. Blade takes Vegas' face in a forceful, passionate kiss, then he quickly leads them out of the little casino wedding chapel, whistles and hollering erupting as they disappear behind the doors.

A strong hand grabs mine, the gentle feel of calloused skin so familiar as I turn into Axl. Wrapping his strong arms around me, he pulls my body close and whispers in my ear, "You look beautiful in black. Leather is hot as fuck on you."

Taking a deep breath, I wrap my own hands around him and run them over his back. "Yeah? I think you're pretty damn sexy in black too."

Axl leans forward nipping at my lips a few times. "Come on, princess, party is moving into the bar."

For most of the night, Axl and I spend time laughing and talking with everyone as an Ed Sheeran song comes on. Every brother runs off the floor like the plague hit it.

Axl grabs my hand while laughing at the mass exiting scene we just witnessed. Bodies rush past us as he leads me down toward the dance floor. He spins me around when *Perfect Duet* starts playing. Grabbing me as I twirl for about the fifth time, his solid chest hits mine. His hands grip my hips and we sway side to side.

He nips at my neck, then starts kissing his way up to my ear. He pulls my body tight against his. We sway together, and I rest my head and hands against his chest. He sings along while holding me close. His warm, soft lips whisper to me and speak to my heart. It's my turn to laugh as he grabs a handful of my ass giving it a tight squeeze.

I say to him, "I was just about to say how sweet you are."

A rumble of laughter vibrates from his chest and I feel it under my hands. Dancing like in another world, we hold on to each other and a little more hope blooms inside of me. That Axl will stick around, stick around with me even when the world crashes around us.

I close my eyes tightly and feel the tears pricking at my eyes as I think of all I've lost. My mom to drugs, men who left when life got real, my dad when I was little.

Gripping Axl's shirt in my fists, a tear finally falls. Axl's hands lightly grip mine to loosen their hold on him. He holds them together with one hand as his other one touches my chin, seeing a tear streak down my cheek. He kisses my pain away. He pulls me closer, holding me to his chest as another one falls.

When the song ends, he pulls my face toward his and his soft lips take mine in a sensual, slow kiss. Giving me promises with his heart through his kisses.

For the second time tonight, another round of whistles and catcalls come from our crowd of onlookers. They drag us out of the magical world we put ourselves in.

Jenn catches my eye as we walk back to the table we were sitting at. She and Solo have a quiet disagreement in a corner. Jenn's hands go up in the air exasperated. Solo shakes his head, turning and walking away from her. Jenn's eyes follow Solo as he walks away and find mine watching her. She rolls her eyes as if it was nothing.

Walking over to me, she says, "He just wanted to hook up, crazy, right?" She says it looking away from me.

"Uh huh, yeah, that's crazy," I answer back, not really believing what she's saying. Even though I know Solo isn't celibate, I know that if he were to go after anyone, I would bet on that girl being Tami. "Are you sure, though? What else did he say?" I question her.

"Does it really matter, Dana? Why don't you believe me?" she barks back at me.

"Just asking. I can't imagine Solo doing that and it surprises me, is all. Why can't I ask?" My voice is rising higher with irritation at her snappy response.

"Girls?" James says as he wraps an arm around Jenn's shoulders and passes her a beer. Just then, I feel Axl slide up behind me and his hand goes to rest on my stomach.

"Sorry, just a long day, you know," Jenn says looking across the floor instead of at me as she says it.

"It's fine." I say it, but I'm feeling at a loss for words right now. Jenn's been different, and I just don't know how to reach her. What the hell is going on?

Allowing a few moments to pass, I watch Jenn move to a table alone, on the opposite side of the bar. I give Axl a kiss on the cheek then follow her, taking a seat next to her with my coke in hand.

Jenn notices my glass and asks, "What, they didn't have a coke in a glass bottle here for you?" she mocks my choice of drink.

"You would think they would, right? What kind of a bar is this? Everyone needs a coke in a glass bottle. We serve beer in glass bottles, right?" I joke back.

"Fuck yeah, we do, there should be that option, totally agree," Jenn says with as much enthusiasm as possible, then looks away from me. She holds on to her cranberry vodka, wiping away the condensation off the glass.

"Jenn, you know that all this shit will work out, right? Whatever it is that has your mind tied up, we can help when you're ready for us to, babe." My shoulder bumps hers.

Jenn looks over to me, unshed tears making her eyes look glassy. "I know you can. My heart hurts so bad. The hollowness there is drowning me." She breathes in and smiles back at me, blinking back the hurt along with the pain.

"I'm holding it in, Dana. If I let go right now, I won't come back as me, as the woman who I know myself to be. I'll know when. I'm holding this together until then. You'll see, I promise."

"I don't doubt you at all. I just want you to know that I'm here, is all. I'll always be here. Even when I wanna punch you."

"What kinda punch are we talking about here?" Jenn raises a scrutinizing eyebrow at me. "Face, stomach, tit, crotch, knee?" she questions.

"Hmmm," I laugh rubbing my chin. This running line has never changed from when we were kids. Where you got punched was how mad we were at the other one. "Stomach, I'm never punching your tit, and definitely not your crotch!" My eyes bug out and I frown at that thought.

"Shut up, stupid. We never did punch each other in the crotch, but the threat was real."

"So real! Hey, no one's been tit punched since sixth grade. I dare you to tit punch Vegas when she pisses you off."

Jenn's eyes open up at the idea. "If I do it, you have to close late for me two times, on call, when I say."

"Deal."

Sorry, Vegas, it's what had to be done for the sisterhood. At least I got my other best friend back, if only for just the night.

# CHAPTER 8

## Axl

"What the fuck is this shit!" I bellow from the garage into the club house. "Solo, Pawn, go grab the brothers, we have some shit to go over. Church! Now!"

Tank, that silly bastard, winks at me as I shake my head at him. "What?"

"You remind me of Kat when you're all squirrely. It's cute," Tank says walking in front of me.

Cute? Fuck that. Balling up my fist, I nail that cocky asshole in his kidney where I know he has a bruise from last night and will hurt like a bitch.

"Motherfucker!" Tank falls to the ground as his knees buckle under him and he lands on them. "Fuckin' dick move, brother," he says, heaving between painful breaths.

Laughing at him, I say, "If you weren't pissing blood before, you are now, *cutie*." I wink and step around him, coming face to face with Blade. He looks amused at Tank on the floor, shaking his head and moving into Church.

Since Vegas and Blade have been away and just got back, we have to update our Prez on business. All the brothers begin filing into the room.

Solo and Pawn begin to walk back behind the bar and I yell out to them, "Oh, no, you two fuckers are the whole reason we have to be in here. Get in here." Their surprised faces find mine and a worried look of what they could be in trouble for crosses their eyes.

Taking my seat next to Blade, he hits the gavel against the table and looks right at them. "What have you two been up to since I've been gone?" Blade questions in a cool tone.

Pawn speaks up first. "Nothing, Prez, that we weren't asked to do. Did our runs south, ran the bar and serviced the bikes," he finishes, sounding confused.

"And you, Solo?"

Solo swallows. "The same as what Pawn just said, and followed Tony like you asked. That was all right?" he questions with a hint of uncertainty.

"I don't know, Solo. Axl," Blade stops to look over at me," Is that *all* we needed for the prospects to do?"

"Yeah, that was all they needed to do. But now we have a problem," I let out a long breath. "Since you two shitheads were following Tony around, we came across something interesting. Tony's been meeting up with our club slut, CC."

"Yeah, I told you that," Solo defends.

"Yep, yep, you did. Now you need to go pick her up and take her to the mine. The bitch has got to die. She sold us out to Tony and you two are gonna torture the info from her. It's your job, we'll meet you both up there in two hours. Don't start, and don't say shit till we get there. MOVE."

Solo and Pawn quickly move to their feet and out the door, slamming it shut hard behind them. Spider cracks a smile. I'm not even going to ask what that crazy fucker is smiling about.

"Dramatic. I liked how you two rolled with it. Are we doing a patch-in party tonight since we have all the clubs here still from the wedding?" Tank comments while taking a big bite out of a red apple. The crunch followed the chew noise and the juice dripping from his chin has us all staring at his dumb ass. Tank picks up his feet, tilting his chair back.

We stare in some sort of fascination at his easygoing, goofy side, but bruises paint his face from the vicious beating he delivered last night.

"Put your boots down for fuck's sake, Tank!" Blade roars. "You act like a fucking teen still. Shit! Anyway, let's take a vote. All those in favor of patching in Solo, after he takes care of CC, and Pawn, after he does a round in Tony's ring later tonight, say aye. If they both hold their own, we'll patch them in tonight?"

A resounding "Aye" is heard from around the room. It's gonna be a long night, but the idea has a smile stretched across all our killer faces.

The entire club walks into the old mine that's way out in the dusty sagebrush filled hills of Nevada. The smell of sage is still strong even this time of year and this far out.

Solo has CC gagged and tied to a chair in the middle of the room. The look of fear in her scared eyes has the wolf lying deep and engrained in us all eager to spill her blood.

Circling around her, one by one we fill the room. There is no hope for this woman to come out of this alive. This pack of killers will be sending her off to hell. Never play with thieves or killers. A lesson these bitches never learn.

Taking my spot next to my Prez, I look around the room taking in inventory. Fuego, the California Prez, Ice the Prez from Elko and, lastly, Stryker. We called them down for the patch-in party later tonight, and they decided to join us for this pre-party activity as well. The timing could not have been better. This girl is truly fucked. There is no way she will leave here without the blood drained from her shaking body. Blade nods at Solo to get to it.

Solo rips the handkerchief gag from her mouth, whipping her head forward with the force of it. Her brown hair is a ratty mess and black makeup runs down her face. Smeared red lipstick coats her face. Her body's shaking from fear.

"Where did you find her at?" Blade questions Solo. His death stare stays locked on CC.

"She was down at the whorehouse, cutting deals with the druggies down there. Paying for their smack to get a hit before they fucked the prostitutes. Those who can't pay, guess who was taking little kids over to Tony to be sold? This crazy ass cunt right here." Solo backhands her across the cheek. Her head whips back with the force. She wilts as far forward as she can, allowing the sobs to wrack her body.

"I grabbed her in the middle of her drug deal, told her I wouldn't tell any of you as long as she gave me head and let me fuck her ass. Bitch was easy. One last ride for the road," Solo smirks when saying that and the men howl with laughter like the wolves we really are.

Blade nods in agreement for him to continue. Solo grabs CC by the hair at the back of her head, snapping her head back. "Got a couple of questions for you, cunt. Where did you get the blow and pills to deal?"

CC shivers and struggles to swallow before she answers, "T-Tony has a supply. He would give me bonuses in supply if I delivered kids."

This time, Solo's face heats up with frustration, and he takes a knife from his boot to cut the zip ties that are holding her arms secured to the chair.

"Undress," he says to her, then watches as she slowly starts peeling the clothes off her body. "Now!"

He barks when she's not moving fast enough, raising his leg to kick her back into the chair.

Quickly, she raises to her feet, shoving and throwing clothes from her body. Once she's bare, Solo walks behind her, grabbing and holding both her arms behind her back. "Lie to me again, bitch." He raises the knife to her chest and starts slicing through her pale skin, drawing crimson lines from her chest down to her navel. Her screams and pleas pierce our ears as blood starts running down her legs.

She pants a breath and shakily says, "I stole it from the club, skimming it off brothers after we would fuck."

"And?" he prompts.

More tears fall as she confesses more, "I told Johnny that Vegas was fucking Blade." She closes her eyes as she waits for it.

Like a ghost, the reaper himself, Blade, is in front of her, knife in hand. He plunges the blade deep into the inside of her leg, cutting from knee to her cunt. He shreds her flesh on one leg, then moves to the other as Solo holds her steady up. Blade loses control to his task, stabbing her stomach and twisting the blade before pulling it back out.

Finally, ready to finish the job, to deliver the last fatal blow, he brutally stabs her in the neck, all the way up through her skull.

It all stops. Everyone is silent as her body hits the floor. "Fuck!" he yells out with his labored breaths breaking the silence.

"*Mijo*," Fuego calls out, trying to stop his manic rage.

Blade throws his knife through the brothers, at the far-right wall. Saying nothing, he continues breathing hard before he storms out. Tires peel out, kicking up sand and rock as Blade leaves.

"What the fuck was that about?" Tank asks.

Stryker's dark eyes look around at all the men standing in the room. "That cunt killed the baby Vegas didn't know that she was carrying. She took that from him. Any of you speak of this again, utter a word of it and I will kill you."

# CHAPTER 9

## Dana

Walking into the office, I see that Vegas is passed out again on top of her desk. I nudge her with one hand and set the coffee under her nose. She perks up with eyes snapping open eagerly, taking the coffee from me.

"Hell yeah, you want to be sister wives? I'll work, and you just take care of me," she batts her eyes my way.

"No, that would make me your bitch," I state flatly.

She smiles around another sip. "I thought you were though, huh? Weird," she laughs.

"Bitch," I squint my eyes at her. "Seriously, though, Vegas, you got to cut back the hours you work. You put too much pressure on yourself. You are going to have a psychotic break one of these days."

"I know, but when do I have the time? I still need income until the brewery is up and running..."

Before she can finish what she was going to say, Blade is barging in through the office doors. Vegas stands as his full attention is on her, storming in her direction. His arms wrap around her petite body, holding on to her and not letting go.

Shutting the door on my way out, I walk over to Jenn at the DJ desk. "Hey, Jenn, I'm guessing it's going to be a hell of a night. Blade just consumed Vegas in the office, so I'm assuming the guys aren't too far behind him."

"Gotcha, boss lady, I got a new track ready for those assholes," she says as she holds her hand up, signaling me to wait a minute. When she steps closer to me in the dimmed light, the dark circles under her eyes are more apparent, but I don't say anything, not wanting to upset her.

"I'm going to head out and grab some food before they get here. You want anything?" She asks while avoiding looking me straight in the eyes.

"A salad or a burger, whatever. As long as it's food, I'll eat it," I reply.

"Kat," Jenn hollers over to the bar. "Food?" is all she asks.

"Whatever you're getting is good with me," Kat yells back.

Thirty minutes later, Jenn runs in, handing us chicken burgers just as we hear the bikes roar up the road. We begin to scarf down huge bites before the night gets caught up around the crazy ass Battle Born parties.

We hear the Suburban pull up and several doors slam shut. All three of us swallow our food down as we lean in sync together to peek out the window, holding our sandwiches midair.

"Patch-in," is all we say in unison as strippers and sluts bail out of the two SUV's carrying all the chicks.

Snapping into action, I take another bite, saying around a mouthful, "Eat, hurry." We keep scarfing down our burgers, and, right on the last bite, the doors open wide and the brothers flood in.

Jenn runs over to her DJ table, finishing her food on the way, then placing her headphones on, ready to start her new mix. Kat and I hurry to take our spot behind the bar.

The girls saunter up and start ordering margaritas. And thank God they do since we have our machine ready to go. Emilia starts her checking on tables and taking orders. These guys mostly want beer or whiskey, easy enough. Tami keeps the glasses clean in the back and stocks the bar with ice and more beer. Vegas is behind the counter helping to push the orders out.

A good hour goes by before we hear more bikes pulling up, and I moan at the thought of how many more people we can cram in here before the fire department shuts us down.

The bikes shut off and Blade whistles loudly to grab everyone's attention. The front door creaks open and the bar is deadly quiet. Solo walks in with a limping

Pawn. Collective gasps sound in the air at Pawn's swollen and bruised up face.

Axl walks in behind them, with Tank and Spider in tow. Axl belts out to the crowd, "You should see the other guy!" The crowd chuckles as he continues, "This pissant fucker gave it back to that asshole twice as hard." Axl slaps Pawn's back, causing the younger guy to wince in pain.

Blade stands up, directing the attention to himself. "Solo, Pawn, bring your scrawny asses over here."

As they walk toward Blade's table, which is closest to the bar, he continues, "You two, over the past year and some change, have proven yourselves and your dedication to the Battle Born brothers. This," Blade points around the room, "Is your patch-in party. Don't be stupid," Blade finishes and sits back down while Pawn and Solo fist bump the air with a "Fuck yeah" from both. They then turn and begin to give each other manly back slaps and fist bumps.

All the guys cheer for the new members when Axl hands them their new patches and cuts off the prospect ones from their cuts.

Tami comes running over with ice for Pawn and pulls up a chair for him. The brothers laugh at her worry and the care that she shows for him. Her face blanches, feeling embarrassed, and she turns around to walk back behind the bar.

Kat turns from handing a beer over the counter and glares daggers at the men. Abruptly, they all get quiet.

Tank starts laughing, "My little kitten has sharp claws, don't ya, Kitty Kat?" he purrs at her. Kat rolls her eyes in response, but winks at him when no one's looking.

Warm hands slide up my sides, following their course and cupping my tits from behind. I jump and yelp from the quick progression, turning around to a cocky faced bastard who smacks a big kiss on my lips and those hands lower to find my ass cheeks.

Giggling with our lips still stuck together, I pull back just a bit to ask, "Did you have a good day or what?"

"The best, princess, but this is even better," Axl says before his lips touch mine. Soon, his lips devour mine intently as they take them in a sweep of passion. His hands crawl up under my shirt. His fingertips graze my skin, and goose bumps pop up all over.

Axl turns us around and leads us back into the office, our lips never leaving each other's, then closes the door shut. Slamming my back against the door, he continues his aggressive pursuit by pulling my shirt off and grabbing my tits, then goes for my pants. He undoes the belt, slides the zipper down, then pushes them off and tosses them aside along with my thong, where they all land next to my shirt.

He growls and tugs me from the door, then tosses me on my back onto the desk. His strong hands grab my knees, lifting them high and wide, almost painfully so. My gasp has him looking from my pussy to my face. His eyes dilate while looking into mine. A small smile plays at his sexy full lips. Stepping a little closer, his fingers dive into me. My back arches at the sudden aggressive intrusion.

He pumps his fingers in and out of my pussy which is coating him with my need for him. His other hand runs up to my tits. His hold grips one of them hard, causing me to wince. He pulls his hand back, and my eyes pop open at the loss of it. Right before a pop and sting come from where he smacked one tit, then the other. I arch my back, craving more from him.

He bends forward, still pumping his fingers in and out of me while his mouth latches onto one nipple, then the other. Squirming on the desk, I pant for breath. I feel my climax almost there, but need a little push.

He tugs at my tightened nipples with his teeth, then lavishes them with his tongue as it flicks across them.

"More," I beg. "Please, Axl, more."

"How, princess? Tell me, what do you need?"

"I need your tongue to lick my pussy, Axl, God, I need your tongue."

"I love your smooth pussy, you keep this bare for me," he requests. "It's so fucking hot."

He kneels in front of me and runs his nose along my pussy right before flattening his tongue and taking a long lick of my lips. He licks over my clit, giving me the attention my mind and body need. Goose bumps spread across my skin. He licks at a fast pace while pumping his fingers in and out of me until my pussy contracts from an intense orgasm.

Panting for air, I start to come back down to earth. Axl continues softly licking, sticking his tongue inside and humming his approval before licking again. Taking all of me with him. He kisses right above my clit, leaving deep satisfaction within my heart.

Standing up, he pulls his pants down to his knees and frees his dick. Pushing my knees up to my chest, he pushes forward into me, crushing me with his weight. I squirm under him, trying to find relief from it. A hand comes down and smacks the side of my ass hard.

"Don't fucking move," he growls again. His fingers, like claws, grip my flesh at my knees, and I still on command. He rears back before ruthlessly plunging back in. I try keeping up with his relentless pace until my body finally catches up with his.

"Princess, make that pussy come for my cock, baby, coat me with you," Axl demands from me. Leaning forward, he changes the angle slightly and I come. I come long and hard for him. He lets my knees go, and his hands grip my waist as he slows down, devouring every last second of his release, moving with me.

After a couple of minutes of heavy breathing, he pulls out, takes my hand, lifts me to sit up on the desk, then tucks and zips himself back up. He helps me to the floor and back into my clothes.

We walk out of the office and that's when Tank starts to clap, then another clap is heard, and another, until the entire bar claps for our office sexcapade. Even Vegas, Jenn and Kat do it!

My face turns beet red as realization hits me that the entire room heard us. Including my mom and dad who are standing just a few feet away. Great.

My dad's arms are crossed over his chest with a very pissed off look on his face. My mom has her hand over her mouth, trying to stifle her laugh when my dad turns to glare at her instead.

I look over at Axl and see that he's not worried one bit as he smacks an 'I don't give a fuck your dad's here kiss' on my lips. I turn to head back behind the bar when Axl decides this is the best time to also smack my ass. That causes me to squeal and rub it, which, in turn, has the entire room erupt into whistles and more laughter.

"Asshole," I murmur to myself as I walk away from him, and from this moment too if I could.

Vegas leans over to me while pouring a beer from the tap into a frosty mug. "It's so hot, isn't it, when they are all worked up from work like that?"

My eyes bug out at her confession. "What?"

"Oh, yeah, you know, Blade and I were in there a while before, uhh, you, and he showed up a little worked up too, and uhh..."

"Okay, stop," I groan to myself. "Don't need to know the details."

Kat chimes in, "But when they go crazy, and they need and crave your body... Hottest sex ever."

Vegas and I stop and turn to look at her, all confused. Vegas just points to her and then Tank. Kat casually shrugs a shoulder, laughing at us as we look back and forth as if the answer will be in the air between them.

Axl walks over with his dad, Maddox, and his mother, Harley, who is freaking supermodel gorgeous. That's because she actually is, or rather was one, and still has the looks to show for it. She was a model for Harley Davidson for years while in her twenties. Axl looks a lot like his mother, with his golden skin tone, her dark hair, green eyes.

Even though I've known Maddox for years since he is the VP to Stryker in the Las Vegas chapter, it feels somehow different since things *are* different now. Will he and Harley see me differently as well?

Suddenly, my face feels hot all over again and the realization dawns on me that they must've been here a little while ago when Axl had his way with me.

Oh God, this was the worst night for a girl to have office sex.

Trying to make eye contact, I smile weakly, since my damn face refuses to fake it for me right now.

Axl's hand grips my own, tugging me into his side, then his arm wraps around my waist.

"Hello, Maddox, Harley, it's so good to see you guys up here," I say, needing to fill with words the awkwardness I'm feeling.

Maddox chuckles, "Honey, why are you so nervous?" Amusement lights his eyes with his question.

"Maddox, you need to teach your son some manners before Ghost, Dana's dad, the other VP, beats it into your son. Of course she's feeling a little nervous," Harley shakes her head incredulously at her husband.

Turning her gaze back to me, she continues, "Honey, this man," she pats her son's shoulder, "is just as bad, if not worse than his dad. Maddox also doesn't seem to think anything he ever does is wrong, only entertaining. I swear, since he was a little boy, they've always been more friends than anything else. Tomorrow they have the hill climb race in Lake Tahoe. That's what we drove up here for, for these two to race their snowmobiles."

Maddox kisses his wife, effectively making her stop talking. She blushes and smiles into his eyes, looking like they hold onto each other's soul. Maddox tells her, "How can I not love him as much as his mother, she's my whole world. Given me the whole world through her love."

He pulls her tighter to him and gives her another hard kiss, then slaps her ass. "Besides, my son had to learn to be the best from me. So how can he be wrong? I taught him everything he knows."

Axl chuckles next me and that has me smile right along with him, until reality hits me. This infectious man will be this way forever. But is that so bad? No, no, I think I would love that kind of forever.

# CHAPTER 10

## Axl

The cold mountain wind in Lake Tahoe whips across my face as I crank the engine on. The hum under the snowmobile ignites the adrenaline pumping through my veins.

Hitting the gas, my old man, Maddox, or Mad Max when he races, and I pull up to the Start line. Revving the engine, we look between us and the other five racers. He gives me a nod, signaling that he's ready to go. My mom, Harley, eagerly waves at us from the stands.

Since I was a kid, my dad would race anything that had wheels and a motor, and, in this case, tracks. He and I would be at every racetrack he could find, racing side by side when we could get away from life and let go. Other than Blade, he's my best friend, the man I trust more than even myself.

Anxiously, I watch the lights up ahead signaling the start of the race. The red light blinks, then turns solid, yellow light, sit and wait, I tell myself. Green!

The sound of machines roar to life as the animal fighter and winner in all of us rushes for the leading spot. A white cloud of dusty snow blows behind us as the stands erupt into cheers for the men riding the powerful machines, competing to be the best.

Our focus is to make it to the top of the mountain first. First place is a few thousand and bragging rights. Pushing my limits, I tail Mad Max as we take a sharp turn around the trail, then again around a steep drop-off down the mountain. Phase one of our plan to win was to block the other riders at this pass. I tailed Mad Max, blocking the other riders from the trail. Mission accomplished.

Reaching the end of the trail, Mad Max and I gun it across the open stretch that leads to the bottom of the mountain. The rest of the race is slick from the sun that melted the snow the day before and iced over this morning. Not like the loose powder from in the shadows of the trees. Straightening our snowmobiles, we start the trek up the steep, slick mountain, dodging trees.

We weave back and forth as minimally as possible. We lean forward, lying almost flat on the narrow seat, our will to lead the way, along with the powerful engines, it all helps to push ourselves further up. The machines grow louder the higher we get from the stress we place on them to go farther, go faster. The beast is coming alive to devour the terrain underneath.

Mad Max veers right, taking on a tougher terrain that needs having an advanced set of skills to navigate through. Another racer follows him, tailing dangerously close. Staying on my course, I focus ahead of me, working on keeping the others behind me at bay.

Almost to the top, Mad Max and I are neck and neck, and I grin to myself that one of us will be taking the win. The racer behind him foolishly accelerates, causing him to lose control and hit the tail end of Mad Max. My heart hammers as I can't see what happens next, but powder flies and my instincts say this is all wrong.

I can't stop here. At this steep of an incline, I'll fall. I can't see what happened behind me either. I have to reach the top. I have to see that he made it too.

Pushing myself harder, I whip myself across the finish line, the momentum pushing me high into the air. The machine crashes to the ground, my hands hold on strong as my heart hammers erratically when my chest hits the handlebars, knocking the wind out of me.

Grabbing the breaks, I squeeze as hard as I can. Jumping off my snowmobile and whipping the helmet off, I hear sirens going off, and the other snowmobiles fly past me. I run through the pain in my chest in the direction of the staff that are running down the hill, and I'm trying not to fall down the mountain.

I see a man trapped underneath his snowmobile. Another machine is caught in the trees, and people are helping that rider stand.

Desperately looking around, I don't see my old man anywhere. Fear ices through my veins, and I pick up my pace to get to the scene ahead of me. An EMT has his radio out calling for a helicopter and some other codes that don't make any sense.

A larger group of men circle around and we all team up to push the machine up and over to the side. Mad Max lies there underneath, unmoving. My breath escapes my chest in a rush, and I can't seem to pull anymore air back in as tears prick at my eyes.

The EMT's attempt to remove Mad Max's helmet snaps me out of it. Kneeling in the snow, I rip off my gloves, looking to help. My mind is numb as I sit there.

My heart is as cold as the snow when I look into the face of the man who has always been my hero. My dad, my Mad Max, my Maddox, and, most of all, my best friend.

# CHAPTER 11

## Axl

Handing my motorcycle helmet to Mom for her to wear, I remain impassive, unfeeling, un-wanting. I didn't want this day, I sure as fuck didn't ask for any of this shit.

Harley jumps on behind me as a long procession of club members follow behind the black hearse that caries Maddox, VP of the Battle Born Brothers, the Las Vegas chapter. I rev the engine and take the lead with all the Club Presidents behind me, the VP's, Road Captains, Sergeants-in-Arms. We are all fuckin here. And not one of us can say shit.

My mom's hands tighten on my cut and I feel her head hitting my back. She can't even look at the road, her heart went to heaven with the man who owned it. My large hand holds onto one of hers all the way to the graveyard where the remains of our souls will be buried.

Since we got off the mountain, I haven't been able to talk. I haven't gone home, I haven't done anything. The pain is so severe that it threatens to kill me.

The look on my mom's face from that day will be permanently etched into my brain, along with his. As soon as I got to the hospital, we didn't even make it to the waiting room. Dead on arrival, the doctor explains in an empty patient room.

Those words. Those words stopped all things in this world that existed within me. I hear people talking to me after that moment. But I don't give a fuck what they have to say. Can you bring him back? No. Fuck off.

Parking my bike behind the hearse as it comes to a stop, my mom wails her pleas to God to take her. She can't move, just like I can't. We're stuck in this pain and in this moment.

We sit there, glued to one another when the man that drove the hearse opens the back. I want to fucking shoot him. Who told him that he could open the fucking car?

Heavy footsteps crunch in the gravel behind me. Soon, Blade stands to my right and grips my shoulder with his hand. I bow my head, looking for some sort of grace to save me. Tank stops at my left and peels Mom off my back as she's kicking and screaming. She starts pounding her small fists on Tank's chest. She begs for him to stop, to leave her alone. He tries to reason with her and console her through her pain as she pounds away at him.

It's all too fucking much, so I yell at her as loud as I can, "Enough, MA! Fucking enough!" Shock hits her at finally hearing my voice after days of silence, paralyzing her. The other Ol' Ladies run up to us to take her.

Looking back toward the hearse, I get off the bike and walk forward, one step after another. Somehow, I make it there. My hands grip the cold poles around the casket. I welcome the cold currently residing inside of me, wanting more of it. To numb me.

Blade, Tank, Stryker, Fuego and I carry Maddox down to his final resting place. The Nevada desert has always been his home and will be his final resting place.

Slowly placing his casket on the mount above the open grave, we step back. Circling around my old man, I hold my hand out for my mom. She barrels into me, and I hold on to her as she sobs.

Stryker starts talking, telling the club and families about the good times he and the man had. How they were some punk kids when they joined the club. My old man's love for Harley. How when they went to a Harley Davidson show, he saw my mother from a distance and stopped. Told the brothers he found his Ol' Lady. They, of course, all laughed at him, saying he couldn't land a pin-up model. Well, he did. One month later, she had his cut, tattoo and ring.

My mom can't even hear the words through her unrelenting crying as Stryker is reminiscing on the story of how she'd met her husband, friend and Ol'

Man. She holds on to me for strength while she gasps for air. Me? I don't even know what I am holding on to. Death, maybe.

Everyone who's anyone takes turns and tells of a memory in his honor. This is it, the end, as Stryker nudges his chin at me, his signal for 'it's time'. So, I say what's in my heart, or what is left of it.

"The best man in the world died. He was my dad, he was my best friend. A once in a lifetime kind of man. Not a fucking person on this earth could ever be him. He taught me to be a man, to be a brother in this club. Everything I do is because of this man. He gave me my first bike, my first beer, my first bud. This man taught me how to be in this world. Without him in it, I don't know what that life is."

I go back to my mom and gently rub her back as she takes a few breaths before she is ready to say her goodbye.

"Hey, baby," she cries, allowing her eyes to close as the tears keep rolling. "You promised me forever, me and you, and I know. God, I know you went unwillingly. Until the day we meet again, I'll keep an eye on Axl, our baby, from here. You watch him from Heaven. Love you forever, Maddox."

Taking a much needed deep breath in that rushes through her entire body, she looks up at the heavens, looking for the man himself. She puts two fingers to her lips, kisses them, then touches her heart and reaches them out to the sky. Reaching for him.

*Don't Cry* by Guns N' Roses blasts through the speakers in my room at my parents' house. No, my mom's house now, I think to myself as the same sharp pain slices through my heart. A room I haven't left in over three days.

Dana walks in and sits next to me. I don't move to acknowledge her. I want to, but the pain hurts and numbs it all. Numbs all the joy and love I had in life. She pisses me off by being here and sticking around for me.

She sees the fucked-up pain I'm in, and here she is to do what? Just give me some weed and go away. I want to piss her off too because it's only fair, right? I light a joint I had rolling between my fingers and take a big drag into my lungs, then blow it all into her face.

I want to fight, to feel something again. Here she sits, taking it. Staring into her eyes, I see the frustration there. I've been ignoring her for days. I can't take her sad pity face for me any longer. Somewhere in my head, my old man is calling me a fool, but I do it anyway. "What the fuck are you sitting around here for, Dana? Shouldn't you be in Reno?"

Her face screws up in pain as she finally lashes back at me, "Shouldn't *you* be in Reno?"

"Maddox died, Dana!" God, saying his name guts me. "What I don't get is why *you* are here."

"I came here for you, Harley, the club and Maddox. They all are my family too, Axl! All you've done is ignore me for days. Maybe I'm hurting here too. Maybe I need you too! You've been nothing but a selfish dick. Thinking only about yourself. What about me and Harley?"

"Does anything you just said even matter?" I lash out at her. "None of this shit is fucking about you. Are *you* really that selfish? None of this concerns you, what I'm going through, because you don't know what it feels like, so fuck off. Nothing lasts forever, Dana. Me and you, any of this shit, nothing lasts forever."

That was the last time I talked to Dana. My memory replays that moment like a nightmare I can't wake up from. Blade heard us fighting and came barreling into the room and saw the pain behind her eyes. He moved Vegas and her into a motel room right after that. That was over a week ago.

I haven't seen, texted or called her since. I'm not good for anyone anymore. Frustration booms through me and wakes a beast that's wrapped my heart up in darkness. These walls and the memories are too damn much.

Getting up from the bed, I begin ripping the posters down from the walls from all the Guns N' Roses concerts we went to over the years. I find a box full of random stuff, pictures, my first pipe and old patches. I toss the whole thing onto the floor, smashing anything that can be smashed with my heavy black boots.

Not feeling the beast lessen the hold on me, I pick up the lamp off my nightstand and throw it against the wall. I need more to fuel the satisfaction of the shattering sound.

I hear the door to my room banging against the wall as Blade barges in and grabs me by the arms. "Axl! Stop, brother! This is your mom's house."

The pain inside of me needs to be freed. I rip my arm from his grasp and punch him in the face. Blade takes the punch, then swings back hitting my nose. Blood spurts all over me. The pain is spurring me on, so I laugh and swing again, needing to hit him some more. Looking for my shot, I nail his side, then cheek. I finally start feeling like the rage is momentarily subsiding with the pain in my hands.

He grips my shirt with his fists and charges forward, slamming me against the wall, pushing his full weight and strength on me. It knocks the wind out of me. One of his hands steadies my body to hold me up. The other hand balls up into a fist and lands another two punches in my face. "Yes, kill me, make it all stop."

Blade stops his assault, bringing his face centimeters from mine. "You want to die? Do it on your own, you selfish prick! You're not the only one hurting!" He's breathing heavy in frustration now. "You have two days to get your shit and get to Reno. Your first fight is scheduled for Friday night. Get the fuck out of your mother's house, you disrespectful asshole." He shoves me forward toward the door, very effectively throwing me out of my own room.

My feet are following the way to the kitchen on instinct. I grab the keys to the Jeep and head for the garage. Mom grips my arm, halting my progress. I can't look at the pain and tears in her eyes as she says, "Come back to me, Axl," then lets go.

Gripping the keys harder, I charge for the door without looking back.

# CHAPTER 12

## Dana

Flipping on the CB radio that Axl had installed in my car, the noise from the static fills the despairing silence. Indecision eats at me as I've tried to reach him for days. My heart sinks when I think back to what Axl said. 'Nothing lasts forever.' The overwhelming doubt creeps into my heart. Maybe he didn't really care for me like I thought?

I push past the pain and hold the button down on the CB mic. "Roger Rabbit, what's your location? This is Jessica Rabbit, over and out." I wait a minute and nothing. Switching to another channel I try again and again to no avail.

Snake knocks onto the window startling me, and I jump in my seat. "For the love of God, Snake!" I screech at him and pull on the handle to open the door. Stretching out my legs, I stand next to a snickering Snake. "What are you doing in there, babe?"

"Trying to reach Axl. Blade said he took off into the desert alone in his dad's Jeep, and I wanted to catch him, and to check in on him," I say as my gaze hits the ground.

"Baby?" Snake's strong hand cradles my cheek as he tilts my face up to his. I can't look at him. I can't let him see what I let Axl do to me. Kissing my closed eyelids, he says, "Baby, let me see those blue eyes, let me see your pain."

My heart flutters after weeks of pain, and I do, I open my eyes into the familiar face of Snake. I yearn for a man's touch to heal the pain inside. I lean in a little closer to the warmth of his strength, treasuring his reliance.

His lips come down and place a kiss on my forehead, muttering, "Dana, you know that he should be with you. He should be here." Kissing me one last time on the forehead, he holds my hand and looks into my eyes.

The bar door slams open as Jenn runs into Spider's back. Holy shit, how long was he standing there listening? An evil gleam graces his face as he walks off the step and heads over to his bike, cranking the machine on.

Snake lets go of my hand and walks over to his bike without saying another word.

Jenn skips on over to the spot to where I'm standing. "Well, well, well, I'm glad I caught you before Spider caught you with your hand in the cookie jar. Or rather Snake's hand in your cookie jar." She smirks and grabs my hand, leading me to her 1982 black Shelby GT 500 mustang.

"Where are we going?" I ask while she pushes me in the direction of her car.

"Picking up Vegas and Kat at the brewhouse," she shrugs back.

Trying my best not to rip her head off, because my emotions have been on the brink of destruction lately, I take a deep breath and calmly ask, "And where are all four of us going, Jenn?"

"Taking you to watch the fight?"

Taking another deep breath, I relax into the leather seat as the big engine under the hood purrs to life, humming under our bodies.

"Jenn, I'm trying to keep my shit together. What fight? Give me the details, please."

"Vegas said there's a boxing fight that the guys fight in downtown to pay off a debt from Johnny, that motherfucker. Anyway, Vegas caught wind of it since the boss bitch keeps her ear to the ground with that shit. She texted me five minutes ago telling me to grab you and pick her and Kat up. Now you know everything."

On some days, I feel like between all these girls and the MC, everything changes so much that I can't keep up. Jenn pulls the car up to the front of the brewery, blasting her horn impatiently. I look over at her, wondering why that was necessary.

"What? I hate waiting," she shrugs.

Vegas walks out the door, Kat following closely behind. Both are decked out in black clothes and biker boots. I get out of the car and hop in the back with Kat.

"Jenn, you two gotta change and we gotta floor it," boss bitch demands. Jenn nods and turns up her track. *Hole* by Violet plays. Courtney Love screams through the speakers as Jenn peels out, tires screeching, rocks flipping in a dusty wave behind us.

Going around the front of the bar, we see a few brothers standing outside, smoking and shaking their heads at us as we head to a destination un-freaking-known.

The four of us, dressed to the nines all in black, walk into the hazy crowd of the underground bar and fight club. Kat whistles low, taking in the ambiance of the dark room filled with all different kinds of smoke. Each of us follows behind the other, fighting through the thick crowd. Vegas goes first since she is the one leading us on this little adventure, then Jenn, me, and Kat last.

Vegas stops, looking around for a spot to stand out of the way as a guy hands Jenn a joint. She takes it from him to take a long pull.

"Jenn, you drove us here."

"It's one hit, Dana," Jenn states, rolling her eyes at me.

I swear to God, if I could get away with smacking her right now, I so would.

Vegas finds a spot for us to see the action and she points at it while moving her feet, hauling ass, and we quickly follow behind.

Tucked away in a darker corner of the room, I take in all the people that surround us. Blonde girls, beautifully decked out in skin tight dresses, walk around. Men in expensive suits turn to look at us. Some in interest, others in disappointment, dawning on me that Vegas didn't want the high rollers to pay us more attention by thinking we were call girls.

Other rough looking men of all likes walk around us to go and stand in line to place bets. A topless woman in a string bikini bottom gets on stage with an announcer. The men holler for her as she smiles and holds up the card with the fight number, walking around the ring.

I blink in surprise and confusion. Kat leans into me, "They are three round fights, unless one of the fighters is knocked out or taps out. If they tap out, they never come back. They bet on the fight, hence the fight number."

My eyes pop at her confession. "Okay. How do you know this?"

Kat just smiles in reply, nodding her head in the direction of the ring.

My breath catches when I see a tormented soul walking toward the ring, shirtless and with his black jeans and boots on. The eyes of Axl are extinguished of the life they once had. His muscles flex as he jumps up and down into the ring. The ring girl slides up next to him, brushing her tits on Axl's arm as she whispers into his ear. He doesn't move away from her and I feel the tears prick my eyes. Kat squeezes my hand.

Vegas mutters, "I'm going to kick his motherfucking stupid ass myself."

The MC starts his introduction. "In this corner we have a new man to the ring, he's six foot..."

The world starts to fade away as my heart beats so hard in my chest until all I hear is the painful rhythm in my ears over the cheers of the fans.

The other fighter and Axl start circling each other. Axl gives his opponent a dead gaze until he jabs, hitting Axl square in his face and blood starts pouring down his nose. A malicious smile graces Axl's face now as he stands there with blood coating his teeth.

"Dumbass better stop fucking around," Jenn says in anticipation.

"It's fueling his psychotic mental state, he wants his blood to pour. Wait, the beast is going to claim him," Kat responds.

As predicted, Axl is hit again in the jaw with a right hook. He spits his blood out and roars, tilting his head back and howling to hell to come and take over him. The roar of the crowd entices him further and Axl charges the guy.

Fists and blood fly from each man. No mercy from the heavens in this room. The crowd cheers from the brutality and sickening sounds of fists hitting flesh. Blood splatters the white ring's floor. Axl lands an uppercut, sending the man flying backward to the ground. He jumps on top of him and grips his hair, then he slams his head into the floor, looking unsatisfied with just winning.

Axl stands and kicks the guy in the head, turning his body in our direction. Vomit is lodged into my throat as I see the man's cut up face from the brutal hits he was given. Blood coats his face and the swelling is so severe that he won't be able to open his eyes when he, hopefully, does wake up again.

"Hello, Vegas." A slick, good-looking Italian man walks up behind Vegas and leans into her. Vegas turns her head, not intimidated by this man at all. Does she know him?

"What's up, Tony? You changed the place up a bit I see. Good for you."

"What can I say? Business has been good." Tony licks his bottom lip, trying to hide the devil's smile that's lurking underneath.

"Yeah, that's what I hear," Vegas snarls back.

"Better run on home before your biker catches you with me," Tony chuckles and tugs on a strand of her brunette hair as he walks backwards. Finally, the asshole turns and gets lost in the crowd.

"Vegas, we need to move out of here," Kat urges. "If Blade catches us, he'll tan all of our hides."

"He knew the second we walked in." She turns and looks off toward the right deep end into the crowd where Blade and the crew stand.

"Why didn't you acknowledge him then?" I ask

"Because he would have sent us home and I wanted to see this for myself. We need to help Axl, these guys are letting him go too far off the rails."

My nerves are shot, and Vegas sees in my eyes that I'm about to explode. Tugging me through the crowd, she pulls us out to the car in the parking lot.

"Why the hell did you take me here for, Vegas? You think I needed to see that?" I yell at her and heave mouthfuls of the crisp night air into my burning lungs.

"Yeah, you do. Because you can't see the reality of what happened to him and how that has changed him. You think that he should just snap back to his old self, Dana. When life fucks you up so bad, it changes you. Changes your heart and mind. If you want him, *any* part of him, back, you're going to have to accept the part of him that is a monster too. Fight your own fears, Dana, and fight for all of Axl."

"You're always just doing shit whenever you want. Not really thinking of anyone else," I accuse.

"Yep, that's me, Dana, only thinking of myself. Wanting to show you the reality of who he is now, so you can find a better way to reach his dark soul. I'm so selfish, that's right," Vegas pops a hand on her hip.

"Fuck this shit!" Angry and pissed off, I storm off to the car alone.

"Guess what?" she yells over to me, stopping me in my tracks and forcing me to turn around. "I'll be here when you stop being stubborn and really see the beast of Axl's pain, and when you pull your head out, I'll be here to help."

Blade walks out from the crowd, storming toward Vegas and swatting her ass in a way that's meant to bruise her. She scowls at him but moves toward where he leads her. I watch as he hands her a helmet from his bike and she climbs on behind him.

My eyes catch the man next to Blade. It's Axl, and his eyes watch mine for a moment. As if he's never seen me before, he straddles his bike and drives right by me. The exhaust from his motor is hitting my nose.

Yanking the door to the car open, I slam my body into the seat and then close it shut. I let out the cry I have been holding just as Kat and Jenn get in the car. Curling forward into myself, I retreat further into my thoughts.

My pride is so strong and tells me that I'm right. That Axl should not be treating me this way, he should be here by now.

My heart tells me to drop my fear and pride and drag him back to me.

# CHAPTER 13

## Axl

Busting through the door of the warehouse, the night sky and the crisp air help to slow down my breathing and the adrenaline that's rushing through my veins. My body hums with desperation to keep killing, the wolf inside never feeling satisfied. He wants loose. He wants to kill all things with a beating, loving heart, including my own.

Like a force, I feel her eyes on me before I see her. I start my bike, anticipation screaming at me to leave before I kill her too. Destroy all the good inside of her heart. I don't want to see her, but the pull to her is stronger in this moment than the beast. I can't stop myself from looking for her.

Some part of me wishes that I could find *me* again. My eyes connect with her broken, lonely ones. I don't want her to see the possessed demon inside of me. The hungry wolf who wants to eat her soul alive only to unleash hell into her like the hell I've allowed the pain to do to mine.

I rip my eyes and my attention away from her. I leave her standing on the cold pavement, alone and better off without the man who only wants to consume her.

The rhythm of the bike's motor and the buzz from the tires on the pavement help grounding me. Reaching the freeway, I let the clutch go and hit the gas. The speed is a drug I can't help but want another hit from. Weaving through the traffic like in a game of roulette, I dodge the other cars and trucks on the road. Horns blare at me as I cut a driver off the road or cut in front of others.

A police siren sounds behind me, exciting me further. I turn around to see the pig has his lights flashing. Smiling, I egg him on in my head, "Come get me, asshole, if you can catch me."

Watching closely the cars in front of me, I race around them. Other cars start pulling over to the side of the road for the siren, and it makes it easier for that cunt to catch up to me. My heart howls at the moon, begging to be brought down by this asshole, make me part of the dirt.

Seeing an exit up ahead, I move the bike to the right side of the road. The ramp comes to a stop at a deadly right turn at the bottom of the off ramp. The cop can't see what's coming from his car. His motor roars behind me, trying to clip my back tire.

Jerking the handlebar to the left, my bike hits the incline back up onto the freeway. The engine screams in unused energy as my bike takes flight, jumping back onto the freeway. My tires squeal as they try to grip traction and I skid back and forth. Loud crashing alerts me that the cop, in fact, like I thought, did not take the turn too well.

Finding my balance on my Roadster, I continue toward the clubhouse at a punishing pace. I pull into the parking lot and park my bike into the garage bay for the night, then I continue to the bar to look for a beer. I sit at the bar and find a woman that I've never seen before eyeing me curiously over the countertop.

"Fuck, bitch, quit staring and give me a beer," I snarl, clearly not in the mood for fucking stupidity from anyone.

Too tense to relax, I wait for the others to get back since I made it back here way before them. I take a pull of the cold beer, holding the bottle to my lips, and smirk to myself at the night I had.

I turn my head and watch Pawn. Now that he's patched in, he's going for some double pussy in the corner. The bitches all want to wear his patch, thinking he's an easy in to become Ol' Ladies.

Pawn stands in the darkened corner with one bitch naked and fingering her own cunt while relentlessly sucking him off, while he sucks on another bitch's face as she rides his fingers. The bitch he's kissing pulls her face away, screeching out her ecstasy. That grates on my nerves.

Taking another pull from my beer, I tilt my head back and start to chug until my seat tilts back and my body crashes to the floor with it. The bottle is thrown from my hand and shatters against the wall, dripping down to the floor from the walls.

Blade is on top of me, pulling me back up from the floor by my shirt only to slam me again against the wall where my beer bottle just shattered.

"What the fuck is wrong with you, Axl!" He roars his anger into my face as his fists dig into my chest.

Throwing my weight forward toward him, I push his hands away from me and step further into Blade. Snarling, face to face, I ask, "What the motherfucking shit are you bitching to me about?" My fists clench and unclench hoping he will swing first.

"Vegas and I were riding right behind you, Axl. I saw how you were recklessly driving between cars. You could kill yourself, and then what? Leave us all here, your club and mom to deal with your selfish choices?"

"What the fuck? Who cares, Blade, we are all going to die anyway."

"You're such a dick, Axl. What about the kids on the road with their families? Or what about the cop you ran off the road on purpose for no god–DAMN REASON!"

Blade heaves from his anger. "He didn't die by the way, and if he did that would be manslaughter of a cop. That's serious fucking hard time, dickhead. Not to mention the heat you would bring down on your brothers. None of us want that shit brought down on us."

Blade takes a few deep breaths, keeping his steely determined gaze into my eyes. Taking a step back, he continues, "You're my brother, Axl. You are my family, my VP. I need you back, by my side. You still have people to live for. You are supposed to be my backup in life. I need you to take care of my back, the club, Vegas and the girls. They are our family too."

I wince when he says *girls*. I know he means Dana, and I can't utter even a word. I know everything he just said is right.

Blade looks away. "I can't have you here, the way that you are, right now." Shaking his head, he turns back to me, and the disappointment there breaks me, right before the Prez continues, "You got to leave Reno until your head is back on straight, Axl. You can't be here with us, not in the living, man. Looking for problems, because your problems, they become our problems. Take some time and leave town while I clean up this mess with the cop."

My Prez turns and leaves. I know my friend, he's hurting, but the Prez, he will protect his woman and his club. He is the man of this MC and his life. And here I am being a fucking clown.

My phone lights up on the floor with a text. Picking it up, I look at it.

**Jessica Rabbit: I miss you, I miss all of you. Will you please come home and just hold me tonight?**

Looking around, I see that the entire club has their eyes on me, looking at me with pity. They see a man in pieces, like this glass on the floor, shattered and fragile.

Pain lances my heart again from my actions. How far have I fallen since my old man passed? My heart squeezes in his memory, and I throw my phone against the wall. It shatters, along with everything else.

Tired of the eyes on me, I walk out through the back to find the dark, and, in the shadows, I can hide from my disgrace.

Finding the old wood bench, I sit down next to Jenn who has an open bottle of whiskey. She hands over the bottle and I take a swig from it, and then another to drown the reality of my actions.

Jenn does the same, taking the bottle back and she asks, "Reality finally hit you, didn't it?"

"Fucking suckered punched me in the nuts," I say as I look out over the dark desert hills and sagebrush.

"You know you are far from okay, right? Even though you finally burst through your fog, you are fucked up," Jenn states mechanically. She takes out a pill from her pocket, pops it into her mouth and drowns it with more whiskey.

Tilting my head at her, I ask, "What was that?"

"For the pain," Jenn says as she reaches into her pocket and offers me one.

I hold the bottle up in mock cheers. "To the pain," I declare.

Taking it from her palm, I too drown my pain in a pill, and the whiskey I drink. Two fucked up souls staring into the night, into what our souls really are, dark and empty.

# CHAPTER 14

## Dana

"Babe," Vegas says holding my hand as I cry. "It's going to be okay, we can bring him home to you."

"He went back to Las Vegas five days ago though, he wants to be there."

"No, Dana, he doesn't have a home in his heart right now. He's in so much grief over loosing not only his dad, he lost a piece of his world. He needs to find his way through a world where he doesn't know who he is in it."

I lay my head onto her lap for a while and give into the hurt as we continue to watch Judge Judy. She has a way of telling people they are stupid that I just love. It makes me smile inside while I take my time to come to terms with my feelings.

"You think he misses me though?" I ask, ashamed of needing to say it out loud. While Vegas plows through her way, she gives me the time to sit on mine.

"Yeah, babe, he does. He just needs to pick one hurt to deal with at a time," she says and places her coke on the side table.

"He doesn't call or text me back, he doesn't act like I'm even alive anymore. He left all his damn shit in my house! I wear his stupid T-shirt he gave me a while back to bed every night. I feel so stupid." My hands cover my face as I cry.

A heavy body sits down and picks up my feet from the other end of the couch. Peeking through my fingers, I see Tank. His large hands begin massaging my feet. Rolling onto my back, I wipe my tears away and take a deep breath in.

"What's wrong, sweetheart?" Tank asks with a pouty face.

"Axl," is all I can choke out.

"Hmm. He is a hard-headed dumbass. What else, baby girl?"

"He doesn't love me," I squeak out quietly and close my eyes.

"He does, little momma. He claimed that pussy," Tank says while dodging the pillow Vegas threw at his head. "I mean, he *loves* that pussy?" He chuckles when the last pillow bounces off his big head and hits the floor.

"What I'm saying is, after he deals with his anger, he'll be back for you. He'll hurt you right now if he comes back, he's really protecting you."

My heart doesn't believe him even though it wants to. They all leave in the end. The people you really love, they all leave in the end. Or they break you.

"What are you doing in Vegas' house anyway?"

"After staying here a bit ago to watch Vegas, I had brought so much shit that I'm just too lazy to take it all back to the clubhouse. It's nice here though. Fresh coffee in the morning with peace and quiet. I don't wake up with those leaches on my dick. It's so nice."

Vegas groans, "You eat like a fucking horse!"

"I will go grocery shopping today."

"I wasn't asking you to."

"I will though."

"NO. You will move your big ass out."

Tank ignores her and sets my feet down. "We good here, honey?"

With a small smile, I say, "Yes, for now."

"You have brothers here to help too, okay?" Tank winks at me before strolling out the door.

Vegas narrows her eyes at the door. "I'm texting Blade to change the locks ASAP, and to have his shit moved out today. Where the hell is Jenn? I'm texting her too, she was supposed to be here hours ago."

She picks up her phone, furiously tapping her thumbs across the screen. I spend the afternoon curled up on the couch next to my best friend, and wondering, does this hurt so much because I *do* love Axl?

I turn up the volume dial on the radio and my mind gets lost in the music as the words run through my mind and heart. Comforting me on my journey of life or work.

My head bobs to the beat as a light catches the corner of my eye. Shit. The siren was partly drowned out by the music. I check my speed and see that I'm going the speed limit.

I turn on my blinker and pull off to the side of the road. I start digging inside my purse to find my license. Leaning over, I open the glove compartment box to locate my registration and insurance too. I feel anxious as I was supposed to open the bar this afternoon, and I don't want to be late.

Finally, the officer taps on my window with his knuckles. Rolling the window down, I hand over my license, insurance and registration.

"Thank you..." the officer smiles and looks down at my license. "Dana Maraschino, did you know your tail-light was out?"

"Uh no, thank you for telling me, I can have it fixed right away."

"Do you have someone to help you with that?"

"Yes, sir." My skin starts tingling in fear.

"I would hate for you to be hit by another vehicle because they didn't see the light. I'm going to run this, stay in your vehicle," he demands as he leaves, and I watch him sit in his cruiser.

Picking up my phone, I text Vegas. **Can you open for me?**

Right away she responds. **Sure, everything okay?**

**Me: I've been pulled over by a cop**
**Vegas: Don't get out of your car, don't say anything, be careful**
**Me: WHAT!**
**Vegas: Don't panic. I just want you to be careful**

"Dana." His gruff voice startles me, and I drop the phone in my lap. The officer hands me back my license and papers. My hand grabs the paperwork to take it back from him, only his hold is tighter. Leaning into the window, he says, "Stay safe, Dana Maraschino." He holds my eyes a moment too long, then he continues, "I'll follow you. Home or work? I don't want something happening to you."

"I, uh, okay. I will just call to my work to let them know I'm running late," I answer.

"When you're ready." The officer goes back to his cruiser.

My hands tremble as I pick up my phone to call Axl. It rings and rings, but no answer. I hurriedly hang up and call Snake. He answers on the first ring. "Babe, what's up?"

My voice trembles as I tell him as quickly as I can what happened. I keep the tears back as best as I can, but the fear laces my voice.

Snake's voice drops low. "You take the long way on the freeway back around to the garage where we take the cars to for maintenance. I'll be there before you, put your phone on speaker. Put your seatbelt on, okay? I'm getting into the truck now."

I do as he tells me and let out a steadying breath when I hear his truck door slam. "Baby, turn your car on. Then your blinker."

"Okay, Snake." Doing as he says, I turn back onto the road.

Snake continues talking to me. "He's just being a dick, Dana, don't worry, I'm sure it's nothing." He keeps the chatter going as I make my way to the garage.

Instant relief floods my veins as I see him standing there, waiting for me outside the garage. He hangs up his cell, pocketing the phone into his pants. I park my car and hear the cruiser pull up behind me.

On unsteady legs, I get out of my car and eagerly walk into his awaiting arms. Snake holds me close, wrapping a protective arm around me, and places a kiss on my forehead.

The officer walks over, eyeing Snake and I suspiciously. "Check her tail-lights, or the wiring may be out."

Snake laughs, "Sure will, I'll take care of my woman, thanks for the special attention to make sure she made it okay."

"Wouldn't want anyone to get into an accident on the road," the officer states before plastering a fake smile on his face. "Ya'll have a good night."

Even though the cop left, my hands don't leave from around Snake's side as my body involuntarily shakes a little from the shock.

"What was that? Why did he pull me over?" I ask, hoping that he will tell me.

"Not here, babe, but Blade wants you back at the clubhouse."

Geez, a lot of dudes cram in here for these meetings. Snake and I walk through the door, finding one seat available for someone to sit in. Blade points to the chair and I sit down.

The angry energy in the room makes this meeting even more claustrophobic like. None of these men have on the happy party faces that I'm used to seeing. That whole night is making a whole lot more sense on why Vegas took me to the fight. I know these men are ruthless, but I have forgotten what lies beneath the smiles and jokes.

Blade slams the gavel on the table, and I feel as if I'm the one in trouble. Snake's hand lands on my shoulder, giving me a gentle squeeze. Looking up, my eyes clash with Spider's, his stare not leaving where Snake is touching me, which is making me even more uncomfortable. My hands grip the seat of the chair to scoot myself forward into the table, losing Snake's hand on my shoulder as I do so.

Blade clears his throat. "Dana, can you tell us what the fuck just happened? And don't leave any details out."

I run through the situation, trying desperately to sound more confident than I feel. My chest moves rapidly up and down with worry. "Why is he targeting me? What is going on? Please tell me something."

"After the fight the other night that you girls weren't supposed to be at, and, while you are here, don't let Vegas go to that shit again, we clear?" He pauses and waits for me to acknowledge his order.

"Yes, Blade."

He nods in approval. Does he not know his wife? *She* dragged *me* there and she didn't even tell me what was going on. Now I'm getting called out for it. Figures. Classic Vegas getting us into trouble.

"After the fight, Axl was racing his bike on the freeway. Pushing cars out of the way." My breath catches and my heart skips a beat.

"He got a cop on his ass who tried to pull him over. Axl baited him to run off the road. I think the cop is looking for him. That's why he left town. He needs to get his shit together and his head on straight and not be causing problems. I sent him down to Las Vegas to stay with Stryker. I think he needs Stryker to kick his ass, he's the closest thing he has to an old man right now."

"So, you are telling me that *you* sent Axl away? And, let me guess, Vegas knew of all this?" I inquire.

"Yes, Dana, to protect the club. And you."

"I don't know who I'm madder at right now, you or Vegas!" Heat spreads through my veins, pushing my body over the top of the table. Anger starts burning from somewhere deep inside of me.

"Vegas does what the fuck I tell her to do, Dana. In case you fucking missed the memo at the wedding, she's not only *your* family anymore. She's the Ol' Lady, *the President's* Ol' Lady, of this fucking club. If I tell her to shut the fuck up, she will. If she can't be trusted by me, we have nothing. Between you and Axl, your insecurities are ripping both of you apart. Deal with your shit, because, let me tell you, if you can't trust your beloved Axl with your life and you with his, this club life will rip you apart. You want to be with Axl? Grow the fuck up, deal with your shit and go claim your man."

Blade stops to make sure I hear this next part. "You fucking dare talk to me that way in Church again, and you will be picking your ass up off the floor. You get me?"

Feeling royally stupid for everything I said, I sit back in my chair and nod in agreement in response.

"Words, eyes, Dana," Blade demands.

I think I would have rather he reached across the table and smacked my ass than taken this proverbial smackdown.

"Yes, Prez, my apologies to you and the brothers," I say and look at him as a tear falls from my eye, and then another.

"Dana, you are loved," Blade states

The room erupts into a resounding "Aye!" as all the men grunt out the word. The deep baritone from the hearts of these men hits a cord deep inside of my sad song that continually plays on repeat.

Something deep within me begs to be free of the torment. I cry. I cry in a room full of bikers. I cry for the little girl who lost her mother to drugs, a father who forgot she existed, and for the man who left her.

Hands upon hands touch my shoulder as my tears continue to paint my cheeks. Standing, I find brothers lined up behind me as each one hugs me and kisses my forehead. By the last hug, my last tear falls, and I feel some part of me was cleansed.

Blade stands firm as he rounds the table. "We are all family, Dana, we will all die for you, we will protect each other. You have us all to carry your burden. You don't carry that shit alone, and never have, you hear me now, Dana?"

"Yes, Prez." A slow smile spreads across my face.

"Good. Now, Tank, you'll be staying with Dana until this shit is settled. Dana, you have a new roommate. Move your shit out of my house today, Tank."

Tank stands at the door smiling and holding his arm out for me. "Hey, roomie, let's go move into your house. You have a room on the west side of the house, right? The sun is a bitch in the morning, and I like to sleep to keep this sparkling personality."

Laughing, I walk into Tank's side and reach my own arm around his back as we walk out, like two friends on a new journey, when it suddenly hits me.

He's never moving back out.

The crowd erupts into fits of laughter from a table in the corner, drawing the attention of those around the bar to where a group of older college kids laugh with each other.

The sound is endearing to my ears. It pulls at long forgotten memories that are coming back to me to be savored and longed for. I love the sound of the careless fun and wish that my life was that simple, that my mind too felt that carefree and light as theirs seem to.

To go back to the days when life was fun, and love was just a crush.

Tami looks across the room and she, like me, seems to be lonely, wanting to be wanted by others. I know this look she wears because I wear it too. Even though our stories may be a little different, we both do feel the same way. I always called it bullshit when a person would say, "You don't know what it is that I am feeling, what it is like to be me." Does it matter if we all go through the exact same thing? I don't think so. Pain is pain, it all fucking hurts.

Earlier today at the clubhouse made me confront some shitty truths. One in particular, that I really hate about myself and try to avoid at all costs, is my need for love. I never believed that another man could ever love me from what happened with my parents as a child. That resulted in me pushing boyfriends I did have away frequently. I was a passive child looking for their attention, and, if I received their attention, it meant that I was loved. This has been my weakness and I don't want it to be anymore. Did I really go to Axl and make him see us? No, I didn't.

I did try getting his attention to come back, so that does mean something special to me. He is different to me than any other boyfriends I ever had were, but I didn't fight hard enough for him, for what we deserve. I thought that if I pushed him too hard, he would leave. I will show him that I can be the woman he needs to fall back on. I am going to bring his stubborn and sweet ass home to me. Any way that I can have my Axl back, I'll take it all. He's mine.

The other thing I learned today is that I am the person responsible for me and no one else. I don't need Axl or my parents to rescue me. I am my own motherfucking badass. I can rescue my damn self *and* him. I am the creator of my own dreams and no one else.

Taking in my surroundings, I look around with a renewed sense of confidence. I promise myself to remember this moment and kick my own ass when needed.

The hours fly by easily and the bar begins to weed out with the joyous ruckus from earlier. Tami has gone home and it is just security and I until we close in the next hour. The front door opens and a cold strong wind funnels through the bar from the strong Nevada winds. A chill runs up my spine from the breeze and also from the man standing at the door that saunters over to the bar with big ideas behind those deep brown eyes.

"You got a beer for me, babe?" Snake's eyes race over my tight black jeans and low-cut t-shirt we had made. He stares at the bar logo that is stretched across my tits a little too long. Shit.

"Sure do." I grab a cold mug from the freezer and grab the handle for the draft beer. Tilting it, I pour the beer until it's full. Instead of handing it over to him over the counter, I walk around and slide the beer across the distance between us as I slide myself onto the barstool next to him.

Snake takes a long pull of his drink with a devilish grin. Taking a fortifying breath in, I ask, "You had a good day today?"

"Mm hm, and I think it's about to get better." His eyes try to capture mine with his unspoken promises.

"Snake, I've been distracted a lot with everything, and I am going to set this weird thing between us straight. We aren't ever going to happen."

"I don't see why we can't." He tries reasoning with me as he's setting his mug down. He turns his body toward me with a questioning tilt to his head.

"We can't because you are full of bullshit, Snake." I try not to laugh, but a little chuckle escapes my lips before I continue. "You want what you can't have and always will. I fell for your games when we were kids. I'm not falling for your shit now. We were always meant to be friends. I'm not going to be your dirty little secret and then you ditch this town and me. Quit toying with me," I finish my speech and stand up from my stool when he grabs my arm.

"I realize you don't want games, who said I was playing around?"

"You haven't seen me in years. None of this matters, I've got a man." I step back out of his hold.

"Fair enough, you can't blame a man for trying, babe. When Axl gets his ass back here, I hope he sees what he's missing."

"He will, or I'll remind him," I assure him as I'm walking back behind the bar.

I won't let the man that lights up my world walk away so easily again. Like I was saying before, I'm the creator of my own happily ever after.

# CHAPTER 15

## Axl

I spray alcohol on a tatt to wipe away the black ink off the brother's back. Last night we had a patch-in party for this new prospect, Audio. Fool plays tracks and reminds me of Jenn, if she had a brother.

My phone rings and I look over to see Dana's calling. I hesitate, and then it is too late. By the time I start ripping off my gloves to answer, I missed the call. Some part of me demanded to answer. What if something happened to her and she needed me?

Shaking my head, I drop that idea, thinking it's nothing and just me being a paranoid asshole. Besides, Blade would tell me if anything was going on with her.

I keep my concentration on this back piece. Audio wanted his whole back dedicated to our wolf patch. Getting lost in the lines and art, I don't realize that it took me eight hours to finish. Wrapping up his tatt with his road name, I finish up feeling a little more at peace inside of myself.

This last week, a burden has been lifted from my heart. Being around Stryker and this old club made me feel connected to my old man in a way that I hadn't been lately. Letting him go has been a little easier at least, even though the pain still lingers and I'm sure that it always will.

"Axl!" Stryker barks from his office. "Get your ass in here, you have a visitor."

I take my gloves off and Audio shakes my hand. "Thanks, brother."

Following him out, I stop dead in my tracks as I come face-to-face with Ghost. Fuck.

He sneers at me with an ugly gleam that spreads across his damn pretty face. You see, Ghost is a big motherfucker, served in the marines or some shit, knows how to kill men about a hundred different ways. He too, like Fuego, is Hispanic, some fucked up hybrid by the looks of his height and built. He's got dark, slicked back hair and a tightly trimmed goatee, dark eyes and skin. Skeleton tattoos cover his arms.

Legend is that the man has a new one done every time after he kills a victim. I'm a total fan, other than in this moment. Because... Ghost is a mean asshole. He is VP to Fuego, who is sitting next to Stryker, and he is also Dana's old man.

The last time I saw him was the night I fucked my princess in her office with the entire club right outside the door, him included. I really fucked up. I fucked up hard.

I may die today, and I need to call my momma, and then Dana, to say goodbye. Fuck.

Stepping into Stryker's office, I see a grin pulling at his lips. "Glad to see you got some color back into your face. White looks good on you. That's how Ghost here got his name. Men seem to know when their past ghosts have caught up to them, and, it seems here, yours literally have. Man, when you fuck up, you really fuck shit up good, son." Stryker continues to laugh but is the only one.

I can't even say anything. Where do you even start? Sorry I fucked your daughter then fucking left her? Ghost and Fuego wait me out a painful minute while I think of something to say. I decide on, "I fucked up."

Ghost raises both eyebrows and looks at me like I'm a weak kid. "No, I know", I say. "Shit went down and I left Dana high and dry. It was fucked up, but so was my life."

Ghost interrupts me with his deep Hispanic accent "Did she tell you about her past growing up?"

"Yes..."

It happens before I see it. My head snaps back as the loud pop from my nose breaking splinters the silence.

"Fuck!" I pinch my nose, willing the pain to go away and the blood to stop running down my face. Stryker tosses me a towel with a smile. Asshole.

"Yes, I knew what happened with you and her past and her mom," I finish my sentence as I'm holding the towel to my nose.

"And you still left her behind like her love wasn't important enough to you?"

"I left her because I was fucked up inside, Ghost. I wanted to kill everything and everyone. I wasn't in a good place. I would have ripped her heart out to feed the pain." I plead with him to understand that I wanted to save her.

"Don't fucking talk to me about pain, Axl. You're a little golden boy, your life has been a cake walk compared to mine. I'd killed hundreds of men by the time I was twenty. Their ghosts are in my dreams every goddamn night," he snarls at me, then continues. "As a young man, I came home to my woman at the time who'd had my baby while I was gone. Shit got ugly. And that's a story your sorry ass doesn't deserve to hear right now." He pauses for a second.

"But I left my baby to save her from a real killer. Myself. You're no killer." Ghost closes his eyes only to snap them open and giving us glimpses of a soulless man.

"I could wrap my hands around your neck and feel nothing from it. I learned there was still love in me for a little girl who pumped life back into me with her pure love. I will tell you this one time and one time only." He pauses to make sure I am taking all this in.

"You go back to her, you better lay your life down for her. If I get a call again to tell me she's crying because of you, there will be no warning. Club or no club, your life will be taken with my bare hands. You protected yourself, not her. You never let her give you the chance to love you back into the living. You fed your pain." Ghost's vacant eyes hold mine with the promise of death.

Bowing my head, I let the pain slice through my heart with the damage I've done to my princess. The realization spreading like fire in my veins that I choose pain over her.

"*Mijo*," Fuego calls me. I lift my head and Ghost is nowhere to be found.

"We all have these *fantasmas*, or ghosts, that haunt our lives. They want to suck us into their hell. You have no excuses *no mas, mijo*. What life do you see for yourself? *Que vida tú quieres?* One where you carry *tu padre*'s life with you wherever you go? Or, *una vida*, a life, rebirthed from your loss? You know the story, *sí?*" He stops talking and points to the chair in front of him. "Sit, *mijo*, let's talk."

Listening to Fuego, I sit and listen as I'm told. Stryker kicks his feet up on his desk after he hands me a beer, then puts his hands behind his head. We settle in together. I toss the bloody towel in the trash and open the beer, then take a drink to wash the coppery taste away from my mouth.

Fuego looks at me and grins. "Many years *antes*, before, *mi hermano*, you know him, Cuervo... *Ese cabrón*, that asshole, he was so in love with his *esposa*. Rosa, his wife, she was a beautiful woman and had grown into a *madre hermosa*, also. He had a son and two daughters as well. Cuervo got careless with his *familia*, he also got into drugs. His bad dealing killed his family and those ghosts of his choices still haunt the man. Cuervo came home to a dead wife who'd been raped and tortured children."

Fuego takes his fingers and touches his forehead, then brings them to his chest and then shoulder to shoulder as he whispers a small prayer in Spanish.

"You cannot bring back the dead, *mijo*. Was your father murdered? No. Was he taken early from you and *tu madre*? *Sí*. But, *mijo*, that man, he lived. He lived for your mother. He praised her beauty and life. He lived for you and for himself, *mijo*. You are now living for his death. He is not happy with you, I know this. I know because I would be sad for my own *niños* to live the way you are. Not *if* but *when* I die."

I open my mouth to say something, but Fuego holds up his hand and I snap my mouth shut. "We all die. There is no way around it. Your *padre* in Heaven wants you to be a man and take care of your *mama* like he would. *Tu padre* would want you to love Dana like he treasured your *madre*. *Tu Padre* wants you to live for you, *mijo*, and live your *vida*, your life, not your death, *sí*?

"*Sí*, Fuego."

"*Bueno.* You have the elders in our MC that are the fathers to you that you have forgotten. Shame. You forget those that came before you and helped raise you. Stryker, *yo* and Ghost, and many others, we all lost a brother on the day that Maddox died. But mostly

Stryker, he lost his VP. You've been neglectful of your family. As one of the Presidents of this club, I am going to tell you this once. You do not deserve to be the VP in Reno, but Blade loves you like a brother. Shit has gone down while you've been gone, and you left your Prez and brothers in their time of need. It's time you stopped using your ghost as an excuse. Pack up your shit and get the fuck back to the living. Stop being a fucking pussy and bleeding your pain everywhere. That shit is messy."

"Mom! You ready?" I yell at her from the U-Haul. I walk around and double check all the doors.

When she doesn't answer, I walk around the two trucks looking for her only to find her staring at the front of the house that her and my father had built as their home. Harley's arms wrap around her stomach and tears stream down her face.

"Momma," I call for her and pull her into me, hugging her and wishing I could take her pain in.

"Hey, Dad is going to want you with me. He isn't going to want you alone anymore. He would kick my ass if he could. I've been a piece of shit son to you since everything happened. For that, I can't tell you that I'm sorry enough, but I'm never leaving you behind again."

Harley smiles through her pain. "Axl, you have his big heart. When he died, it broke you. I think your heart stopped with his. Your dad was a man who lived, Axl, he lived and learned from love and from his mistakes. Live and learn, baby." She then pauses, only to ask, "Have you talked to Dana?"

Shame and sadness wash over me at hearing her name. "No. I really fucked up. I'm going to get her back though. I didn't want to call her. I want to hold her again when I talk to her."

My mom smiles at me. "Good. I have something for you then. I've been holding on to these, waiting for you to be ready."

She hands me a picture envelope but stops my hands with hers before I open it.

"Remember, Axl, things always happen for a reason. Your dad must have known deep down that his life would be cut short, so he lived each moment to the fullest. I'm so happy he chose me and the life we had together. When you open this envelope, remember that things happen for a reason. Live your life like your dad taught you to. It's not too late for you. You look at every picture really well, then we'll leave. Holler out when you're ready."

She smiles as she walks through the front door of our home one last time. I sit down on the front porch step and open the envelope.

The first picture is of three cute young girls making faces at the camera. Two brown haired ones with a blonde in the middle. I start browsing through them all. Some are of them together at the pool with some boys. Who *are* these girls? More of the same goofy pictures follow.

Until my heart stops at the sight of the beautiful blonde–haired girl kissing a young wannabe rock star in front of a stage with a Guns N' Roses concert in the background.  He holds up the camera, snapping a picture of them, of a night he should have never forgotten, but somehow his heart already recognized.

"Hahahaha." I roll back onto my back and laugh for the first time in months. I look at the next one. She smiles back at me, the young man behind the camera. In the next, she's watching the concert with hands up in the air, singing along with a group of rough young men. The one after that, I laugh harder at seeing the young blonde girl flashing her tits to the band as she sits on top of the young wannabe rock star's shoulders.

Laughing to myself, I hold the pictures to my heart. Blood and love finally explode life back into me. Pumping fresh air into a deserted body.

"Good pictures, right? I couldn't go far. I had to see your face," my mom admits with a smile.

"Pictures that helped to wake up my cold dead heart, Mom. How did you get these?"

"The day after you trashed your room, I was cleaning and found this old disposable camera under your bed. I had a hell of a time finding someone to develop the film, but it was well worth the trouble."

"Yeah, fuck yeah! Let's get the hell out of here. I have shit to do in Reno. There's this beautiful blonde waiting for me."

I take off running over to the truck, love pumping vigorously in my veins. I turn the engine on excitedly, then the CB radio. Holding the button down on the CB mic, I try the first channel.

"Roger Rabbit to Jessica Rabbit, hey, princess, I'm coming home, I'm coming home, 3's and 8's. Love and Kisses. I repeat, Roger Rabbit to Jessica Rabbit, hey, princess, I'm coming home, I'm coming home, 3's and 8's. Love and Kisses. Over and Out."

# CHAPTER 16

## Dana

"Hey, you wanna go buy some..." I immediately stop talking as my CB radio bursts to life. Quickly, I turn it up to hear over the static. "I repeat, Roger Rabbit to Jessica Rabbit, hey, princess, I'm coming home, I'm coming home, 3's and 8's. Love and Kisses. Over and Out."

Vegas looks over to me and me to her, our mouths hanging open and we both start crying. My phone pings with a text, and thank God that I had her drive us to the store as I wasn't feeling well this morning, or the last few mornings.

Taking out my phone from my purse, I see a text from Axl.

**Roger Rabbit: Hey, princess, you remember that concert from when you told me about where you lost your virginity? Did that guy who popped my girl's cherry, did he beat the shit out of the guy she was with that night?**

**Jessica Rabbit: How do you know that?**

**Roger Rabbit: Did my princess actually pop her blunt berry with a wannabe rock star that night?**

**Jessica Rabbit: Axl, how do you know this??!!!**

**Roger Rabbit: Because you've been mine, Dana...See you soon, I'm on the road.**

"Dana, what is he saying? What's going on?" Vegas impatiently demands answers.

"How does he know about that night, Vegas?"

"Dude, slow the fuck down and breathe, backup a decade. What night? And he's coming home!" she starts screeching.

"He's coming home!" I squeal back. "But that night when I snuck out when we went to Las Vegas for spring break with our parents, and my dad said no, even though I was nineteen, remember?"

An evil smile spreads across her face. "Yeah, I remember the cherry-picking night. Why?"

"Listen to this." And I start reading his texts out loud to her.

"He can't be your cherry-picking blunt berry popper, can he?! Dana, think hard for once in your life, woman! Is Axl your blast from your past that you obsessed over?" She bounces around in her seat excitedly.

My face falls and I squint my eyes. "Think hard for once in my life? Did you really just say that to me? No, Vegas, I think I just love to live my life in mystery," I deadpan, then yell back, "I was drunk before I met him, we blazed till everyone's faces looked the same, and, after, I don't know, like, ten years have passed, it's hard to remember, you asshole!"

"HA! Good point, but what if he *is your cherry picker*, Dana?!"

Vegas' eyes water with mine while we look at each other. What if this whole time Axl has always been mine, and we finally found our way back to each other?

"Mom!" I throw the door open and run into her arms.

"There's my girl!" She jumps off Papa's bike and drops her helmet at her feet, racing toward me too. We collide into a heap of hugs as Papa gets up and joins in with us in my front yard. Pulling us apart, he tosses me into the air, then hugs me into his strong frame. Mom laughs next to us.

"I didn't know you guys were coming today!"

Papa puts me down. "I had some business to take care of down south, but as soon as that was done, I drove up here to check on my baby. We got some *carne asada* for dinner. I'll cook you some dinner, spend time with you tonight, *sí, mija*?"

"*Sí, papa!* Vegas is already here. You want me to call Blade, Jenn and James over too?"

"*Sí, mija*, if that's what you want, *mi corazón*."

"Come inside," I ask as I lead the way. Reaching the kitchen to put the meat away, we see that Tank is standing there, chugging milk straight out of the carton, only in his boxers, in all his man glory. If I didn't know him already, it would be quite a sight.

Mom's face spreads in a humorous expression while Papa's not so much and he grunts. "Why the hell is this *pinche* asshole in your kitchen in his chones for, *mija*?" he booms. "Does he not have a job to go to?"

Tank chokes mid gulp and Vegas laugh-snorts from around the corner, flipping Tank off.

"Sorry, Ghost. Dana, or *Vegas*," he turns and glares a promise of death and torture at Vegas, "didn't tell me there were visitors coming by today, or I wouldn't be standing around in my underwear," he explains a half heartfelt excuse.

"Do I look like a fucking visitor, *cabrón*? Do I need to call ahead of time to come to *el casa de mi hija*? Doesn't answer either goddamn questions I asked."

Ghost pointedly stares at Tank, impatiently waiting. Try being a teen and living in his house. It sucked.

"I am protecting Dana since the cop incident until it's resolved, so I'm staying here."

"In your chones, sleeping in on duty? You're doing a damn fine job, son, I can't thank you enough," Ghost deadpans. Huh, that's where I get that sarcasm from. Oh God, I am my father!

Vegas snickers at Tank as his face grows red. "If you would excuse me," he grinds the words out while slamming the milk back into the fridge and taking off down to his room. Poor Tank, Ghost is no BS twenty-four-seven.

Vegas walks out from around the corner and Papa keeps a pointed look at her now. "Always stirring the shit when no one's looking still?"

Vegas points to her chest, "*Moi?*" and leans in for a hug, "Love you too, Papa."

"Love you too, Vegas, and your brass balls," he chuckles at her.

Vegas was always the tomboy and scheming with Papa for war tactics, would even go shooting with him. Which really helped him out as far as he was concerned, because that also got me to hang out with them too during a time when I was very pissed off at him. I also think she did it because she wanted me to give him a chance. I am happy she did, because I don't know that I would have ever given one without her prodding.

"Hey, Katie! Man, woman, you are looking fly. I want to be you when I grow up. Keeping it tight for your man, girl. Respect." Vegas moves over and hugs her too. She loves Katie just as much as me.

"Girl, your BS is on high alert tonight," Katie mocks her.

"*Moi!*" Vegas laughs and touches her hand to her chest astonished. "Let's get this BBQ going before my hungry man shows up."

The four of us work together preparing the food and laughing for the rest of the afternoon. Slowly, people start trickling in. Since it is a Wednesday, everyone is off from the bar because it's closed.

It's getting closer to eight and I start worrying that Axl isn't coming here tonight. My heart sinks at the thought.

I set down a fruit bowl and head back into the house when I hear a knock at the door. Excitement races through me as I run to see who it is. Blade is standing on the other side of the door with Snake, Spider and Cowboy.

"Hey, guys," I push for a nice greeting, but the enthusiasm isn't selling it. "Everyone is out back."

The guys head past me, and Snake winks at me as I shake my head. The asshole will never learn I think shaking my head at him as he laughs at himself. Blade stops in front of me and carefully considers what to say.

"Dana, you have to have trust in Axl. He will come through. He had a few delays on his way up here. Flat tire and other club shit. Patience, you've made it this far," he says before catching sight of Vegas, and I become an afterthought. I'm surprised, even though brief, the man does show the ones he cares for small tokens of friendship.

Taking Blade's advice, I head back to the BBQ turned party. I see James alone across the yard and head toward him. James holds a Corona up to his lips and takes a long pull from his beer, the sadness and loneliness radiating from him. I can't help myself but wanting to hug him.

James sees me coming and opens his arms up to me reading my mind and wraps his non-beer holding arm around me. "What's up, babe, you okay?"

I hug him a little closer. "Everything is getting better."

"Oh, yeah?" A hopeful smile plays at his lips. "Why is that?"

"I just realized how much love I really do have all around me. You know that too, right?" James nods along with me. "I'm sorry I haven't been a good friend. What's going on with you?"

Waiting for James to answer, I see him watching Jenn mess with her phone as she plays songs for us. "I don't know if holding on to someone is worth hurting me. Or if it's time to let go, Dana."

Holding him a tighter, I try prodding him further. "Are you planning on leaving us, James?"

"Not you and Vegas, I just don't know if I should work at the bar anymore. It's been a long road, I need to rest, a new start, but not leave you girls." He finishes on a sigh.

"I see. Can I be gone the day you tell Vegas? She's gonna flip her shit. I'd rather deal with her after, when she calms down, I will totally support you. Jenn's been quieter and more distant. The more we try to engage her, the more she pulls away."

"I know, she's been doing that to me too. It's why I'm leaving."

"We'll get everything figured out, you'll see."

"You are feeling better, happiness looks beautiful on you, babe."

The sliding door flies open, and Axl comes barging through, with a round of *hey*'s coming from the brothers who are trying to give him hugs.

He blasts straight past them all, heading straight for me. James gently pushes me forward. One step turns into another and then my feet are running toward Axl. The light is back in his face, and his eyes light up in the same excitement as mine.

In the middle of the yard, we collide. My legs wrap around his waist and my hands in his hair. Axl's large hands grab a hold of my ass and he holds me tightly to his body.

We stare into each other's eyes for a second. My fingers run under the bruises around his black eyes and my heart aches. What happened to him?

Before I know what is going on, Axl's lips claim mine in a long passionate kiss, our lips and teeth fighting for dominance.

He pulls back, his breathing labored, and pecks my lips softly. His forehead rests against mine.

"I'm sorry, I'm so damn sorry I left you alone, princess. It won't happen again, believe in me, baby. I want to be the one to stick by you in this life." He brushes his lips against mine.

"God, Axl, I need you too and I will never let you leave me again either. You're mine."

His chest vibrates with a barely audible laugh. The feel of his strong body and heat envelopes hope and desire back to right where it was before.

"I got work tonight and shit to square away, but I couldn't spend another night without touching you, feeling you. I'll be back for you, and this time nothing will keep me away."

He lets go of me and my feet touch the ground. Then, he bends over and whispers into my hair, "I love you, princess. This will last forever, my love for you will never end." Grabbing my face with his warm hand, he pulls me back to his lips, sealing his words in a promise.

He then lets go of my face, kisses my hand and steps away, saying, "I'll be back, Dana! It won't be long, but I'll be back for you tomorrow."

With those last words, he walks back through the sliding glass door, Blade and the men following closely behind.

# CHAPTER 17

## Axl

My skin prickles alive with awareness, a renewed energy, as I sit among my brothers, next to my President, Blade. The brothers feel the promise of death in the air. Solo and Pawn are the last ones to walk in. Once the door is shut, the gavel is slammed down on the table.

Standing, I say, "I've let my brothers down, my club and oath I forgot. I'll take my penance to show my dedication to the MC."

I move to stand in the middle of the room. Man after man throws a punch at my face, stomach or back. The pain conjures the living beast within me to come to the surface. A few knees and kicks punish me for my disobedience to always remember that my MC brothers come first. I howl out in pain and sufferance as the last blow is delivered by Blade. His right fist comes down onto my temple.

On one knee before my brothers, I struggle to keep at bay the beast inside of me that begs to be freed and kill the others that stand before me. Taking in a fortifying breath, I raise to my feet. I feel the strength in my gaze as I stare each one in the eyes.

"I want to keep my place as VP." I hold my fists at my sides and wait.

Blade asks the room, "Anyone contesting his spot?" The death of silence is a gift among my brothers. "All in favor to leave Axl as VP, say aye."

A resounding "Aye!" vibrates off the walls with their yells in agreement.

Blade's lip curls up in satisfaction. Pulling out the knife from his shoulder holster, he twirls the blade around with ease as he's looking around the room. "In the last year, we weeded out those who betrayed our club"

"Aye," the men agree.

"We have our crew here now, brothers you would bleed for, yes?" The devil twinkles in his eyes.

"Aye," we echo through the room.

"Then, we pledge ourselves in blood that we move forward as one and blood we will spill to protect what's ours"

"Aye!"

The twirling of the blade stops, and he holds it over his right hand to cut a cross into his skin. Snarling as the blood dribs from his own cuts, he hands me the knife and I do the same, sealing an oath to these brothers and this clubhouse. We all take our turns, marking our flesh with a cross.

The last brother, Pawn, sets the knife back down in front of a now sitting at the table Blade, with me to his right and Tank, the Road Captain, to his left. Nodding toward Pawn, Blade continues the meeting.

Looking at me, he says, "The cop you ran off the road came looking for you, and pulled Dana over with some bullshit about a broken taillight. Since you've been gone, Tank has been staying with her. That cop has been driving by looking for you, the asshole still thinks you're in Las Vegas. He tried to go into the bar and brewhouse, but we've had shit locked down tight."

Shame washes over me again as I realize that Dana must've called me when that prick was looking for her and that I left her alone. A sigh escapes me, and my head looks up at the ceiling, amazed at my own stupidity.

"We've been going to the fight tanks like normal. We haven't caused any waves. Yet. Tony had that cop following you. Spider pulled up his cell records, and, before the fight, they had contact. A transaction's been made in cash to the cop by Tony's security. Solo and Pawn have been running detail on them. The cop is building a case against us. He wants to take us down to gain this territory. We haven't been moving cash like the others before us did with the diamonds and the sex trafficking. That cop that followed you was going to arrest you. Looks like your crazy ass had some luck that night. Now we have two problems. To kill a pig *and* a man highly influencing in the sex trade."

Anger rolls through my body to think that this entire time this asshole had his eyes on Dana and the club.

Tank interrupts my thoughts. "Shit is in the past, Axl, leave it there, brother."

Blade continues, "I have the Black Widow with him now." He raises his hands to answer the murmurings of who that is. "You don't want to know the woman. Her job is highly skilled and paid to off serious players or law enforcement. A black-market secret, and none of you will ever meet her. She's paid to keep her mouth shut and she likes it, so everyone's happy. Right now, she has our cop strung out on drugs in a motel room downtown. Only Axl and I are going. The rest of you go back to business as normal."

Blade and I park our bikes outside of a bar downtown on Fourth Street. Walking through the bar, Blade hands a security guard a handful of cash on his way back out the back door. He lights a cigarette, and I'm following him until he stops in the alley way.

Taking one last long drag of his smoke, Blade stomps it out, then we continue walking. Whoever this bitch is has his nerves up, which means he doesn't trust her. Grabbing a key card, he opens the door to room number sixty-nine. Classy bitch.

A woman covered in black and gray tattoos, long black hair and dressed like a hooker turns her gaze to me and I stop in my tracks.

The Black Widow is Kat. Tank's Kitty Kat. Kat that works at the bar with our women.

I feel the heat flushing my body as I'm overcome with anger when she pulls her silenced nine-millimeter on me. She sits in a chair by the window, cool as a cat playing with her mouse that's tied up on the bed.

"What. The. Fuck." I feel like I'm on autopilot. "How are you the Black Widow?"

"You'll never know, Axl, so ask the questions that really matter right now. I have other shit to do, and the longer we drag this out, the more your Prez pays," Kat says while holstering her gun inside her boot.

Blade, the sadistic fucker that he is, has a gleam in his eye as he says, "What did you come up with?"

"You mean what did I fix? I met him on the street, had pictures of him 'picking me up'. We went on a few dates. Texted myself a few as "blackmailing" the hooker to suck my little dick threats. Pictures of him stalking me at the bar, of him beating up drug dealers on the street. He's a real dirty pig."

The cop starts twisting, trying to free himself from the bindings, yelling something under the ball gag that's strapped around his mouth.

"Point is," Kat says, rolling her eyes in annoyance, "He is a really dirty dick. Between Spider and the pound puppies, you can kill him any way you want. Drug overdose would work because he had a habit to shoot up with hookers. Or shoot him in the head, he made enough enemies. When the cops start digging through his shit, thanks to Spider, they won't know what the hell to think of this dirty fucker. I left you a bag of toys. Have fun, boys." Kat throws on her jacket and heads for the door.

"Hey." She grabs the doorknob and looks at me with her cat shaped eyes over her shoulder. "Who's the pound puppies?"

An amused grin covers her face. "Solo and Pawn, little dogs that are learning to run with the big dogs," Kat winks and opens the door then shuts it behind her.

Blade looks over at the man tied to the bed, his body laid out for us forming an X. He grabs his blade from his boot while I head over to the bag that was left for us.

Taking out the needle and syringe filled with heroine, I ask the cop, "You know, they say this drug is like epinephrine, one shot can keep your adrenaline running for hours before you can pass out from the pain."

His screams go on unheard as I plunge the needle into his arm. He squirms, trying to fight it, but it's of no use. A few seconds later, his body is relaxing from the high.

I get ready for the show and step back a bit as Blade starts walking forward with his knife in his hand. I punch the asshole on the bed across the face and his eyes snap open so that he can see Blade coming at him.

With hands of a surgeon, he places the knife to his victim's skin and the sharp blade of the knife slices like through warm butter, rivers of crimson following. His arms and legs get covered in long cuts.

The gagged cop screams and screams, shaking his head back and forth. Tears run out of his eyes as they shut.

I take the knife from Blade, then I smack the asshole one more time. Grabbing the handle of the knife with both hands, I lift them above my head and plunge it through the side of his breast plate, aiming between his ribs. The force behind my weight and strength break his bones and crack underneath my hands. I raise my hands again to strike the other side.

With both lungs collapsed, he gurgles under the gag and the blood is flowing out around it. His arms and legs twitch for about another thirty seconds while we watch. Grabbing the fucker by the hair, I rip the sharp blade across his throat.

The wolf pacing inside of us runs free and howls.

# CHAPTER 18

## Dana

My phone pings early in the morning with an incoming text. Only someone who's in danger of bodily harm would dare to text or call me before ten a.m. Rolling over, I leave my face buried in my pillow while my arm flies out and my hand slaps around until I locate my phone, which, as it turns out, was on my pillow by my head. I figured that out when the phone slid down the pillow and hit me in the nose.

Growling to myself, I open one eye to peek at the message. I see Axl's name and, as I perk up, the other eye opens to read his message.

**Roger Rabbit: Morning, princess, sorry, I know it's early for you. Last night I had to drop my mom off, then the rental truck. I wanted to come to you last night. It was really late to talk. Today I'm finding my mom a house to rent and have some club shit. Don't know when I'll be available to see you today. But be**

**ready by 7 tonight for our date. I'll meet you at the bar.**

**Jessica Rabbit: I'll see you at 7, and your MOM moved here!**

I'm uncertain at where this day will take me, but I'm ready to see where it ends up.

A smile plays across my lips at the old crew of the Battle Born MC members that pack the bar here at The Black Rose. I miss Vegas coming in and bartending by my side like we used to in the past, but I also get that the woman is driven and her creative spark leads her to be a gypsy at heart.

My poor Jenn is closed off and needs some help. Finally, feeling a little more at peace with life around me, I see that my pain has been blinding me with what is going on around me.

Walking past the tables I see Papa and lean down to give him a kiss on the cheek. "Hey, Papa, you boys starting early tonight? Where's Mom?"

"*Hola, mi corazón*, we are headed out soon. *Tu mama* is helping Harley with something they have going on tonight," Papa winks at me.

Why is Papa winking at me about their plans? Patting him on the back, I walk away to the back office to put my purse away and start to work on our finances.

As I set my purse down in the desk drawer, I find an old photo of the three of us, Vegas, Jenn and myself, laying on top of the desk calendar. I sit in my chair and pick it up. I flip the photo back and forth and look at the back and front repeatedly, hoping there would be a clue to where this photo came from, but nothing. It's a memory I vaguely recall, but I don't remember seeing this photo in here before.

I set it up against the newer framed photo of us three from the day we opened the bar. I decide to take a walk and go ask Vegas if she knows. Stepping out the back door, the warm sun heats my cheeks, and I look over to see Axl watching me from his bike at the other end of the building. Anxiety hits me as I remember the last time I saw him on his bike outside on the night of the fight.

He yells out, "Hey, princess, see you at seven."

A few other members come out from the tattoo shop and he waves. Little butterflies swarm my heart and words lodge in my throat with my feelings. I wave back and tuck my head down while I keep moving toward The Brew House.

Walking in, I stop to look around at what Vegas has done out here. The floors she glossed over the concrete with a deep cobalt blue. The walls that have a texture of dark gray with logos that Blade must have come out here and hand painted for her. On the middle wall is large sign of painted letters that spells "Battle Born Brew" around a large wolf. A large brewing kettle sits underneath the logo in the corner.

I couldn't be happier for her as she creates a new world with her own touches. Classy and a little flashy, but very much my Vegas.

"Yo, ho, what's up?" she yells as she walks out from her office, carrying some supplies in a brown box.

"This place looks so good, why didn't you tell me about it?"

"Dana, girl, you were hurting. Paint and flooring I wasn't going to bother you with," she scolds me.

"This," I point around the room, "is a whole lot more than a little paint and flooring. I've been in my own world," I agree with a sigh. I wasn't in the right frame of mind to hear about it. "I'm here now, so keep me in the loop."

"You got it. Hey, I found this old t-shirt of yours at my house, I thought you might like it back?" Vegas places the box on the floor before I have a chance to answer. She runs to her office and back, holding out a ratty and worn out Guns N' Roses t-shirt from the night I lost my v-card at the concert.

"After what we were talking about the other day with Axl's text messages, I thought to myself, 'I bet I have that t-shirt from that night'. I thought that I had it packed away in the garage when we all moved up here, and I did." She grins, so proud that she brought me something comforting.

"Yeah, I do." My hands hold out the shirt I haven't seen in years. A little light shines from some little dark place that's still hiding a secret away, tucked in the back of my mind. The dark holds up some memories that want to come back to me about that night. A guy that wore a red bandana. It starts coming forward from the back of my mind. Like a flash, the rest of them are pulled back under and like a dream it escapes me again.

"I thought, since we talked about that concert, that you would want to see it after all these years. We really should see what else is in the garage. The three of us have tons of boxes in there. We need to get together and go through all that again one day."

"Yes, we should, it would be fun. Hey, I was going to ask if you left a picture on my desk?"

"Nuh uh," she shakes her head no and goes to pick her box back up.

"Okayyy, well, I got a few things to take care of. Talk to you laters."

"Laters, *chica*," she says over her shoulder, back to her mission of taking on her little world.

Back at my desk, I hold onto the shirt and stare at the picture. I sit and think but nothing will come to me. Frustrated, I set the shirt down and start to work on bills. After hours of work, I walk out to check on the floor before Axl gets here.

Stepping out of the office and into the bar, I see that the bar lights are off. But white twinkle lights are spread across the ceiling.

Axl is standing directly across the bar from me, wearing his cut and a red bandanna. He's so handsome and appears to be so much more relaxed today.

The bar is completely empty of people, just he and I stand here looking at one another. At a table to the side, there's a small pitcher of beer and two plastic cups.

His smile hurts my heart and I don't know why. A tear starts to roll down my cheek. All the pent-up agony pools in my eyes and it bursts open from deep within me.

In quick strides, Axl is in front of me. Holding me to his chest, he rocks me back and forth while I cry all over his cut and black shirt. Taking in a few deep breaths, I gain some control.

"Dana, I was wrong to push you away, I never left you, princess. Please believe me when I say that I never left us. You have always been mine. Sometimes, we need some time on our own to figure things out. I shouldn't have done the things I said and did. I'm going to get your trust back, Dana." Axl holds my face in his hands and gently kisses my lips.

"Nothing stays the same, Axl, we can't go through that every time something happens. We have to lean on each other."

Axl nods along with me before he softly says, "Dana, nothing lasts forever, this minute to the next is never the same. I learned from this, and I know that I never want to have another moment without you in it again, good or bad. I want you at my side for them all. *That* I know will never change. Our love will never be the same, but it will last forever." Axl kisses my lips, then my cheeks.

"These tears," he kisses my eyes as I hold onto his forearms tightly, "Tell me how much love you have for me, they tell me that you know you are mine too, princess. They tell me how much I hurt you, my woman. I'm sorry, Dana, stay with me?"

Axl kisses my lips one last time before pulling me in tightly to his body. With one hand around my back, the other holds my head as he rests his head on top of mine.

"You'll see, Dana, this is our life and I'm going to worship you and the love you give me from it."

Whispering back, I choke out, "I'll always be beside you, forever, you're mine too."

Letting go, Axl wraps his hand around mine, taking me to the table that's set up for us and scooting me in. He pours us a beer and sits down next to me.

"Fancy pitcher you have here," I chuckle at his romantic choice of drink.

"Only the best for my woman," he beams back.

Getting comfortable in the wooden chair next to me, he asks, "How was your day?" while resting one arm on the back of my chair.

"Axl, what happened to you? You're more bruised up than yesterday." I can't help but worry that he's still getting into reckless trouble like before.

"Nothing like that, princess, club stuff. Tell me about your day," he vaguely responds.

Knowing that I will never really know what's happened, I continue. "Good, really. Papa was kind of weird, then I found this old picture on my desk that I don't know how it got there."

I watch as Axl starts playing around with his phone and I'm about to say something before I realize that he started a song. The room fills with the sounds of *November Rain* by Guns N' Roses.

"Sorry, go ahead, princess." Axl looks at me as he puts his phone down. "What weird picture?"

Holding my finger up, I race into the office to grab the old picture and race back to show it to him.

He takes it from my hand, and I sit back next to him. "This you?" he asks as he squeezes me with the arm that was around my chair.

"Yeah, me, Jenn and Vegas."

"Tell me about it." Right as he finishes talking, Mom and Harley come walking out of the kitchen. Axl grabs my hand from under the table. Mom sets a plate of shrimp scampi in front of us and Harley sets down a breadbasket. Neither one of them says a word, trying not to interrupt our dinner.

Mom kisses my forehead, and they both walk out the front door, waving at us. Kissing my hand, Axl says, "Eat and tell me about the picture." Setting my hand in his lap, he starts to eat while watching me.

"I was nineteen, my family went down to Las Vegas for spring break. We went along with Vegas and her parents. Our parents always took Jenn with us wherever we went. This trip, I begged Papa to let the three of us go to this concert, but he kept saying no, that he had business and couldn't go with us. The girls and I were so disappointed because we had already bought our tickets. We ended up at the pool that day and met some guys there. I really wanted to go. So, Vegas asked this guy to go with me." I stop for a minute to get a drink and a bite of food.

"I went along with it, mostly because I had packed for this trip, I was ready for this concert, and if I had a chance to go with this guy, I would take it. Turns out, this guy was a total dumbass."

Taking another bite of food, Axl watches me with a twinkle in his eye.

"Let me guess," he says rubbing his chin. "This guy got knocked out early into the night?"

Nodding my head, I agree, "Yes! He was so drunk and was bumping into everyone. If he wasn't holding onto me, he was hitting the person next to him."

"What happened next?" he questions.

"This hot guy kicked his ass and then he asked me to hang out with him and his friends. I was so in love after one punch with this hot badass, I couldn't say no. It's hard to remember the details after that, but we uh..."

"What?"

"You know..."

Axl turns up the music a little, and *November Rain* continues playing on repeat. He pulls my face close to his, then whispers in my ear, "He took a picture with you, actually several. You two spent the night dancing, drinking and buzzing. Until you pulled him into the bathroom, and you gave him your virginity at a concert while listening to *November Rain*?"

Looking around, I feel paralyzed in my spot, my eyes darting around as I look at Axl in his red bandanna, hearing the song that's playing, and I can't say a word. My pulse rushes through my veins, my mind spinning with the memories, clashing with my reality.

Axl starts laughing and hands me an envelope. I don't touch it and he continues holding it out to me until I take it. I open it to find a stack of pictures. I thumb through them and each picture tells the story of that trip.

My fingers stop and run over the one of a young man resting his chin on my shoulder as he holds me from behind. In the next one, he holds out the camera as he's kissing me.

I close my eyes, and feel the memories flooding me even clearer as the song plays in the background. I try to slow my mind down from the onslaught of memories that are on replay in my mind, just like the song. I see us talking and laughing and singing together. Then me flashing the band from on top of Axl's shoulders! My eyes snap open.

Pure love and amusement are covering Axl's face. "You remember something interesting?"

"Oh. My. God. It was you all along, it was you! And you let me flash my tits to the band!" I accuse Axl of what *I* did.

"Dana, I was just standing there with you on my shoulders. You did that all on your own." He shakes his head at me. "Look at the next picture."

I look at the next picture and there's a profile of my body with my tits out. "Son of a bitch, who took this picture?!"

"I had asked Tank to take a picture of us, and, right before he snapped it, you flashed the band." Laughing, he takes the picture out from the stack. I try to get it back, but he swats my hand away, tucking the picture inside his cut.

"Where, or how, did you get these?"

"My mom, after Maddox died," Axl swallows before he continues. "I threw shit around, trashed my room, she went in there to clean up. She found this disposable camera and developed it for me, and out of curiosity."

I run my hand over Axl's face, and the pain in his eyes breaks my heart for the piece of himself that left with his dad. Kissing his cheek, I want to kiss his hurt away with it.

"I'm happy your mom is here with us in Reno," I tell him earnestly.

"Me too, Maddox would want her with me." And a little more conviction reinforces my belief that Axl will be okay, that *we* will be okay.

We laugh some more while reminiscing of that night. We finish the pitcher of beer and then another two. By the end of our own Guns N' Roses party, we are slow dancing when an idea pops into my head. I start pulling Axl from the dance floor, down the hall to the public bathrooms.

Chasing behind me, he follows me in, and we lock ourselves into a stall. Axl's hands run up the back of my thighs, pushing my skirt up as his fingers trace the hot pink thong I have on. "Princess, I love you in pink." His fingers rub my clit, tracing his fingers along my folds, he pumps his fingers in and out of my pussy.

I devour his lips with mine needing him inside of me, needing to feel whole again with our bodies. I unbuckle his pants and push them down his legs along with his boxers. Lifting one of my legs over his hip and then the other, he pushes into my hot, wanting cunt. His weight helps to hold me up against the door while he sinks his dick further into my aching, needy body. I moan out in bliss as he rears back to slam into me.

Axl uses his need of me to heal a tear that was broken between us. This man worships my body. His hands hold my ass while he kisses and nips up to my ear. He watches in amazement as he pushes inside of me and growls out at the sight of our connection.

"I love you, Dana, we were meant to last forever."

Our hearts and bodies ravage the other until we both come together, and our future welds back together. I hold Axl's face to mine, our foreheads touching.

Best fuckin' night ever.

# CHAPTER 19

## Axl

I stir from a deep slumber, my body feeling warm and relaxed wrapped around Dana's petite one. My arm and leg possessively claim her body. Spooning her from behind, my face is buried in her golden hair. The slight smell of vanilla and coconut linger around me. She stirs a little in my arms, and I hold her protectively against my chest as I thank God or whoever that she stayed with me even though I hurt her so much.

My hand slides under her arms and in between her breasts. Reaching up to her collarbone, my heart beats a little harder at the thought of losing her. I take a few moments of her peaceful serenity and beauty and let it creep its way into my heart, tattooing her permanently there. Taking up some of the dark and pushing it out, making room only for her.

"What's wrong, baby?" She whispers in her morning raspy voice.

"It scares me what I could have done to us. I could have pushed you too far to ever have forgiven me. I know that I need to earn your trust back. My view of life went dark, and thank God you see me, princess, you see my soul through all the pain I put you through."

"Baby, whoever said that I forgave you? I haven't forgotten shit either. You still have a lot of work to do." Dana chuckles at the little admission of her own darker confessions.

"I have faith in you and in us, Axl. I have faith that you will deliver on your promises. We may stumble along the way, but you will come through for us." She says it as she rolls to her back and brings her hand to my hair to brush back the overgrown pieces that have fallen forward.

"I like this repayment request, I can repay you in many ways, princess."

"Yeah?"

"Yeah, and I'm going to start now," I say as I pull the sheet away from her firm body. My lips kiss her enticing plump ones, kissing down her jaw and throat. My princess moans for me when I suck on her neck. My hands grab hers and I lift them above her head, holding them there with one of mine.

Following the seductive lines of her body, my lips stay on course, kissing down. I leave a cherishing kiss over her heart. Dana's restless body stretches under me.

"Keep going," she demands of me, her legs rubbing together in anticipation of my touch.

My thumb grazes over her nipple. Ever so lightly, I caress her skin on the way down to her waist. Goosebumps prickle as she tries to stifle from laughing.

"Behave," I growl at her, "or I'll stop."

Taking her nipple between my teeth, I graze them across her sensitive flesh. Dana moans and tries to bring her hands down, but I hold her there, needing complete submission from her. My other hand picks up her knee and I rest her leg over mine. My fingertips caress over the arch of her foot, up the inside of her leg and she shivers from my delicate touch.

Reaching down to her pussy, I stroke her delicate lips there, and find her hot and ready for my dick. My fingers pump in and out while my thumb caresses her little clit. Moaning, my lips find her ear and neck, and I deliver nips, tasting her skin as I stroke her. Priming her pussy further to take more from me, my desire wants to bring her to ecstasy with me.

My submissive princess arches into me, asking me to give her large breast attention. My tongue swirls around one nipple and then the other. I bite down on her delicate flesh and she starts tensing as an orgasm rushes through her. Her legs open wider for me, inviting me inside her compliant body, inside her tender heart.

Slowly, I suck at her breasts and pump my fingers until she fully comes down from her blissful state.

Dana's chest rises and falls as she takes in deep steadying breaths. Releasing her hands, I position my body between her legs. My goddess lays before me, her legs spread wide for my enjoyment.

"I will consume all of you," I warn. "I am not the same man as before, Dana, there's a darker version that was never there before. If you take me, you take the demon that's inside of me too. I don't want it to take away from your light."

"Axl, all of you belongs to me. All of you that's good or bad. I can't live without you. I *won't* live without you. Take whatever light you need from me. I want your dark, too. I want it all."

Leaning forward, I take one long lick of her pussy. Having missed her scent, touch and taste, I devour what's always been mine, what I took all those years ago without knowing what it was when I had it.

Somewhere inside of me, I knew this woman was mine. I savagely hunger for her and won't allow her to stop me. She is mine.

The taste of her intoxicates me, taking me to a primal level of need. It is a need that overrides my senses to fill her with my life and my baby. I flatten my tongue over her clit, and, with hurried strokes over and over again, I bring her to another quick but powerful orgasm.

Moving up her body, I place one hand beside her chest as my other hand drags my rock-hard dick through her folds. I coat her on myself and moan out with the need to fill my woman.

With a determined push, I connect us as one. I bring my body forward, my chest to hers, and I kiss her lips.

"I need to mark your skin with my brand. My baby stretching and marking your body. Mine," I rasp over her lips.

I savagely nip and pull at her lips with my teeth. I want to destroy her and take her to heaven or our hell with me. Make her the reflection of who I am, of what my love is, of us. Whatever it is, it's us together.

Dana licks at my tongue and I lovingly rub mine back over hers. Rearing back, I begin to stroke my dick in and out of what is mine. I love the slick tightness of her, it sends tingles through my body. Needing more, I increase the speed of my thrusts.

Fire ignites into my body as I pound out the release into my woman and her pussy convulses around me.

Dana reaches up, in her skin-tight Levi's, to place some dishes in the cupboard above her. I have to close my eyes to resist the urge to rip her jeans off and fuck her in my mom's new kitchen. Groaning to myself, I take a tentative couple of steps toward the living room with some boxes in my arms.

"Axl! Why are you walking around with your eyes shut! You almost ran me over!" Mom screeches at me. I pop my eyes open, startled to hear her voice so close.

"Fuck, you don't wanna know, Ma," I say and walk around her.

"He was popping a semi for the princess in the kitchen," Tank helpfully tells her. "I saw the same thing, but I didn't close my eyes," Tank teases.

"Shut the fuck up, Tank, I will fuck *your* ass up if you stare at *her* ass, it's MY ass," I warn him, scowling.

"Easy, boys, and I really don't want to know about her ass, I've already seen her tits," Mom confesses, and a glass is shattered onto the kitchen floor. Mom chuckles as she walks away. "Dana, that's a nice set of tits too, girl, my boy did good."

"Axl! Where is that picture? I'm burning it." Dana comes storming out of the kitchen and stands her ground firmly in front of me.

Setting the boxes down, I reach around her to grab handfuls of the ass I was eyeballing a little bit ago, and say, "Never handing it over, it's mine. Losers weepers, finders' keepers." I kiss her nose and let go, then I walk away with Tank as he whispers to me, "Can I see it?"

"What the fuck is wrong with you? Besides, they are my tits. You remember that concert, the one where you took the picture with the girl on my shoulders and she flashed the band?" I question, shaking my head at his dumbass.

"Kind of, yeah. Are you telling me that was *her*?" Tank says in disbelief. Then realization hits him. "I've seen your woman's tits." He smirks. "I may need to verify it was me who took that picture. I never forget a pair of nice tits."

I start reaching into my cut to pull out the picture... Instead, I pull my hand out empty and flip Tank off. "Fuck you, asshole. Like I said. My. Fuckin'. Tits. My eyes only."

"You're a selfish fucking bastard, you know that? Jesus, was that really her a whole fuckin' ten years ago?" Tank's face is priceless, his mouth opened so wide with disbelief.

"Believe it, fucker, I found my princess after all this time. I'm Prince fuckin' Charming in my own fairytale," I tell him with a cocky grin.

"What? As in she lost her dick and you helped her find it again? So," Tank laughs, "You slipped your dick in all the maiden pussies in all the land, searching for the right maiden pussy that was lost all those years ago. Some pussies fit too small and some fit too large," Tank chuckles.

"But this one was the fairest maiden of them all, she slipped on the lost cock, and it was a perfect pussy fit after all?" he finishes while holding his stomach from laughing so hard.

"Fits like the finest fuckin' princess pussy in all of the land," I say and grab my crotch, thrusting my hips forward.

Tank's hand is over his mouth, laughing with his eyes on the kitchen window. I turn to look at my right, and Dana is at the window where it's obvious that she heard the whole conversation.

"I love you, princess!"

"He loves your princess pussy!" Tank yells after me to make sure she heard it. Dana's eyebrows raise and she slams the window shut.

"Fuck, Tank," I shake my head at my best, dumbass friend.

"You're also like Humpty Dumpty," he snickers. "She had to go put your broken dumbass back together again."

Glaring at Tank, I say, "At least I have princess pussy. Say whatever you want, my dumb humpty dumpty ass gets all the humpin' pussy. Fuck, never mind, this shit is stupid."

Walking around to the back of the U-Haul, I spot a black sedan parked a block over, with the ignition running and facing us. I grab a box and continue back into the house. I set it down in the living room, then continue into the spare room, signaling for Tank to follow me.

Tank shuts the door as I call Blade, placing the phone on speaker. I wait until he picks up.

"Axl," his deep baritone voice echoes in the room.

"Outside of my mom's house there's a black sedan with the engine running, facing the house. I don't want to be paranoid, but can we get some eyes and

Spider on it?" I ask as an uneasy feeling crawls up my spine.

"Aye, how long will you be there?"

"Most of the afternoon, moving shit, why?"

"Keep the girls in the house, but keep your eyes on it. I want to look around town, see who's here. I don't want the car to move until I get a head count," Blade states.

My phone beeps off as Spider calls and instructs me to get a few pictures. Opening the door to the room, I find Dana and my mom standing with their hands on their hips and eyebrows cocked.

"What? We had a club call," I explain, and Dana raises her eyebrows higher, not believing me. "We did," I say again.

Walking into the clubhouse, I find Blade in his office looking out the window. "That bad of a day, huh?" I ask him.

"I think Tony has been following you still, along with the rest of us," Blade answers.

"Why?"

"I called Fuego and Stryker. Tony has a deal with *Los Reyes Malditos*, The Cursed Kings, to transport drugs and diamonds up here. Since we took over, or killed off his connections for transport, he's fucked."

"How close are we to paying off the Club's debt with him?" I ask.

"One fight to go." Blade takes a long drag off his smoke. His thoughts swirl around the space along with the smoke as he exhales.

"This isn't over, is it?"

"Far from over, brother," he replies and shakes his head.

"What did we find about the car at Harley's house?" I don't want to have to worry about my mom's safety on top of everything else.

"One of Tony's guys was watching the house," he says while exhaling smoke.

"Fuck, maybe I shouldn't have brought her up here," I say and run my hands through my hair.

"No, her being closer to you was better. Down there she would've been left more vulnerable. This way, we have eyes on her. We will finish this last fight and get some answers. Stryker has a call out to *Los Reyes Malditos*."

Blade's worried eyes find mine. Stryker never asks for help from *Los Reyes Malditos*, and we all know why.

Cuervo.

The music blares, pumping the crowd with fake energy for the fight. They all cheer as Blade jumps into the ring, shirtless, like a predator. He surveys his surroundings and takes a walk around the ring. The MC eyes him as he is announced. Blade doesn't give one fuck other than to drop the other fighter and then get the fuck back to the clubhouse.

The other fighter turns to face Blade. He is also one of Tony's guards. The fighter pops forward, lunging at Blade, looking to get the first hit in right after the bell. Blade dodges left and jabs the fighter in the stomach, who, in turn, falls forward with the blow, and forgets to cover his face. Blade brings his fist up and catches him on the chin, his head whipping back. His body follows, falling backward onto the ropes and then the floor.

A man that's sitting in the front row seat stands and quickly walks by the fallen fighter.

"Snake, follow that asshole who just left the ring."

Snake takes off into the crowd, and, just as I suspected, the fighter stands, fisting a small knife in his hand. Blade's eyes zero in on his hand. Lifting his leg, he reaches into his boot and he pulls out a butterfly knife of his own. Flipping the handle around in his hand, he firmly grips the knife with an evil gleam in eyes.

The fighter steps forward, looking for an opening to sink the knife into Blade's flesh. Lunging for him, Blade brings his size twelve boot up into the man's face. The knife misses Blade's throat but nicks his arm. Blade slashes across the man's stomach. Blood pours from the cut across his abs.

Polices sirens blare from down the street. Blade grabs the fighter's hand that's holding the knife and pulls him toward him, only to plunge his own knife into his gut. He twists the knife as he pulls it out. He rapidly stabs him several more times and the room erupts into chaos. People rush for the exits before they end up getting arrested.

Men circle Tank and I as fists start flying and more knifes come out to play. Tank and I are stuck in a knife fight with four other guys. Odds aren't good. A blast of a gun goes off behind us and scares the shit out of me as I jump and hit the floor. Tank turns, and I see sparkles lighting up his eyes. I look over my shoulder to see Kat dressed all in black, walking over our way, double fisting two Glocks.

"There's my Kitty Kat. Just in time, baby!"

"Shut the fuck up, Tank!" she scolds him.

She tosses him a gun, then stands in front of him. Reaching behind her back, she tosses out another nine in my direction. I catch it in midair and jump to my feet.

Tank's hand slides around her stomach and he whispers into her ear while grinding his dick into her ass. She fires her gun just as Tank does the same, holding his arm out over her shoulder.

Real *Pulp Fiction* mixed with a twisted *Kill Bill* kind of shit is happening and I see dead bodies drop. Taking their backs, I fire and hit three more men that were coming from the same direction Kat just came from.

Blade jumps down from the ring with his hands covered in blood from the four guys who are bleeding out up there. Trapped in the warehouse, we look for an exit and we start running back toward the offices. Kat hands Blade a small canister of lighter fuel and a lighter.

"Tank, Kat, run into the rooms to find papers or shit to burn. Axl, watch the hallway!" Blade yells and runs into another room.

Holding my Glock straight out in front of me, my legs are spread wide and I'm ready for the first fucker to pop his head around the corner. One unlucky motherfucker notices me too late since he came barreling around the corner, and I pop him in the head.

Blade runs back and dumps a trashcan of papers onto the floor. He is followed by Tank who's carrying a few boxes and Kat brings an oxygen tank.

"Fuck yeah, light this bitch on fire," Tank high fives a demonic looking Kat. Blade pours out the small container of lighter fluid around the items, tossing the lighter on top of it all. Flames rise high around us, making a circle of fire. Three cops appear from down the hallway.

Tank, Kat and I raise our Glocks and fire through the flames. Three more dead bodies hit the concrete, dead cold. We jump out and take off down the hallway to the back office, locking the door behind us.

Blasting the window, I hold my hands together for Kat. She sticks her boot into the step I made, and I lift her up to the window so she can crawl through. Blade helps me to heave Tank's fat ass up. I help Blade up through the window, too.

Tank yells from the other side, "Move your ass, Humpty!"

I jump up, gripping the windowsill. With a loud grunt, I pull myself up to find Tank waiting.

"Get your ass down, Dumpty, before you crack your ass on the concrete."

As I'm lifting my leg up and stick it through the window, a loud boom shakes the walls and floors from the oxygen tank blowing up. I lift the rest of my body as smoke and heat envelopes the room. I drop to my feet, coughing and dry heaving from inhaling all that shit.

Tank and I jump into the back of the Suburban with the rest of the crew. We peel the fuck out of the death trap we just escaped from, thank fuck.

# CHAPTER 20

## Dana

"Jenn!" I yell for her outside of her house as I bang my fist against the door for the tenth time. "Son of bitch, what's wrong with you?" I mutter to myself while walking around the house to the back.

I walk up the steps to reach the back door, and then bang on it too a few more times. She doesn't answer. I am annoyed that she can't bother to show up or call us anymore.

I get back to my car, then drive the twenty minutes over to The Black Rose. I'm hoping that I can find her there, lost in her music, and that she didn't blow me off again. Emilia opens the door to the kitchen with Tami trailing out behind her, carrying cleaning supplies.

"Have you guys seen Jenn around today?"

"She called in sick last night, we haven't seen her in a few days," Emilia answers, looking concerned.

"I haven't seen her either, is she okay?" Tami asks, and starts wringing her hands together in front of her.

"I'm sure she's fine. I just thought we had made plans for today." I pull my lips up into a smile and try to seem unaffected that Jenn didn't show up for work. Jenn lives and breathes for her music, so the news is making me feel even worse.

"I bet she's over at the brewery, I'll go check over there. If you do see her, give me a call, okay?"

"Okay," they both answer, sounding unconvinced.

I leave the bar through the back and head over toward the brewery, even more worried now than I was before. I find Vegas behind her desk, with her black rimmed glasses on as she types away on her keyboard.

"Vegas," I say at the same time as Tugg barks all excited to see me and wanting to play.

She jumps in her chair and hits her knee on the desk. "Jesus, you asshole, what's with the tone? What's going on? You just scared the ever-loving shit out of me," she says, taking her glasses off and setting them on her desk.

Reaching over, I pet an anxious Tugg as I tell her about my problem. "I was supposed to go shopping with Jenn today. I went to go pick her up over an hour ago. She hasn't been answering her phone and she wasn't home." If anyone will believe me that something is wrong, it'll be Vegas.

"I thought maybe she was working on her music again, but she wasn't at the bar, and Emilia and Tami said she called in sick. What the hell's been going on?"

Vegas holds up her hand and walks around the desk, all while putting her leather coat on. "Don't panic, we know she wouldn't go too far off the grid. Let's go talk with Blade and Axl. Let them know we are running off to go find Jenn. Come on, Tugg, let's go."

"We have to go tell them?" Tugg and I follow Vegas out of the building. He jumps all around my feet, asking to go play.

"Yeah, we do. The last time I took you on an impromptu field trip, I couldn't sit down for a week, and Blade turned into Sandman, cold bastard, and that was boring as fuck."

"Sandman?" I ask as we jump into her black Tahoe.

"Yeah, you know the song *Enter Sandman* by Metallica? Dude kills people in their sleep, takes them off to Neverland to never return."

She starts the car and drives us over to the tattoo shop. "He's a prickly bastard when you piss him off," she casually states about the killer sleeping next to her every night.

Leaving the car running, we jump out with Tugg in tow, and walk into the Battle Born Tattoo shop. Vegas is on a mission, not seeing anything but her destination in the back room where Blade is working on a guy's arm piece.

"Babe? Sorry, can I interrupt you for a minute?" Vegas asks so sweetly.

He rolls back in his chair, with his eyebrows raising at her tone. "Give me five?" Blade asks his client and rolls his shoulders back to stretch. The guy nods, and Blade grabs his smokes with one hand and plants his other one firmly on her ass as he starts leading us out the front door.

Once we're finally outside, Blade lights his smoke and looks at Vegas. "What's going on, baby doll?"

"We think something's wrong with Jenn, so Dana and I are going to go find her."

Just as she finishes her sentence in one quick breath, Axl pulls up on his bike and parks in his designated spot. He comes and stands next to me, then, bending down, he gives me a big kiss.

"Vegas and I were just telling Blade how we can't find Jenn. She's not answering her phone and called in sick," I fill Axl in on the situation.

"Is that all? Maybe she doesn't feel good and is sleeping off a hangover?" Axl questions as if we are overreacting. Vegas and I turn to look directly at him, both of us surprised at his statement and reasoning.

Vegas' eyes squint at him and points a deep red polished finger at him, "What do you know, Axl?" She takes her pointed finger and rests her hand on her hip. I cross my arms over my chest waiting for Axl to explain himself.

"Well, she likes to get lit every once in a while, nothing wrong with it."

"Axl, I'm losing my cool with you, get it out and tell us what you know," Vegas demands. Blade sits back, smirking at the pile of shit Axl just slipped in.

"Before I left for Las Vegas, I was at the clubhouse and Jenn and I were both sitting outside having a few drinks of whiskey, and she and I popped a pill, is all. How would I know or think she has a problem?"

"What kind of a fucking pill, dude?" Vegas shrieks at Axl in disbelief.

"I don't know, a Percocet, I guess, some kind of prescription painkiller," he shrugs.

"So, let me clarify this situation here so you and I are on the same page. One," Vegas holds up a finger, "It's totally cool with you to have Dana get, I don't know, what was the word? Oh yeah, *lit*, with one of your brothers, alone, without you there?"

"No. I did not say that."

"Nope, you didn't, but, hey, what's good for you is good for her too."

Axl opens his mouth to protest, but Vegas brings her thumb and fingers together in a 'shut the hell up motion', then continues.

"Two, you don't find it alarming that Jenn is carrying around prescription pain pills to drown in hard liquor and is getting shit faced while taking them, Axl? *Pinche cabrón.* Stupid asshole," Vegas shakes her head at him.

"And, three, you don't even tell one fucking important person in her life that shit may be wrong with her? Are you really that selfish lately? Fuck, Axl,

I know you went through some shit, but a fuckin' text would have been really cool. Makes a whole lot more sense where my pain pills went. You remember that at all?" Vegas' face scrunches up at Blade.

Axl just stands there, frozen in spot, afraid to move or say the next wrong thing. I would too if I were him.

"Vegas," I stop her to get us back on track. "We've got to figure out where she is and check on her. Even though Axl didn't tell us then, we have a clue of what could be going on now. Where would she go?"

"I can think of a couple of places. Blade, keep your phone close by, love." Vegas leans over and pecks Blade on the lips. "Keep Tugg too, please?" she calls over her shoulder while storming back to her car. "Let's move our asses, Dana, we've got our girl to find."

"Aye," is all Blade says as he watches Vegas' ass and hips sway from side to side.

"That shit was always fun to watch, her rip into your ass, brother," Axl says while shaking his head. "All too funny until it's you the she-devil digs her claws into."

"You fucked up, brother, you fucked with her girls. If she held that information from you about one of the brothers, you would feel the same." Blade drops his smoke in a canister and heads back into the shop with Tugg following closely behind.

Axl grabs me around my waist and tugs my body into his. "Sorry, princess."

"I know, Axl, see what you can do to find out what's going on with her?"

"Dana! Let's move ass!" Vegas bellows and slams the driver door shut.

Axl kisses my lips, "I'm on it, princess, your wish is my command."

I book it over to the car, afraid of the wrath from Vegas. Waiting for me to snap my seatbelt on, she peels out of the driveway.

"Dana, I pray to the heavens up above that you rip into Axl's ass later when you get home. I wasn't even done yet with my ass chewing. It feels so unresolved in here," she points to her head.

"I just wanna tell him all the ways he's been a little shit lately. Girl, you better promise me right here and fucking now that you make his ass pay. Promise me."

Vegas is a hundred percent serious too, or she will finish this for me later. "I promise a full ass chewing report by tomorrow. Would you like this in an email or an office debriefing over your morning coffee to get you pumped for your day?"

"Morning coffee debriefing is best. Thank you." She thinks for a moment and taps her nails on the steering wheel. Her eyes dart between me and the road. "How are things with you and Axl now that he's back?"

I tell her honestly. "Even though him pushing me away while he was going through all of that hurt like hell, I don't think I could ever turn him away, Vegas."

Shame covers my features and I look out the window, not wanting Vegas to see the truth in my eyes.

"Dana, you don't have to push him away to prove shit to anyone, and sure as hell not to me. If you two had a rough patch, I'm going to support you, no matter what, okay?"

"I know."

"Then hear it and fuckin' believe that shit." Vegas smirks over to me before her eyes go back to the road.

"He wants me to get a tattoo," I blurt. "I'm scared of needles, Vegas. What kind of an Ol' Lady has fears of getting a tattoo? We were born and raised in this lifestyle. How am I going to tell Axl no when he's ready to brand me!" I panic looking for Vegas to help me.

"Do you trust me? And do you *really* want a tattoo," she asks with a glint of mischief in her tone.

"I don't know, your devious tone is freaking me out!"

Vegas turns her head toward me again. "I got you, Dana, I got this. I will make it happen for you, but I need a reassurance."

Fucking hell, what kind of help did I just ask for? "What the hell are you asking for?"

"Send me a text, a waiver of sorts, stating that you want a tattoo and you have put your trust into me to help you make it happen."

I start typing... **I, Dana Maraschino, of sound mind and sound body, do hereby...**

Vegas and I went and checked Jenn's house again, she wasn't there. We checked the gym, the grocery store, Kat's apartment. We both are at a loss of where she could be, alone in the city. We cruise up and down the main streets thinking while we listen to music.

**Roger Rabbit: Spider can't find her phone, she has it off.**
**Me: Thank you ; )**

"We fucked up, Vegas. We should have pushed her harder to come to us."

"I don't agree. If we would have done that, then she would have taken off for sure. It is her choice, Dana. We did ask her a few times what was going on before all this shit. It's up to her to let us in too. She also knows we are here, and we will always be."

"I see that too. I just wish that there was more we would've done. I just don't feel like this is it either."

"It's not it. Jenn is struggling, and we will find out what it is and help her through it. Out of the three of us, she had it the worst. I keep reminding myself of that," Vegas finishes.

We continue driving in silence until I hear her gasp. "Hey, I think I know where she went. You remember that little bar that did an open mic night? I bet she's there."

Vegas takes a sharp right, speeding down the back streets to get to the place she's thinking of. She parks across the street from the small bar.

Together, we run across the busy street and walk into the bar. Walking around the tables, we find Jenn sitting in the corner. We both halt at the same time and our faces drop at the sight in front of us. Jenn. Alone. She just sits there staring into space as she's stirring her cocktail.

The bar is busy with laughter and the singer belts out a beautiful melody that can't even engage the beautiful Jenn. Her long, blond hair is falling around her face. Deep, dark circles haunt her complexion. She looks haunted, just existing amongst the rest of us.

Vegas grabs my hand and pulls me with her through the crowd. Jenn doesn't register us walking toward her or even us standing in front of her. The waitress comes by with her tray and notepad, curiously eyes us up and down, then asks, "What can I get you two girls?"

Jenn's eyes come up and she startles at the sight of us in front of her.

"I'll have a coke," I smile back at the waitress.

"How about a water with lemon for me. Jenn, you ready for a refill?" Vegas asks her casually, trying to mask her concern.

"I'll have a... no, thanks, I'm good. Thanks, though," she responds and looks back down at her drink.

"Be back in a few then." The waitress pops her gum and heads back to the bar.

Vegas and I slide into the empty seats next to Jenn. "Dude, this place is pretty nice. It's been a while, you should have called, Jenn. We would have come with you."

"Definitely, no one should drink alone." Vegas looks at me worried.

Jenn looks up at us, anguish covering her face. "You guys came looking for me?"

"Jenn, we know something is wrong. We didn't want to push you too hard before, but we know you are not all right. Did you even remember we had plans to go out together today? I was worried about you. Why are you pushing us away?"

"No, I must've forgotten that we were hanging out today. Sorry, I should've texted you," she mumbles, then goes on. "I feel so lost in this world and I don't even have the words to explain it all."

She exhales deeply. "I've felt like I have lost it all lately. I've lost touch with myself mostly, and I've tried to ignore those feelings and get lost in my music. Even that has not been helping. I feel so dead inside. I feel as if I have been gutted out. I don't feel like any part of me fits anywhere."

She pauses before looking at us. "How can I be around anyone when it's so hard to be around me? I wasn't ready to talk about it."

Jenn goes back to stirring her cocktail as the waitress stops by and sets down our drinks. I place a ten on her tray and she thanks us, then continues to the next table to drop off their drinks.

"You are not alone, Jenn. Not ever. We are always a team. If you sit in pain, then we all sit here in pain. If you want to talk, then we do too, okay?"

Jenn doesn't say anything one way or another, and I fear we lost her. I fear we are too late to reach her, and that thought terrifies me. I will sit here with her as long as it takes. Vegas and I watch the crowd of happy couples and friends talking and enjoying their night. We listen to songs and drown into the abyss with Jenn. We are staying, whether she wants us to or not.

After about an hour, Jenn scoots her chair back and heads toward the door. Quickly, Vegas and I follow. We reach the dark sidewalk of the River Walk downtown. The cold air feels welcome to our somber moods. Lights string along the pathway of the sidewalk.

Picking up our pace, we catch up to Jenn and flank her on each side, as a team. We walk the streets together, listening to the cars that bustle by and honk their horns as they go by. Aptly showcasing what Jenn must have been feeling this whole time. Watching us live, thrive around her while she drifts alone, just a voyeur.

She stops in the middle of the bridge, her feet guiding her to overlook the calm river. She places her hands on the railings and deep breaths override her calm exterior.

"I've lost a lot. When I was a little girl, my mother was raped and murdered in front of me. My sister and I watched as men took her flesh and abused her for their desires. The memories haunt me. Her screams still run through me."

Tears flow down her chilled cheeks. She doesn't bother to wipe them away. They are a welcome part of her that she is intimate with.

"Memories I can never erase because of him. My father. He is the one responsible for her death and our torture. I have so much hate for him and those men for what he did. Then he leaves me and my sister with my aunt to deal with this alone. My entire life, all alone. Ashley was just a toddler when this happened, her mind doesn't remember, but she knows of what happened. How fair is it that she gets to have a normal life? Why would that asshole leave his kids behind, all alone? Why?"

"Babe, what happened to you? What happened last year that has brought all this back now?" Vegas implores her.

"Those men came back looking for me."

# CHAPTER 21

## Axl

"Hey, Mom!"

Where the hell is she at? I walk around the house and check each room, but I can't find her. Anxiety crawls over my skin, worried that something's happened to her. Racing from room to room, I look for her. Pacing to the back patio, I finally see her in the hammock, curled up in a blanket, next to a small fire.

"Mom?" I call to her as I open the sliding glass door. She turns her face to me. Puffy swollen eyes find my own. "Momma, what's wrong?" I pull up a chair to sit next to her.

"I'm trying to find my way in this world, sweetheart. Without him in it. It's suffocating. It helps being closer here with you. The lonely days and nights are so hard without him."

I reach under the blanket to grip her hand. I give it a tight squeeze. "Keep going, Momma, I want you to tell me all of it. I'm here for you."

"I need him, Axl. I need him to hold me. In the past thirty-five years, I never slept alone, without his arms around me. Every day I heard his voice, and now... nothing. I go to the store and go to grab his favorite foods, only to find myself crying at the checkout line because I have to go put it all back."

She sobs, and my throat hurts so bad that I can't even say a word.

"I will go on. It's just learning to live without him, to forget living with him, that's hurting me the most. Forgetting the way he feels, and his voice. God, I miss his voice. I haven't, and can't, erase his voicemails on my phone."

"You have one?" My throat loosens barely enough to get those three words out.

"Yeah, baby. Listen." She pulls out her phone from under the blanket and pushes play.

"Hey, Harley." My dad's deep voice comes through. "Axl and I are at the clubhouse. We are waitin' for you here. Hurry up with the girls, I miss my woman." She smiles and plays the next.

"Have you heard from Axl? That little shit is going to get a boot up his ass if he doesn't get here. Tell him to hurry the hell up."

I remember that day about a year ago...

*"Dad, what the hell? Quit blowing up my phone, I'm not even late. You're fuckin' early. Jesus..." I tell him as I put my kickstand down and meet him in front of the tattoo shop.*

*"Well, I've got other shit to do today too, you know?" He says it as he's hanging up the phone after I hear him bitching to Mom about me being late, again. I swear, if his ass wasn't so impatient...*

*"Uh huh, like what?"*

*"You don't want to know," the devil grins back at me.*

*"You're fucking right about that," I say as I open the door to the tattoo shop. "I wanted you to be my first client here. You pick it, I'll stick it."*

*I set up my room while Dad scrolls through his phone until he finds a picture of a skull with a crown, and behind the skull there's a bright red rose.*

*"A skull and a rose, huh?" I ask him to tease.*

*"Aye, it's for your mom. In this life or the next, our love will last forever. Put it right here on my forearm. Is there enough room?"*

*Grabbing his large arm, I move it side to side, eyeing how much room I have. "Let's do it."*

An idea sprouts in my mind. "Get up and get ready, you and I are going to have some fun today!" I stand up and hold my hand out to help her out of her little sad cocoon.

Mom nods, and I see a little life coming back into her eyes. "Yeah, let's go get into a little trouble, just like Mad Max would!" She fist pumps the air.

Less than an hour later, we walk through the Battle Born Tattoo shop.

"What's up, Sunshine?" I greet our receptionist.

"Nothing, Axl, is this your first client with you?" Sunshine has been working as a receptionist, but is also working with us as an apprentice.

"Sunshine, meet my mom, Harley."

"Hello. It is so very nice to meet you. How old are you? I mean you are so gorgeous and, holy fuck, seriously, Axl cannot be your kid!" she exclaims.

"Yes, honey, this meathead is all mine," she says, slapping my back.

"Damn, you are one fine cougar then."

"She was a Harley pin-up model, it's how she got her road name by the old man," I brag just a little, wanting to help put some more light into her pretty green eyes.

"That was a whole lifetime ago," Mom blushes.

"I bet you could go back to it today," Sunshine compliments her, and I know it's genuine because my mom is a cold stone knock out, even in her fifties.

"Sunshine, please cancel my appointments for today. I've got a whole date day planned with Harley."

"Sure thing, boss."

In my room, I riffle through my drawing binders until I come across the one I was looking for. Taking it out of the plastic sheet, I hand it over to her.

"Is this the last tattoo you did for your dad?" she asks with shiny eyes. Her fingers run over every line, then looks up at me.

"Yes, it was. You know that message you just played, Dad telling you to tell me to hurry the hell up and that I was late? I wasn't late, the man was twenty minutes early, as always. But anyway, it gave me an idea. You want the same tattoo?"

"Hell yes, I do! Where are we going to put it?" Happiness lights up her voice.

"It's pretty big, so I would say it would have to be a thigh or on your back to work. If you want your thigh, I'll call in Blade or Tank to do it, because yeah, I'm not going there."

She sits and thinks about it for a few minutes before she says, "I want it on my right shoulder, right next to the brand your dad gave me. Will that work?"

"Yes, I can do that. It's going to take me about thirty minutes to draw it and set up. You can go over to the bar and chat with the girls while I get it all ready, and then we will stick it!"

Hours later, Mom looks into the two mirrors opposite of each other. Her eyes begin to water and a smile spreads across her face. She originally had a tattoo of a heart and a rose together, with Mad Max scrolled across the top. I added to the words as a surprise, it says now, 'Mad Max, from this life to the next, our love has no bounds', with more vibrant red roses and black leaves that intertwine around a black and gray skull with a crown.

"It's beautiful, sweetie!" She is standing there, holding her gaze to the mirror, when Tank comes barreling through. He stops, staring at her back.

"That is beautiful," he smirks.

"Don't be a dick, Tank."

"What?" he smirks at me, feigning confusion.

"You know what. Get the fuck out so she can put her shirt the rest of the way back on."

"Fine," he winks at her. "I hear that we are having a date day. What else are we doing? You know what, don't tell me. I want to be surprised." He looks at me again. "I'm going to go grab Dana for our double date because I don't want you to feel left out."

"Why the fuck would I feel left out? Just fucking get out, Tank!" I say pushing him out and into the hall. He skips his big ass down the hallway and out the front door, then over to The Black Rose.

Ten minutes later, Dana, Harley, Tank and I are out on our double date. I told him before we left that his flirting better not go too far with Mom. He just laughed at me and said not to be stupid. Fucking dumbass.

We've arrived at the mall and Tank groans, "The mall, dude? Come on!"

"You wanted to come, so shut the fuck up. And you're paying for half of everything," I inform him.

"Okay, I have more money than you anyway. That's fair enough."

"That's not what I meant."

"Sure you didn't," Tank says and holds the door open for my mom, and I do the same for Dana.

If there is one thing I know about these women, it's that they love their boots. So that's what I do. I grab Dana by the hand and take her to her boots.

"Wow, feel how soft these are," Dana says to Mom handing her a pair of Harley Davidson boots that lace up the side and stop at her calves. "These are nice, I could wear them to work too."

"They *are* nice. Look at these ones, Dana!" Mom races over to a pair that you would think would have disappeared if she didn't get there fast enough. "These remind me of a pair I had years ago." She holds them up with a faraway look on her face.

"Get them. Everything we do today is on Tank and me," I say as I'm flagging down a salesgirl. She asks them for their sizes, but Dana's isn't in stock.

"Don't worry, princess, I'll pick yours up when they come in." I kiss her lips and swat her ass out the door.

"It's pedicure time. My ladies need some pretty toes." Grabbing Dana's hand and then Mom's, we swing our hands back and forth. Tank takes my mom's hand on the other side, and the four of us stroll down the mall walkways, forcing people to walk around us, but I don't give a single fuck.

We arrive at the pedicure shop when Tank says a little too loudly, "This place is like Chinese takeout but

for feet. It's cool though, let's get our pedicures on."
He slaps his hands together ready and leading the way.

Dana whispers, "Did he really just say that? Now they're going to be mean to us when they aren't really nice to begin with, and is he really coming with us?"

"Easy, princess, if those bitches are mean to you, you let me know and I will take care of it. Okay?" She nods back. "Go pick your color for whatever bullshit and I'm grabbing a drink."

An hour later, we are at the little mini racetrack for kids. There are two lanes and several drivers, but there will be only one winner.

Tank and I decide to be gentlemen and allow Mom and Dana into the go-karts in the very front. I'm still determined to beat them though. I said I was a gentleman because I gave them a shot at the front.

I rev my little lawn mowing sounding engine. I let out a "RRRR" and Dana and Mom turn around and eye me. What? Don't they feel the need for speed?

I grip the stirring wheel tightly. The light starts to count down, red, yellow, green! I slam my foot down only to bump the back end of Dana's kart. "Go, woman, step on it!"

Mom and Tank hackle at me as my woman finally gets the idea of why we're here. I push on the gas and bump her into the corner, laughing manically at my maneuver. Dana flips me off, but it's better that she learns this now.

I zero in on my next two targets, Tank and Mom. Tank and I take turns brutally slamming each other into the side rails. Mom knows well enough and just gets out of the way.

I'm so close to winning, it's the last lap, and I'm screeching tires coming around the corner when I'm hit, and I spin into Tank. Mom hits the back end of his kart, so we are now facing each other, and those sneaky girls take the win. Son of a bitch.

Dana parks the kart and jumps up and down with Mom, giggling the whole way to the mini golf course arm in arm, and later again on our way out.

"Alrighty, ladies, last stop of the day, go ahead and look." Mom's out of the car before I even tell her that we are at the pet store, and runs in.

Taking Dana's hand, we walk in and find Mom sitting on the floor with two puppies, playing with them. Dana lets go of my hand. "Oh my God, a playpen of puppies!" She steps over the gated circle. She sits down on the floor too and starts playing with a little labradoodle that keeps licking her face. His little paws rest on each of her shoulders.

"Dana, I think I want to take two of these little babies home!" My mom squeals while playing with two small King Charles dogs. "They are just so fluffy and cute, and they are the only two in here, like a little set. Aren't you a little set?" She's baby talking to them now.

Tank and I grab two carts and a saleslady. We follow her around as she loads our carts full of puppy shit. When she asks if I want this or that I just say, "Just throw the puppy shit in the cart, please," followed by a, "Thank you." As I mentioned before, I am a gentleman and shit.

We check out and head over to grab the girls. "Mom, grab your fur babies and let's take them home."

"Best day ever! Now I've got to name you and take you to the vet. Then we can go to the park." She keeps rambling as she kisses both of their heads on her way out the door.

Dana pets the little labradoodle and picks him up to kiss him on the head before setting him back down on the floor. "What are you doing, princess?"

"I'm putting him down...?" She sounds unsure as she turns her answer into a question.

"Princess, get the dog. We are taking him home, too," I tell her.

"Really? I get to take Charlie home as mine?"

"No. He's our Charlie. Let's take him home. You girls are a lot of fucking work. All this excitement in one day, I need a damn nap from it."

# CHAPTER 22

## Dana

Jenn swings her feet back and forth over the arm of the chair she's sitting sideways in while sipping on her coffee. Aimlessly staring at the wall.

It's the morning after my day date, and I've given my full update from yesterday. Vegas sits across from me, sipping tentatively from her own coffee while listening to the day I had.

Feeling guilty, I stop talking and look over at Jenn to see that she probably didn't even hear a word I had said.

"Jenn, are you going to come over later and see Charlie at Harley's with us? I want you to see him too."

"Why is he at Harley's house?"

Patiently I repeat, "Since Axl got her two dogs as well, she said that she would house train Charlie while he's so little since she has to do that with her little dogs anyway. I think it's been really good for her. Axl gave her two of the sweetest little puppies to help her heal and keep her company. It was a great idea he had since she lost Maddox."

"Really, that's so nice for her," Jenn says in a dead tone and takes another sip of her coffee.

"Hey, I know! We can go get you a puppy today too, then we can plan playdates and stuff," I perk up ecstatically at the idea.

"Wow, thanks, Dana. But I think I'll pass." She sounds all bitter as she's rolling her eyes at me. "Tell me, what else has Axl said? Did he tell you to get me a dog, too?" Jenn coolly asks while turning her body and setting her feet on the floor.

I snap my mouth shut and the embarrassment covers my face at her cruel words back to me. I am so taken aback by them that I can't even think of a single thing to say back to her. Jenn's eyes appear more dilated and bloodshot as she refuses to lose eye contact with me. The sight of her like this saddens and shocks me further.

"What the fuck, Jenn?" Vegas defends me. "She was telling you about her goddamn dog, and we know that shit's been hurting you, but do you have to rip her heart out over it?"

"Fuck off, Vegas. Tell me why, then, out of blue, you two suddenly came looking for me? You two have only given a fuck about what has been going on with your men lately, not me."

"No, Jenn, fuck *you* and your poor little '*Everyone, feel so fucking sorry for Jenn*' attitude. Get over yourself,

Jenn. We've been here, you've just been lying to us the entire fucking time!" Vegas throws back at her.

My stomach feels sickened over the words they throw carelessly at each other, so I try diffusing the tension a little. "It wasn't out of the blue, Jenn. How many times do we have to ask you what's wrong? We want to help but we can't keep bugging you and waiting for you to let us in either."

Avoiding what was said, she asks, "What was it then that made you go looking for me that day?" She looks at me dead in the eyes.

"Fuck it, fine. You want to push this? Let's rip into it then." Vegas demands Jenn's attention back to her.

"We know you're taking pills. We are worried you have a drug abuse problem and wanted to check on you because we never know lately when we will see you." She sets her coffee mug on the office desk, readying herself for battle now. "We found out about it, and, because we are your family, we came looking for you!"

"Who told you? James?"

"What the hell? NO."

Jenn yells at the top of her lungs, "Then who!"

Having enough, I tell her. "I went to Vegas because you didn't show up to work or for our shopping trip. We went to tell Blade and Axl that we were worried and heading out to look for you. Axl only said that he thought that you might be sleeping off a hangover, then we asked him what he meant. Axl said that you and he took pills together once, okay? We were already looking for you that day. Not that any of this information matters, because, clearly, you don't trust us anymore." My heart is shattered from laying out the truth into the open with the words I never thought would be said between us three.

"I don't have a problem," Jenn firmly states, standing up rigidly from her seat.

"Yes, you do, Jenn. We want to be here for you and help you," Vegas says with an eerie calmness in her voice.

Jenn loses her cool and throws her mug with all her strength in her body, shattering it against the wall to the left. The explosion is mirroring what has been building for a long time.

The office door bangs open and James barges in. "What the hell is going on in here? Is everyone okay?" That's followed by Blade and Axl charging into the office behind him. The atmosphere is suffocating with anger and pain in the tiny space and even more with their presence.

Jenn ignores the guys and James' question, staring us down and picking up where we left off.

"I don't need you guys, *any* of you guys, following me around and talking shit about me. Fuck this, I'm out of here." She picks up her handbag off the floor and goes to storm past the guys on the way out.

James holds his hand out, gently gripping her elbow. "Please don't leave, Jenn, we all love you. We all just want to help you." Tenderly, with a sincere voice, he pleads with her.

Very calmly, in a low tone, she says, "I don't want to be helped." She looks James up and down. "You can't help what I need help with anyway." She rips her arm away from his hold and storms out the front door of the bar.

The five of us look at one another as we listen to her starting her car and ripping away from The Black Rose and the people who love her most.

# CHAPTER 23

## Axl

We have Church in a few minutes. I sit here, looking around at the men who are filing in and those who have gathered around the table already. And, for the first time since I was a kid, do I wonder what if this was what it's like to be a grown up. I can say that, after years of acting irresponsibly, now I truly feel the repercussions of how my choices affected my life and have brought me to this point. Yes, I lived free. Partied and fucked with the best of them.

Maybe it's my age finally catching up with me and seeing Jenn so lost and drowning with regret that I feel fortunate my life is the way it is now. That sounds a little fucked up even to me. Maybe it was my old man's passing or a combination of them both, but I feel fortunate that I did make it back from the hell I just walked through. It makes me think back to all the times my old man was there to reel me back in when he could see that I was going too far off the deep end with drugs and booze. I can clearly see how much the man, and my mother, really protected me from my choices.

Slam. The gavel hits the table and I snap back to reality. I look up and straight into Blade's eyes. I recognize a clarity in them that I've never seen before. Blade was made to be the President, and I'm now just catching up. He recognizes the same thing as me and nods my way. He sees that I'm back and better than before. Whatever we have lost between us is now back.

"First order of business, we have a new prospect with us that I'm personally vetting, but I'll open up the room for a vote. All those in favor to have James, the security guard from The Black Rose, prospect for membership say aye."

"Aye!" the room erupts into agreement.

"Any nays?" The room is deadly silent. "Alright then, someone call James in from the bar."

James walks into the room as Solo holds the door open for him to come in. Blade and I stand at the head of the table, our faces impassive along with the rest of the crew's.

"James," Blade calls him forward. "Take this cut with a prospect patch on it. Wear it wherever you go. You now are prospecting for the Battle Born MC. Once that cut goes on, you represent your brothers. You fuck up, you're out."

James takes the cut and shrugs it on over his shoulders, then runs his hands down the front. "I know what it means to wear this cut. I won't let you or the brothers down."

"What you hear, see and do is a bond between brothers," Blade reminds James. "It's a pact made in blood. And death, should you betray your family. And it's a consequence of death to protect our secrets that you will take to your grave."

James stands a little taller as he's addressing his new Prez and brothers. "I will do what you need of me and protect my club."

"Good. Now, you start your initiation into the club. You will still be a security guard on the floor at The Black Rose until we find a new one to take your place. You will also bartend here. Wait outside for me. We will head over to The Black Rose and speak with Vegas and her crew," Blade instructs him.

James turns to leave and, on his way out, he is congratulated by the brothers with back slaps and handshakes. The room settles down from the excitement and Blade's mood drops to an icy chill to update the brothers on the trap set the other night at the fight tank.

"We had an issue after the fight we had over at Tony's. We suspected that he was after something more and we were correct. We knew that he'd been following us and looking to get us busted with the cops. At the fight, he had his own warehouse raided. It's his second attempt to take us down. Tony has the cops in this town on his payroll. We will need to take Tony out."

Blade stops to think and light a smoke before he continues. "I never wanted to get into paying off the cops here to cover for us, but bought loyalties and blackmail are going to have to happen in order to protect the club. Fan out and find some dirt on the members of the police department and any other government official. Snake, you and Tank are in charge of this project."

"What do you think he's after? More young bitches?" Solo asks, looking all pissed off while spitting his words out.

I take this one. "I don't think he is in it for the girls himself, I think Tony is running the girls and the diamonds now that we took Johnny out and the previous members here that were helping him. He has an agreement with *Los Reyes Malditos*, The Cursed Kings, and we didn't agree to haul his shit for him. The only answer was to take us down to get his products moving again. If he got us caught up with the cops, he was hopeful to blackmail us into it, and he's probably still working on it." As I speak my thoughts out to the group, an ominous feeling crawls through my body and Blade confirms it.

"Aye," Blade agrees. "The only way around this is to get into bed with *Los Reyes Malditos* ourselves, and cut Tony off, and his throat too. We just can't kill Tony until we know exactly what their deal was."

"This means getting into bed with Cobra, their Prez. It's a dangerous fucking situation, man. That shit from the past is going to sink its fangs into the club again," Spider says.

"Aye, brother, but you can't run from the past. We have to confront it and clean it up before the past becomes a future none of us want to live in or die from. It's time we called Stryker and Fuego in on this," Blade declares.

He hits the numbers on his phone and connects a conference call with Fuego, from the Cali chapter, and Stryker, the Las Vegas Mother Chapter President.

"We have a situation our club wanted to bring you all in on." Blade gives them the update about the cops and Tony.

"We know he was transporting shit with *Los Reyes Malditos*. It's time we meet up with those fuckers and resolve this shit with them."

Just the mention of the name has the room and the phone line silenced. Not a single one of us wants to step in on their business or bring them in on ours.

"How do you know? We can't contact them on a hunch," Fuego responds, warning lacing his voice.

"We have the Black Widow. Since last year when we came up here to take over and we found out that we were dealing with the Mexican MC, we contracted her. She has the information."

"Are you fucking kidding me!" Stryker's voice roars through the phone. "She could get you *and* us killed, Blade!"

"You don't think I know that? What other play did we have? We had to get intel, and on the down low, to get ahead of this. I made a choice and I'm standing behind it," Blade defends.

"She isn't coming out until the time is right. She's agreed to work with us. She has her own agenda and will collect from me when this is over."

"Fuck!" Fuego's heavy breathing hits the line. "I hope you're fucking right, Blade. I can imagine the shit she knows about us now."

"Fuego, start asking yourself what it is that I *do* know about her. This shit ends now. I'm not living my life looking over my shoulder, afraid of the past. It's here and it's time. Get your men on board. We meet in Las Vegas. Stryker, can you make contact with Cobra for a neutral meet?"

"Aye, get your fucking ass down here so you can answer to me face-to-face." Stryker hangs up.

"I'll be there in the morning to ride out. Be fucking ready, *pendejo*." Fuego hangs up the phone.

We all exhale a long breath and sit back in our seats. Blade looks out the window as he says, "Drink and fuck your bitches. Some of us may not come home."

The brothers are amped up for the meet in Las Vegas and with *Los Reyes Malditos* later. Not all of them know the back story of those crazy fuckers. But Blade, Tank,

Spider and I do. They've been at odds with our MC for generations of bullshit. Only the really old fuckers of the club remember all that. I'd prefer it if we could bury it *and* them all, but that shit will never happen.

I sit and drink a beer at the table in the corner of the room with Blade, Tank and Spider. We want the guys to relax and let loose, but we keep the situation on our mind. We replay the scenarios and strategies over and over, stressing our minds with the importance of it all. Life or death. We keep our focus to protect the members.

Vegas, Kat and Dana come wandering into the room. Dana spots me and heads straight over to sit in my lap. Vegas and Kat head to the bar to grab a drink. She wraps her arms around me, giving me a flirtatious kiss. I can't lie. I love how much she openly shows me her desires and love. I crave her touches and kisses just as much. These last few months we've bared every ugly part of ourselves to the other. We have connected in ways I never knew possible.

Wrapping my own arms around her slender waist, I take her kiss and welcome her comfort. Only she can make my world worth living in and fighting for.

"What's wrong, Axl?" she asks and pulls back to look at me. Her eyes wrinkle in the corners ever so slightly, but I see them. My thumb comes up to run over the little, barely there lines.

"I have to head out tomorrow, princess, for club business, and I don't know when we will be back. I don't want to leave you here since I just got back, and things got back on track with us." My pride doesn't even care if my brothers hear me.

"Oh, I see. Baby, we'll be okay because you *will* come home to me."

My head drops to rest on her chest as I think about Maddox and the possibility of never coming home to her again. The thought of leaving her alone in this world like my mom is now is crippling.

"Baby," she says and tilts my chin up with her tiny, soft hand. "We can't go there every time you have to leave. When it is our time to leave this world, it will happen. Doesn't change how we should live in today. What should we do tonight to make this moment last forever?"

Crushing my hungry lips to hers, I take her love and support deep inside and feel another small crack heal. She is my heart. In this world of chaos and death, she keeps me alive. My mouth consumes hers in a salacious, dirty kiss.

"I love you, Dana. Every moment with you is worth fighting the darkness for."

Dana leans forward, her lips brushing sweet tender kisses over mine before she whispers back, "I love you, Axl. I will walk through the darkness with you."

"Vegas. Pst." Damn woman can't hear me. "Vegas!" Lightly, I punch her shoulder and her drink spills on her boots. Oops.

Blade gives me an irritated look of "Did you just shoulder punch my woman?"

Vegas grabs her drink with her other hand and wipes off the wet one onto her Levi's. "What, asshole?" the she-devil speaks.

"Sorry, but I have to hurry and tell you this before she gets back from the bathroom."

Interested, Vegas moves closer, eyeing me suspiciously. "What's that?"

"I want you to help me get Dana to the tattoo shop tonight. How do we do that?"

She laughs in my face. "Good luck with that." She snorts then continues, "I've known her for, well, ever. She will not sit under the gun, for anyone, not sober. Why should I do this for you anyway?" Ah, Vegas is out to play tonight.

"What do you want?"

"Well, for one, I don't ever want to see you push her away like you did again. Two..."

"Why do you always count shit off to me?"

"Shut the fuck up and listen," she snaps at me. "*Two*, you owe me help with some painting."

"Painting what?"

"Does it fucking matter?" the bitch counters.

"Fuck, you're a cold bitch. Alright, I'm in, but my tatt has to be on her by the end of the night."

"Then it's show time, and you," she points her finger at me again, "better stay the fuck out of my way. And you're buying hangover burritos tomorrow."

All of a sudden, Vegas smiles sweetly, and I turn around to see my princess walking over to us. Fuck, what have I done?

"Hey, Vegas, what are you guys talking about?"

"Oh, nothing much. Axl was just volunteering to help paint the outside of the brewery for me! He is so sweet!" That fucking she-devil plays off her innocents. I see Blade smirking over his cigarette to keep from laughing. Tank dives his face into Kat's shoulder while his body shakes with unheard laughter.

"Baby," Dana beams at me, "God, that's so sweet of you! That building is huge and tall. I can't believe how sweet you are." Her arm comes around my side and her other hand rubs at my chest.

"Yep. I'm really fucking sweet like that, princess." I try really hard not to come unhinged and hit a bitch, but, God, Vegas, she makes it hard. If I ever had a sister to hate, it would be her.

"Well, love," Vegas turns to Blade and asks, "Should we tell them?"

Blade puts two of his fingers to his mouth to whistle loudly over the laughter and music before he belts out, "I'm gonna be a dad! Vegas is having my baby."

That fucking bitch.

Cheers erupt into congratulations and champagne is popped and passed around to celebrate the occasion. So, she knew, and she played me hard.

Dana leaves me to jump into Vegas' arms, hugging her. Vegas winks at me over Dana's shoulder and I flip her the fuck off. She rocks her glass back and forth and tells us, "Cranberry juice." Dana's face glows from the happiness she feels for her friend. She steps back into my side and curls into me.

Vegas is passed from person to person as she collects hugs and congratulations from around the room. Hugging Kat, she whispers something into her ear. They part and I watch Kat leaving the room. Vegas continues on to the next person. Kat is back in and walks over to us to stand next to Dana, handing her a glass of champagne.

After every hand has a drink, Vegas yells over the crowd, "Toast!"

Blade says, "To not knowing what the future holds, but betting on forever." He pulls Vegas into him for an intimate kiss.

Out of the corner of my eye, I see Dana's eyes shine with love as she's watching her friend. In this moment, I know that there is nothing else in this life I want more than to give her every possible experience of love and happiness that she deserves.

Kat clinks her plastic champagne flute with Dana's and the girls drink together as I take a pull from my beer. Dana holds out her glass in front of her, eyeing it suspiciously. "That was a little bitter," she comments, and I groan. They better not have laced her drink, but with what?

The Black Widow mouths a smile over her flute, "X," and proceeds to down the rest.

My jaw ticks from anger and anxiety that I got her into this mess with these crazy ass bitches. When she wakes up tomorrow and realizes that we drugged her, *and* with a tattoo, fuck, my balls are going to be ripped off.

An hour and three more drinks later, Dana giggles at everything that anyone says. The other club sluts have showed up by now. The room is packed with booze, bud and ecstasy. Dana watches one of the naked club sluts start stripping for Pawn and she stares in amazement. Pawn's greedy eyes watch her from the couch he sits on. *Toxic* by Britney Spears starts playing. The rhythm entices the girls to bump and grind on each other. The smell in the room is heady with sex, and dark promises lurk in the air.

Dana gasps as another girl gets onto her knees. Pawn rises slightly, and she takes his pants with her to the floor. The slut takes his rock-hard cock into her hands and pumps him lightly a few times before we lose sight of his dick into her mouth and she sucks him with slow strokes, wanting to bring him blissful pleasure.

Wrapping my arms around Dana as she's watching the scene has my dick aching to be in her silky pussy. As if her watching this is making her wet and wild for me and for my cock, she begins to sway her ass, rubbing it into my crotch. My cherry pie is definitely fucking hot for my cock. This whole thing was a bad idea, but then again, why does it feel so right?

My hand runs up under her shirt and I pinch her nipples. She gasps and stills in my arms. Pulling her back against me, I whisper into her ear, "Does my princess' pussy need her king to take care of her?"

"Yes." She rests her head back on my shoulder, arching her ass into me.

I drop my hands from around her body and pull her down the hallway to my room. I slam the door shut behind us and turn her to face it, kissing down her neck. My hands eagerly pull her pants down, then mine.

Leaning into her body, I warn her, "I have other plans for you right now. You're going to do what I tell you. Right, princess?" I ask as my fingers find her pussy and pump in and out of her

"Yes," she gasps and submits to my demands.

"Good girl," I whisper into her ear and nip the flesh with my teeth. Her body shivers and the reaction increases my need to fuck her sweet pussy.

Removing my hands from her silky hot cunt, I place one on her back and push her forward until her hands are resting on the door and I can see her pussy from behind. Grabbing my dick, I pump it a few times, then run it through her soft folds. She moans and pushes back against me, arching her back.

"That's my princess, take it all." I grab her waist and impale her onto my dick. Reaching around, I rub quick circles around her clit.

I push our limits together, racing for a quick and hard release. Her fingernails scrape the paint on the door. I hammer myself into her body.

If this is love, then I love her body hard. She was made to take my cock. I pump and fuck her as fast as I can, racing against time until she moans out her release, her cunt gripping me. I feverishly pump a few more strokes and explode my own pleasure inside of her.

Our racing breaths mingle together as I hold her to me before turning her around. Kissing her lips, I pull up her pants and then mine. She buttons hers up and I take her hand to pull her out of the room. The brothers catcall when they see us walking back into the main room. Dana's face lights up red with embarrassment. Kissing her again, I tell her, "Don't worry, we're leaving."

Do I really want to go through with this? I ask myself over and over as I hold the tattoo gun in my hand. Kat and Vegas helped me get a buzzed Dana into the car.

By the time we got here, I think I underestimated how much of a lightweight my woman was. She is now drunk and passed out on my tattoo table.

"Well, all I can say is, I held up my end. Tattoo her or not, Axl, the rest is up to you from here," Vegas comments while picking her bag up, ready to walk out.

"Shit, what if she's not ready for this?" I plead with the devil, and she starts laughing.

"How do you know though? Vegas! This is not a joke. I've never done something this fucking insane. I know you do crazy ass shit on a daily basis, but the rest of us don't live in your fucking world of fucked up mind games."

"Easy, asshole. You're just being bitchy because I kick your ass at mind games. It's not your fault you're a dumbass pretty boy. We all can't have it all, smart *and* beautiful. But I'll give you this because it's important to Dana." She finishes the ass chewing and pulls out her phone to send me a text. She then looks at me expectantly, waiting for me to read it before she leaves.

**Mega Bitch: Show this to her in the morning if you have any doubts of where your balls are at, you lame ass little pussy.**

If only I could punch Blade's woman without getting my ass kicked again this month.

"I'm out, I want my paint done within two weeks," Vegas says as she walks away holding two fingers up in the air. Not having a comeback, I flip her off behind her retreating back.

Bitch.

# CHAPTER 24

## Dana

Waking up, I start stretching my aching body as I remember all the fun and sexy times we had last night. I roll over onto my back and feel startled by a memory and a little bit of pain. I jackknife straight up in bed at the thought as I screech, "Axl!" before diving back under the covers.

"Oh my God, oh my God," I chant as I throw the covers back off me again and get myself out of bed. I take off toward the bathroom and run straight into Axl's chest just as he comes barreling out the door in a towel, dripping wet. His hands drop the towel from around his waist and grab a hold of my shoulders to keep me from bouncing off him and onto the floor.

"What happened last night?" I push past him to get into the bathroom so I can look. Pulling the mirrors out, I look at my naked reflection in the mirror and my eyes focus on my back. I pull my hair over to the side to see covered clear plastic in the center of my back and bellow my neck. Axl comes up behind me and turns my body so that I'm facing the mirror. Gently, he starts pulling off the tape and plastic.

"Did you tattoo me, Axl? Did you brand me last night?" I ask in a panic. *How did this happen?*

"Yes, princess." Lovingly, Axl kisses above my tattoo as he reveals his brand for me. He turns me to the side so I can look into the mirrors.

In an arch, it's written in script, *Axl's Princess.* Under the writing, there's a beautiful pink heart, and on each side are a partial black and gray rose and an angel wing opposite to it. The tattoo was done in light colors and shading with the effect of what would look like water coloring. Under that, it is also written *Battle Born* in an arch.

Tears prick at my eyes at how pretty it is and the minimal coloring he used shows me how much thought he put into it for me. "Oh my God, Axl! It is so beautiful. I have a tattoo! I have *your* tattoo! Is this your tattoo?"

Axl's fingers run over it. "Axl's Princess." His finger traces over the writing as he says it.

"The heart is for you. You are at the center of everything, Dana. The rose is what you have built with your girls, the wing is for me, for taking care of me with your heart. And Battle Born, princess, you may not know this, but you are a warrior, you are Battle Born." He kisses me again on the back of my neck and I turn around to face him.

"You think I'm strong?" My lips quiver as I'm trying to get the words out.

"Dana, who helped her dad find love in this world and loved him back? You stood by Vegas and helped her with The Black Rose when her life was falling apart. Just because you aren't front and center, that doesn't make you any less. It makes you the one your people go to because they know you're strong. Battle Born."

Axl picks me up by the back of my thighs and sets my ass on the counter. "I have to leave, princess. I'll call you when I can, okay?" Axl holds onto my face, looking deeply into my eyes.

"Charlie and I will be here... oh shit, where *is* Charlie?" I start to panic and jump down from the sink. I grab one of Axl's shirts and throw it on to cover my body.

Axl throws on his pants and shirt also. "Babe, I just put him in the back yard, he's fine. I got to run and get Vegas some burritos before I leave. Do you want me to bring you one?" That stops me right in my tracks.

"Why are you taking Vegas breakfast, Axl?" What the hell is going on? Then it dawns on me. "Why do you OWE her, Axl?"

His face turns ashen as he quickly shoves his boots on. "She just helped me out, is all."

"With what? And then you're just going to paint that big ass building out of the goodness of your heart and I wake up with a tattoo on my back and a very sketchy memory? I'm not buying your bullshit, Axl, fess up."

"Fuck, okay. I asked Vegas to help me get you under the gun. She and Kat put some kind of ecstasy in your champagne. After you had three more glasses, you were so hot, so we fucked in the room. Then I took you to the tattoo shop and I tattooed you. You even fell asleep and did your princess snore through the whole thing. That part was kind of cute because you are cute when you snore, and no one has ever passed out on my table like that."

"Kind of cute! Axl! Drugging people and them passing out is not fucking cute, you dick! I'm going to kill you *and* Vegas." Holding my finger in his face, I threaten.

"I'll take X with you next time, princess," Axl bites and sucks on the end of my finger.

I pull my finger away from him. "I'm never taking drugs again," I growl the words out. "Never, you hear me?"

Axl stalks closer and closer, crowding me, until my legs hit the back of the bed and I fall back on my elbows. The shirt is raising up over my stomach. Axl growls and hovers over my body with his.

"I did what had to be done, so quit bitchin' over it. You know you love it. This body and pussy belong to me." Axl shoves the shirt up over my tits before his teeth claim each one, scraping and pulling on the sensitive flesh.

"This belongs to me," he says again as he's shoving his fingers into my pussy and his thumb starts rubbing my clit.

"Give me your dick," I plead with him.

Axl shoves his pants down around his thighs, and, without any care, shoves his dick into me. My back arches from the bed as he mercifully fucks me into the mattress. He grabs my hair and pulls it back, exposing more of my neck. He bites and sucks and fucks. I feel so close as pressure starts building deep inside when Axl roars out his release into me.

Releasing his hold on me, his body collapses over mine. His hands are resting on each side of me. He whispers into my ear, "Every time you talk to me like that, Dana, my princess doesn't get to come." He pushes his ripped body up and tucks himself back into his jeans.

I sit up, annoyed with the current situation, and feeling mind fucked. Yep, that's an accurate description of what I'm feeling. Mind. Fucked.

Axl steps in front of me and grabs the shirt at the hem, ripping it from my body and over my head. Bunching the shirt in his hands, he brings the shirt up to his nose and takes a deep inhale.

"Fucking perfect, smells like your pussy." He opens the shirt and puts his arms inside and over his shoulders, covering his perfect body.

"Well, at least we fucked in a bed this time, and I will actually remember it," I deadpan.

Axl throws his head back and the deep laugh vibrates through his chest. "Aye, princess," is all he says, gathering his wallet and walking over to me to kiss my lips. "Love you, stay out of trouble till I get home."

"Love you, too, Axl."

Finding another shirt and sweats, I go looking for my baby. Opening the patio door, I find my black, fury, little labradoodle come barreling for my legs. "Charlie! Come here, baby."

I scoop him up in my arms and give him kisses as he gives me one of his signature hugs with each paw on my shoulders. "You're getting too big, little man," I tell him, and we walk back into the house. Rubbing his head, I sit him down on the bathroom floor to stay there while I shower.

I remove my clothes and jump into the stall, enjoying the hot water while trying to keep the water off my back. My tattoo! I'm so excited to be his Ol'Lady. My muscles loosen, and I close my eyes, taking in deep breaths to calm down.

I'm lost in thought when the shower door flies open, and I shriek as I'm trying to cover my tits and girl parts with an arm and a hand. Axl laughs at my girlie scream. "What the hell are you doing here now?"

"Brought you breakfast, cranky princess." He grabs my arm from around my tits and pulls me to him. He gives me a long, sweet kiss before he playfully smacks my ass. "Later! Answer your phone when I call, love you," and he's gone in a flash.

I rub my ass and mumble to myself, "Is this what I have to look forward to?"

"Yes, yes, it is."

Grabbing my throat, I jump back and slip in the shower, barely steadying myself on the wall and the door. "How are you still here! Quit sneaking around, it's creepy!"

"Sorry, forgot my phone, I'm gone, bye."

I sit and wait. Uncomfortable with the silence, I crack open the shower door only to find Axl's face peeking at me from around the corner of the shower stall, staring at me. "Hey!" Charlie jumps up and down wanting to play and barks at Axl.

"For fuck's sakes! Slam the door shut and get out! You ruined my morning, now go!" Charlie barks even more excited at my anger.

Laughing, Axl watches me watch him leave. I carefully sprint across the floor to lock the door. The lock won't turn, and I put my weight into it. Axl's muffled menacing laughter comes from the other side. I go to grab the handle and I can't turn the knob.

"What is wrong with you, Axl! GOD!" My fists hit the door. Completely annoyed with his antics, I yell, "Fine, don't leave! Whatever, asshole."

I turn back toward the shower, determined to finish washing what I can when two strong hands circle my body. "I swear to God, Axl, I'm about to shoot you myself, and with your own gun, too. Do. Not. Fuck. With. Me."

"I'm sorry, princess, I couldn't help myself, and I couldn't leave you alone. Forgive me?" he asks while licking the water that's running down my neck.

"Yes, but I need you to leave now because I'm freezing my fucking ass off."

Axl turns me to face him. Kissing my lips softly, he says, "Be safe, okay? Call me if anything comes up, anything."

"I will, promise."

"Okay, love you, princess."

"Love you, too, but I don't like you right now."

Smiling, he responds with one last kiss. He backs up while looking at my face and I see a shadow of doubt masking his face. He locks the door, and, suddenly, I want to cry. I wish I knew what's caused it, but maybe it's best that I don't.

Walking back into the shower, I start shampooing my hair. The water goes from warm to cold.

It is official. Today sucks.

Showered and dressed in a hoody and jeans, I sit on the couch with my feet under me, scrolling through my phone and reading the news when a text message from Axl pops up. I open the message, but he only sent a screen shot. Tapping on the picture, I open it larger to read the words.

**I, Dana Maraschino, of sound mind and sound body, do hereby enter into this agreement to give Vegas, aka Alessia DeRosa-Johnson, full legal authority and custody of my body to help me procure by any special means necessary for placement of a tattoo. Dated this day and shall be noted and effective hereinafter.**

No way! Vegas did it! Throwing my head onto the back of the couch, I laugh out loud that Vegas pulled it off. And I'm so happy that she did.

Charlie starts whining in my lap while looking at the door when I hear a knock. Setting him aside, I walk over to the peephole to see who it could be.

Excitement floods my system at seeing Mom and Papa at the door. Swinging the door open, I throw myself at my parents.

"What are you guys doing here?"

Papa holds me close to his chest. "I wanted to spend some time with you. Fuego went with the brothers down south, and someone needed to stay here, so I volunteered. What are you doing today, *mi corazón*?"

I step back through the door and my parents follow as we walk together into the kitchen. Grabbing a few mugs from the cupboard, I fill them with coffee and say, "Just work."

"What is it, *mija*, what's got your heart sad?" Papa asks, taking a seat with Mom on the kitchen bar stools.

"Axl ruined my shower..." Papa holds his hand up to halt my words and I snap my mouth shut. "Do not mention that *cabrón* and a shower in the same sentence to me. Besides, I can tell that's not it. What is wrong, *mija*, in here?" Papa points to his chest.

Taking in a deep breath, I try, I try really hard to be strong for him, but I can't.

"It's been a rollercoaster lately. Vegas went through losing her baby. Then I let Axl get close and his dad died." I hiccup my words out as tears spring into my eyes. "Then he comes back and things got back to okay. Then Jenn has been popping pills and ignoring me and Vegas. Then James quit our bar to go prospect for the MC. Then Axl left me today after he gave me his brand last night. And I didn't have a hot shower."

I finish in a long, whiny breath as I'm wiping at my eyes. I can't look into his face. I don't want him to see me cry.

"*Mija*, look at me."

I shake my head no.

Walking around the counter, he takes me into his chest and wraps his strong arms around me.

"You know, I never did give you enough of these when you were a little girl. I didn't protect the most valuable thing on this earth. You, *mija*. I failed at protecting the heart of you. Of all the things in my life that I've done, that's the only thing I've failed at. I'm sorry, *mi corazón*. Tell me, tell me how it made you feel. Let me carry your sadness, baby. Tell *tu papa*."

Shaking my head no again, I manage to mutter, "It's okay, Papa, I know you're sorry. It's okay."

"*Mija*, no, it is not. I need you to say the words, for you to tell me, *mija*."

"Why?" I step back to look at his face.

"Everything you just said, those are hard things or normal stress of life and relationships. All of them have one thing in common. They all left, *mija*, or they died. You can't trust others because of it. So, tell me, *mija*, let me have your fears and heartache."

Mom sits there, quietly listening, not wanting to come between us. I look over at her and she nods to me in encouragement. I look back at the floor and take a deep breath. I close my eyes, inhaling and then exhaling all the hurt, before I can allow the words that have been trapped for so long to finally come to the surface. They've been locked away in a safe place that no one can touch. My eyes find my Papa's and I let go. I let go of the past and pain. I let him have the words and all of the rest.

"I loved you and Momma so much. I would go to school and try so hard to be the best student so when you would come see me, I would have all good things to tell you. But whenever you would come, you and Momma would just fight, and you wouldn't even talk to me. I would sit and wait for hours for you to see me, but you never did. Then, as I got a little older, she got worse, she did more drugs except for when she knew that you were coming. She would clean up for *you*, not for me. You only came for her. You didn't come to see me. The worst part of it all, I wanted to hate you so badly, but I never could, because I loved you too much."

Papa swallows and I see his Adam's apple moving with the movement like he swallowed razor blades. "Keep going, *mi corazon*, give me your ghost, give me your pain."

Nodding at him, I sniff back my tears and continue. "I took myself to school. Learned how to live with no one by my side because the people I loved the most couldn't even see me. I walked this earth alone. My mother chose to kill herself with drugs over being here for me. Other than Vegas and Jenn, no one cared about me. When Vegas loses something, I feel the loss too. When Jenn is lost, I'm lost too, because they are my family, my blood, my sisters that have stood by me and have never left my side."

I stand tall. I stand up for the little broken girl inside of my heart who I protected all these years. That little girl will always be a piece of me.

"*Sí, mija*. They are your *familia*, they are your blood sisters. You are right, *mija*. I was a shit father and I did those things to your heart. But, hear me, baby girl. Your tears and sadness are not weakness. You are still standing with a beautiful, beating heart. I may have all the strength in this body. But it is nothing to your beautiful heart, *mija*. Nothing compared to you. *Mi corazón.*" Papa's eyes mist over. His show of emotion paralyzes my thoughts and movements.

"*Mija*, I think you are ready to hear a story. What I mean is, your mind and heart are ready to hear it. Come sit with me on the couch."

Papa turns and heads toward the living room. Mom and I follow him. She sits on the loveseat and Papa and I sit opposite from each other on the couch.

"You know that I was away at war when your mother was pregnant with you. As a young man, I came home to my woman at the time, who had my baby while I was gone. Shit got ugly. We were high school sweethearts, but time away changed us and we didn't know each other anymore. I was a Marine and she was still the girl I left behind. I thought I left my baby to save her from the killer I had become. I was ashamed of the things I had done with these hands, and touching something as beautiful as you felt wrong."

Papa hangs his head in shame. "It was never you. I was wrong and really fucked up in my head." His eyes close only to snap open as a soulless man. "I can wrap my hands around a neck and feel nothing from it. I learned there was still love in me from a little girl who pumped life back into me with her pure heart. You never gave up loving an undeserving man, you brought me back, *mija*. Katie helped me see it. I'm sorry, baby girl. I'm sorry your parents weren't parents at all. You keep fighting this life, bad shit is going to happen. You remember that your papa and all your family will stand by you. But you are strong enough to stand on your own."

Battle Born.

The phone rings and rings, then eventually goes to voicemail. Disappointment fills my mind since I haven't been able to get a hold of Jenn. We've texted her and called in the past few days, and still no answer. I'll keep trying until she has no other choice but to answer me.

**Me: So, today sucked, I got drugged by our friends and then tattooed last night. I guess I'm an Ol' Lady now. Not the Ol' Lady part, that doesn't suck. The part where I woke up with a headache and then ran out of hot water because the man you live with is a child. That part sucks.**

Vegas and Kat barge through the office door at The Black Rose.

"Show me your tatt," they both demand at the same time. Placing my phone on the desk, I turn in the chair and pick up my shirt at the hem to lift it up my back to show them.

"Damn, girl, that tatt is beautiful and very pretty, very you," Vegas awes over it.

"He did good, girl, really good," Kat agrees. "He put himself and you in it."

"I agree, I love it. Although, I can't remember some things and it surprises me I did it. I only had a few drinks and we all know that that's not enough to get me in the chair. So strange," I feign confusion, tapping my chin.

Vegas' eyes beam with pride. "I date raped you." Excitement pours from her.

"Is that normal to be proud you date raped your friend?"

"I think so. Axl asked me for help, then I asked Kat to give you X," she shrugs. "You're welcome too, that tatt is tight and you're too much of a sissy to get it on your own, and now you're a claimed woman." Vegas claps her hands together. "The way I see it, you owe me too."

"Oh, I see, you drug your friends and get them tattooed and then they owe you, Vegas?"

"Yes?" She smiles at her own logic.

"No, you're not taking credit on this one. The way I see it, *you* owe *me*, and I will collect a favor."

My words trail off as Gabe, my little brother, comes walking through the door. He's a handsome little devil. He could be my father's twin, but with a slightly lighter coloring from our mom, Katie.

"Gabe! What are you doing here? I didn't know you could come!"

Even though Gabe is only nineteen, he's built and very tall. He picks me up as he spins me around before setting me on my feet again.

"I'm on leave before I'm put on duty. I'm staying with you for a few weeks. Mom and Pops are staying here too before I leave, so we can all stay together. I don't know when I'll be home again."

My throat constricts, and, all of a sudden, it's hard to breathe through the idea of not seeing him again. "You will do great in the Marines, I know it. And you'll come home soon. And you'll write often, right?"

"You know I will write you. Pops can't be the only badass in the family," he tells me as he's standing a little taller.

After I introduce him to Kat, we spend the afternoon hanging out.

# CHAPTER 25

## Axl

On the drive down south, all I can think about is leaving Dana and Mom home alone with that slimy little fuck, Tony, in town. After we settle shit with the *Reyes* we can get the fuck back home and get back to something normal for once.

Ice, the Elko Prez from the north eastern corner of the state, is also headed this way for this meet up with the *Reyes*. We are bringing all the firepower that we can with us. He's going to cover our backs in town while we talk with Cobra.

The Reno and California chapters rode down together for this meet before we call Cobra, the *Reyes* Prez. We pull up to the clubhouse gate in Las Vegas. I can't wait to stretch out, take a hot shower and find some food after a six-hour drive on our bikes. The tall, long gate rattles open allowing us all entrance.

This clubhouse is like a second home to us. Blade, Tank and I grew up here. The brothers and sluts start trailing out of the club at the sound of our bikes. Stryker stands on the walkway from the gravel parking lot, with his arms crossed. He's not happy with Blade, and I can't say that I blame him.

We park the twenty plus bikes and walk toward the door and the club's main President, Stryker.

"Bitches, move the fuck on until notice. I want the Presidents and the VP's in Church, now."

Not a hello or nada. Stryker turns and knocks a few bitches out of the way with his bulky body as he's plowing through the front door of the Mother Chapter's clubhouse. He is followed by Fuego, Blade and then the rest of us walk inside.

"Lock the club down until Ice gets here. No one fucking leaves," Stryker bellows, stomping down the hallway to Church.

"Some shit I was hoping to never have to revisit in my motherfucking lifetime, and this was one of them, goddamn it."

We take seats around the table and the door is locked behind us.

"Let's get this shit over with. Why the fuck is the Black Widow up in Reno with you?" Stryker looks pointedly at Blade.

"We all knew the previous President was up to shit and we all knew he was dealing with diamonds. We just didn't have all the connections. The sex trafficking was his side profit, but the diamonds... The diamonds were worth millions and with less risk. With the intel Cuervo brought us, we hunted until Spider found the Black Widow. Cobra is her father, her *estranged* father, and she wants him dead. She can't take him out herself directly," Blade explains to his old man.

"Blade, she could be playing us, only to deliver us right to him in the end," Stryker theorizes.

"I don't think so, we have more, and I'm going to give that information to her when this shit is settled. She's working for us, or she dies along with everything she's trying to save. She knows the score."

"Cuervo came down here with you, Fuego?" Stryker asks.

"*Si*, but he rode alone down to Tijuana to keep an eye on the streets. He's set up, ready for direction."

"So, we call Cobra and ask for a meet. He's been waiting. I have no doubt he's been putting pressure on Tony for a while. Who has eyes on Tony?"

"Ghost is watching Tony with a small crew and prospects up there," Blade answers. "Tony wants back into the game. The only way to do that is through us, dead or alive."

The red and orange sunset here in Tijuana, Mexico, is beautiful over the horizon. Horns blare from taxis and the locals yell back, cussing the asshole taxicab drivers for almost running them over. Men and women sell food out of the trucks or carts that line the streets.

This place in the slums, deep into the city, stinks. Children run up to us, wanting to sell jewelry or drugs to a bunch of thieves as their whore mothers offer us their bodies. Bitches would be fucking us no doubt while their fucking bastard kids would rob us blind. We left most of our credit cards and cash at the clubhouse in Vegas. Tucking my wallet in my cut, I tell the hundredth little shit, "*No, gracias.*"

I swear these little bastards only bother the white boys, leaving the darker ones alone. Must be a taught trait; go for the white, naive guys first. We round the street corner and come up to a stop in front of an old Catholic church. Here in Mexico, the drug lords are considered heroes, even though thousands of people go missing every year. Not to mention the beheaded bodies found in ditches or the ones that swing from the bridges.

I guess you protect the strongest, and here, that's the criminals. You protect or help them, and they help keep you fed, or you die. A vicious reality. Even in the ranches, it's not uncommon to find the wealthiest drug lord living with his family that will praise him. Listen to the songs of their native bands. They'll tell you stories of their infamous drug leaders, selling drugs and doing drugs.

Stryker, Blade and I, along with a handful of men, wait outside the church and are ordered to wait until a nun is supposed to allow us entrance. The hot sun and humidity sticks to our clothing, making standing here out in the open heat very uncomfortable, not to mention, out in the open in Tijuana.

A few more minutes pass before a tiny little nun comes to the large front door. "*Entren*, come inside," she greets us and shuffles her old body along in her black sneakers. We follow her down the rows upon rows of pews. The smell of musty, old wood assaults my nostrils.

She stops abruptly and, turning to us, she says, "*Espera*. Hold on." Putting her hand up, she nods and walks away, only to disappear into a side door. Our nerves are shot as we remain quiet, listening for any movement and sounds. Our eyes scan the room and the landing for the seating above us.

A door cracks open to the left and we see Cobra walking through. A little ranching looking man, weathered, with a long mustache and wearing snakeskin boots and belt, cowboy hat and collared shirt. He doesn't look like a flashy criminal, but, to the underworld, he is deadly.

Cobra wears an MC cut over his shirt, the only indication of who the man really is. To our right, another door is cracked open and more of *Los Reyes Malditos* crowd the room. Five on my count to the right. My hand twitches in instinct to shoot all these motherfuckers.

Blade and Stryker are at my back, watching the left side that Cobra just came through.

"*Hola, mi amigos* from America are here. So nice of you to come visit. Long time, aye, Stryker? I think Fuego came home for a visit to his people too, no?"

"If we are friends, then, Cobra, you can ask your men to stand in front of us and not at our backs?" Stryker's low growl warns Cobra.

"Sure, *amigo.*" The rest of his men move out behind him. "*Bien*, good? So, what has you all the way down here?"

"You know why, cut the shit. Tony. We know you were transporting the diamonds through the old Prez in Reno and, after he died, through Johnny. I'm sure you heard they both died by now for their betrayal to the club. We have one last rat to clean up, and that's Tony," Blade bluntly states, sounding annoyed. "Stop fucking around and let us know what you have going on with Tony. We are here out of respect because he works for you. If I drop him, I would rather not have you on my ass. So, what is it?"

"*El hijo de Stryker, verdad?*"

"*Sí*, Cobra, he is my son and the Prez in Reno," Stryker responds.

"*Que bueno familia, no?* I had a sister too once. Rosa. She ran off with a *pendejo* to America. I hear she died a horrible death. But, after she left *mi familia*, she was already dead to me."

Stryker and Cobra hold each other in a silent war while the rest of us wait the tension out.

"A story I'm sure to be continued for another *día* perhaps? This man you speak of, Tony, yes, he works for me, he's behind on his shipments. How he acquires these shipments is none of my concern. What are you offering me for him?"

"Nothing," Blade states.

Cobra tsk's his tongue in response. "*Mijo*, this doesn't work that way. I'm a businessman, I need money and diamonds for my customers and suppliers. He's made me look bad. If you're willing to transport, I'll give you Tony." The little motherfucker smiles with laughter in his eyes.

"Not good enough, Cobra, and we don't have any intention of transporting the shit for you either. We'll give you passage at a freight fee, that's it. It's more than we've given you in a decade. Technically, you should be dead for moving shit across my territory without coming to me and ask, motherfucker. I'm tired of your games, Cobra. After years of living with this bullshit with you, it's over. Take it or leave it." Stryker's impatience grows thick with each word he speaks. Blade's hand slowly moves at his side.

Crack! A gunshot comes down from above. The men and I dive in between the pews as more gunfire goes off. Looking over the bench, I see that our men have spread out and glass is flying around from the windows. My hands come up to cover my head and face. Shouting and gunfire from both sides create chaos. My ears start ringing from a gun that's firing next to my ear.

Fuego and his men storm above us, shooting down below at Cobra and his crew. Crawling my way over to the side, I aim my gun and pull the trigger at a man who was pointing his gun at Stryker. Memories assault me, and all I see is Maddox's dead eyes staring back at me.

Crawling over to Stryker, I give him cover with gunfire as we both stand and run behind a nearby wall.

An enraged Cuervo shouts from up above, "You will die today, *pinche cabrón*. Today you will fuckin' die by my hands!"

Cuervo jumps down from the seating level above, and, with a machine gun, he starts spraying fire left to right when a bullet suddenly hits his leg. It slows him down, but he keeps moving forward. Blood paints his pants crimson.

The brothers take out a few more men, gaining ground. Cobra's men drop to the floor like flies. Cobra raises a gun at Cuervo's head. Blade pops out from behind the bench and shoots his arm. Standing, Blade and the rest of us inch forward with our guns aimed at the last few men standing, Cobra included.

"Toss your guns," Blade demands, but no one moves. He shoots one in the head and the other man tosses his gun to the floor, leaving Cobra standing there alone.

"You think this will avenge the *puta*, that slut, you married, Cuervo?" Cobra laughs in his face as Cuervo drops his machine gun at his side and charges Cobra, taking out a knife from his thigh holster as he goes.

Cuervo stabs him in the gut and he continues charging forward until they both hit the wall. Holding him there, he pulls the knife out and goes to stab his gut again, then his neck. Cobra's body slides down the wall, leaving it painted in a haunting red in its path.

"*Puta madre*, Cobra." Cuervo spits on his body and starts walking for the door. Without looking at us, he throws over his shoulder, "Get on your bikes, assholes, and make it over the border by sunrise or your corpses will stay in Mexico forever."

# CHAPTER 26

## Dana

God, not again. There's a banging on the door, and I've felt so tired. There's never enough time to sleep to satisfy me. Axl has been gone for four days and I wish he was home already. I feel restless and extra cranky over it even though we've talked. But I won't be happy until he's home.

The persistent knock gets louder, and I drag my ass out of my warm bed to get to the front door. Peeking through the peephole, I see Vegas standing there impatiently. I unlock the door for her, swinging it open, and the cold breeze winds its way around my bare legs like a lover's caress. I pull the flannel tighter around my arms, wishing I had put on more than shorts.

"Vegas, it's early. I know you rise at the crack of dawn! But I love my sleep."

I keep ranting as I walk into the kitchen, with her trailing behind me. "No more visits before ten a.m., that's a new rule," I declare and make my way to the coffee pot in the kitchen. I find Mom pulling out a fresh pan of cinnamon rolls.

"Yes." Vegas and I fist bump at the same time.

She sets her grocery bag on the table and grabs a plate, setting a hot roll on it and inhaling it just as fast as I do.

"Mom," I say around a mouthful of food. "This is great, and I love your cooking, but you cannot keep cooking this for me. I think I've gained ten pounds these last few days. I need you to stop. Really, I do." I complain, but it does not stop me from taking another bite.

"I don't care what you say. Your dad and brother love my food. You don't have to eat it. No one is making you eat it, sweetheart. But I'll take the compliment. Thank you," Mom grins and gives me a side hug.

Gabe barrels around the corner, following the smell of bacon and rolls. His hair is a mess and he's only wearing his boxers. He grabs a roll with one hand and takes a big bite out of it, then stuffs half of a piece of bacon in his mouth with the oher.

"Holy shit, bro, you're all grown up. Really, go put some clothes on. I can't look at your manliness. It just got weird," Vegas tells him, pointing her finger up and down over his exposed muscles.

"Like these arms," he says, flexing his arm.

"Yep, still a dork, but in a man's body," Vegas tells him.

The front door slams open and Papa comes walking through, packing in orange juice and milk in each hand. "What the fuck are you doing, *mijo*? I swear to God, I will beat your ass if I catch you in the kitchen with no clothes on again."

Gabe's mouth drops open in explanation before Papa barks, "Did I fucking ask you to tell me why? Fuck no. Go."

"Yes, sir," he says as he's grabbing one more roll, and heads off after kissing Mom on the forehead.

"Baby," Mom says with puppy dog eyes at Papa, "Do you have..."

"Yes."

"But he's just..."

"Yes, Katie, I do. Because he's going to be a man, not your little boy forever," Papa says as he's placing the orange juice and milk on the counter. He kisses her and does the exact same as Gabe not two minutes ago. He grabs bacon with one hand and a roll with the other. He takes one large bite of his roll and then half of the bacon is gone.

"He's a man, alright," Mom comments sarcastically.

The three of us laugh together as he chews, scowling at us. He takes his food and leaves us alone in the kitchen.

I turn to look at Vegas. "What's in the bag you brought?"

"You're going to think I'm really weird."

"I already do, so what?"

Vegas rolls her eyes at my sarcasm. "I'm scared I'm going to lose the baby again. So, I bought a couple tests to check," she admits with a hint of sadness in her voice.

"Vegas, that was a freak thing that happened. You'll be okay. You can't control this. It will happen for you. I know patience is not your thing, but let it go, okay?" I reassure her.

"What if the first test was wrong?" she asks.

"Oh God, I can tell you're not going to let this go, are you?"

"No." She tries to stop the grin coming, but she fails miserably.

"I'll prove it to you." I grab a box and take it with me to the bathroom.

A handful of minutes later, I come walking out with the peed-on pregnancy test in hand. Shaking it back and forth like a thermometer, I tell her, "See, only one line, not pregnant. The test works fine." I hold the stick out to show them.

Mom and Vegas' eyes pop out and Vegas points at the stick. Flipping the stick around, I look at the small window seeing that there are *two* lines!

"What the FUCK!" I yell out and toss the stick toward them like it was gonna bite me. Vegas and Mom jump out of the way.

"Dude, you threw your piss stick at me!" Vegas yells back.

"I'm not pregnant!"

"Yeah, you are!" she yells in excitement.

"Mom, go take the other test, hurry!" I beg her.

Mom laughs and says, "Your papa was fixed, honey." She grins with her hands under her chin. "I'm going to be a grandma!"

"I'm gonna cry," I admit.

"I *am* crying," Vegas says.

"Princess?"

Startled, I turn to find Axl, Blade, Tank, Papa and Gabe all staring at us from the living room.

"You're having my baby?" Axl's eyes beam with pride at his question.

Words fail me and I just nod yes.

Axl steps forward toward me when Gabe brings his fist back and punches Axl in the nose. Blood sprays everywhere. Papa, Tank and Blade belt out a boisterous laugh.

"What the hell is wrong with you, Gabe?" I yell at him, grabbing a towel from the sink.

"Nobody leaves my sister and then gets her knocked up is what, Dana," he states calmly.

"He didn't leave me! Damn it, his face was just starting to heal!" I yell back.

"Oh," he looks at Axl. "Sorry, dude, I didn't get the update," Gabe shrugs.

Walking over to Axl, I place the towel on his nose, and he pulls me close. "What the hell is it with you and your dad? He hit me in the face, too."

"See that, Katie, that's our boy," Papa says, beaming at Gabe.

"When did you hit, Axl?" Mom asks him.

Papa opens his mouth to answer before he's cut off by Axl. "Dana, you're having my baby." He's not asking this time.

"Yeah, me, you and a baby. I don't know how. I must've forgotten to take my pill a few times right after you left?" I look at him a little unsure.

Axl grabs his phone from his pocket and starts dialing. He places it on speaker as soon as it starts ringing.

"Hello?" Harley answers.

"Hey, Ma, guess what?" Axl exclaims to her while still holding the towel to his nose.

"What, sweetie? You sound weird."

"You're going to be a grandma. Dana and I are having a baby!"

There's no response from her and I start to worry. Then I hear sniffles coming from the other end. "That's great, I'm going to be grandma."

We all know she's happy but also devastated because Maddox can't be here with her to witness this.

"Hey, Momma, this little one is bringing some of him to us, okay? Dad is right here with us, because he's in our hearts."

# CHAPTER 27

## Axl

Blade and I sneak around the ritzy neighborhood, dressed in all black. We dodge the house lights that pop on in the back yards. We stick to the shadows as far back as possible. Quickly, we run between two houses with a large gap between them. The neighborhood security guards zoom by in a cart, looking around, surveying the properties.

"Ready?" I ask. The house we came here for stands a few more yards away.

Blade texts Snake the go ahead. A few minutes later, Snake texts that the guard is at the opposite end of the block checking on an alarm in an empty house. He will keep the guard busy and set a few other alarms off for him to check. We have about thirty minutes to get in and out with the security bypass.

The doors on the house have a security code keypad to unlock them. Spider set up a new code for us. I punch in the numbers and the door unlocks. Following the floor plan we memorized, we creep through the house as quietly as possible. We come to the master bedroom door, slowly open it and walk in with our guns drawn out. Blade points his at the bed as I look around the room.

Walking up closer, we find Tony in bed with one of the girls that he keeps around at the Casino. Pointing our guns, we each take a shot at the same time. One shot through the skull and one through the lung with our silencers on. Practically soundless. Her body jolts from the bullets ripping through her small body.

Tony wakes up from her movement as her body convulses from the nerves, uncontrollably shaking her. He pulls on her shoulder, moving her over onto her back, still not noticing us standing and watching in the dark. "Anna, what is wrong?"

Her lifeless heavy body barely moves toward him, but it's enough that he now sees the bullet hole in her head as the blood pours out. Soaking the sheets. A manic laugh rips from Blade, and I see Tony's horrified realization. That fucking whore is dead. Blade flips the light on, still pointing his gun at Tony.

"Sandman is here, motherfucker," he snarls at him.

"You dirty fucking biker!" Tony roars at Blade, jumping from his bed to charge at him. His fists fly, aiming for Blade's face. Blade tucks his gun in his holster, dodging a few, but one lands on his jaw.

The pain brings the wolf completely to the surface. Gone is Blade's sanity. He thirsts for Tony's blood as he howls out. His fists come swiftly for Tony's head. He punches him with a right, then a left blow from down up, under his chin.

Tony's body flies backward and he stumbles before he hits the floor. Blade and I charge forward. Our boots kick unrelentingly from his head, down to his legs. We stomp this dirty fucker into the floor.

"You will never touch what's mine again, Tony. Vegas belongs to me," Blade roars, bringing his boot down and breaking the bones in Tony's hand. Tony wails out in pain, clutching it at his chest and curling himself into a ball.

"I never touched her," he pleads for mercy.

"No? Who started this whole fucked up mess?" Blade seethes. "Who put her in the hospital? Who touched her at the fight? You, motherfucker!"

The light has completely left Blade's eyes as he walks over to the closet. He slowly pulls the sliding door open. He reaches in and pulls out a golf club. A menacing smile covers his face as he saunters over to the pussy that's cowering on the floor.

He raises the club over his head with both hands and, with all his strength, he strikes Tony's body over and over with the club. Tony twists and turns with each lethal blow, roaring out in excruciating pain. Blade swings the club for his face and his jaw breaks from the impact.

He laughs as Tony is now unable to move his jaw. "Cry for me, be my little BITCH, Tony, and cry at my fucking feet. My dirty ass biker feet. Cry, bitch," Blade taunts him.

Tony shakes his head back and forth with his eyes shut, and I'm sure he's praying for heaven or hell to claim his soul. Blade finishes his job by beating the life out of him, making his prayers come true. Blood splatters the walls and our clothes as he beats his head in with the bloody club.

I take out the envelope full of pictures of him with the dirty cop. Bribes and other documents are laid out to incriminate him to the crimes of the underworld. No one, including the cops, will give a shit that we killed off this fucker. We'll leave him right here for his maid to find and call it in.

Tony's body goes limp as the devil came and claimed him as his for eternity.

Battle Born.

"James!" I yell from my bike as I park it, then we both walk into the house. "Did you pick up what I needed?"

"Is this the same shit that Pawn and Solo had to do for a year?" James complains, handing me a box.

"What, you don't like burying dead bodies at three a.m. or running to the mall for me?" I question him.

"That would be a no. Here's your boots. I've got a bar to stock inside the clubhouse."

"Bro, really, what's up with you?"

"Jenn skipped town, man. She took off to Cali and didn't say goodbye to any of us. It's hard to understand why."

"James, Jenn's been fucked up for a while. Maybe some space will help her get her head on straight. For now, take care of you, yeah?"

"Yeah, brother, I need to start over," he concedes.

"Normally, I would be your man to help you get back into the pussy scene. You'll have to hit up Tank for that. He needs a new wingman now." I set the box with the boots on the counter. "See you at the bar later. Thanks, man."

James throws up a two-finger salute on his way out the door. I call Spider and he answers on the second ring. "Axl."

"Did we find Jenn?" I ask him.

"Yeah, man. She overdosed in her aunt's house. We had the Cali members pick her up. She's in rehab for now. Fuego will take care of her."

"Don't mention this to anyone but Blade for now."

"Aye," Spider says, and he's gone. Fuck. What the hell happened to her?

A little bark comes from the back door. Grabbing the boots, I open it for Charlie, and he jumps up to my side. Patting him on the head, it amazes me how big he's got. "Come on, Charlie, we've got to set these up for Dana."

Together, Charlie and I set the boots by the bed. I drop something inside and smile to myself as Dana walks in through the front door a moment later. Perfect timing.

"Axl, you here?" she calls out for me.

"Yeah, princess, in the bathroom." I move to stand by the bathroom door. When she comes in, I walk toward her.

Kissing her lips, I tell her, "I picked up your boots today, they are by the bed. Go try them on?"

"Baby, you are so sweet! Thank you." She eagerly tosses her sneakers off her feet and sits at the end of the bed. I should feel bad, but I don't.

Walking over to her, I kneel next to Charlie as he wags his tail next her. I pet him and we both watch when she slides her right foot into the boot. She stops and pulls it out.

"There's something at the bottom." Holding the boot upside down, she sticks her hand in. A small black box drops into her hand.

Taking the box from her, I open it and show her the ring inside, which has an infinity diamond band.

"Princess. Will you ride with me through this life? Be by my side when things are great. Stand by me when they are hard. Dana, will you be my wife?"

My poor woman nods yes, unable to find her words, then she starts crying with fat tears that streak her face. Using my thumbs, I wipe them off her beautiful face and I tell her, "We were meant to last forever."

She wraps her arms around my neck and holds me tightly to her. I kiss her neck up to her jaw and then mouth, "I love you." I take the ring from the box and slide the band onto her finger.

"I love you too, baby. It's a gorgeous ring, Axl," she tells me as she's touching the ring with the other hand and spins it around her finger.

"I can get you another bigger one if you want? You can pick it out."

"No," she stops and places her hand on mine. "This is perfect." She leans forward to kiss my lips.

"Okay, we have to meet the guys at the tattoo shop before dinner. Put on something nice and let's go out," I request, taking us out of our moment, for now.

Thirty minutes later, Dana is ready, and she takes my breath away. She's wearing a skin-tight halter dress with her new black boots. Her long blonde hair in contrast to her black dress is fucking hot. She did a loose braid to the side. Walking up behind her, I kiss up her shoulder from behind, then the other side to her tattoo.

"I love my brand on you." I kiss her back between her shoulder blades. I grab her left hand and spin her around to face me. Kissing her ring finger, I tell her again, "We were meant to last." I take her hand and lead her out of the house and toward our future.

The parking lot is packed at The Black Rose, with cars and bikes parked out front. Getting out of the truck, I walk around to her side of it.

I help her out and lead her to the front of the building when she tugs me to a stop. "Axl." She looks around, scoping it all out. "What's going on?"

"Princess, these people are here for us. They are here to see the start of our future."

She blinks in shock, so I continue. "We're getting married tonight, Dana. Everyone is here, and your brother leaves in a few days. I wanted him here for you."

"What about Jenn? Is she here?" Her hopeful eyes search mine for answers.

"No. She is okay though. We will bring her home to you, okay?"

Katie and Vegas come out the front doors and wait patiently at the steps. "Hey, I'll see you in a few. Go get ready."

Kissing her lips one last time, I walk back to the brewhouse where the wedding will be.

# Dana

"Baby, you ready? Mom calls out.

Breaking myself free of my thoughts, I turn to look at her and Vegas. They hold out their hands for me to walk over to them. Excitement catches up with my reality. I run over and hug them both on the front steps of the bar.

"Let us see!" I put my hand up to show them the small diamond band.

"He definitely knows you, sweetheart," Mom says as she's brushing a hair back out of my face.

"He does, Mom."

"Good," she reassures my own happiness back.

Together, we walk into the office and they hand me flowers, then I put a blue garter on. My phone vibrates in my hand and I swipe to the screen to read the incoming text.

**Roger Rabbit: Get your ass over here, five minutes!**

Laughing, I remember the night Blade and Vegas got married, and I text back: **Easy, tiger, we are headed there now.**

**Roger Rabbit: Right the fuck now, not in 15**

The dots appear on the screen and he sends back: **I'm serious, woman. RIGHT. THE. FUCK. NOW.**

**Me: Copy, road boss, love you, over and out.**
**Roger Rabbit: copy, love you, princess, over and out.**

My mom, along with Harley, follows Vegas and Kat out the back the door of The Black Rose. We walk up the back to find a million lights trailing up to the brewhouse. Behind the building, the mountains give a beautiful backdrop to the golden rays of the setting sun.

Meeting Papa at the back of the chairs, my eyes look over him in so much love. He wore a black collared shirt for me that's tucked neatly into a nice pair of black jeans. Standing on my tiptoes, I kiss his cheek.

"Love you, *mi corazón*."

"Love you, Papa."

I hear the soft melody of *Perfect Duet* by Ed Sheeran filling the air. A smile plays at my lips as I remember Axl and I dancing to this song at Vegas' wedding.

Vegas, Kat and Mom walk first down between the chairs toward the open double doors. Standing at the end are Axl, Blade and Gabe, all dressed in black. A little part of me melts that Axl dressed all in black for me. He knows how much I love to wear black, and especially when he does.

My heart swells at the sight. As soon as Mom and the girls reach the end of the makeshift aisle, Papa takes my hand and places it on his elbow as he leads me down. For the short walk to Axl, a million memories of us flash across my mind, and I know this man is meant for me.

When we reach the end, Papa gently kisses my hand and places it in Axl's before giving him a warning glare. An older pastor steps forward to officiate the ceremony. He runs through the customary ritual.

"Who takes this man, Brian Adams, to be their lawfully wedded husband, for better or for worse, until death do you part?"

"I do," I giggle at hearing his name, "take you, Brian Adams, until death do us part."

Axl blinks back an unshed tear before winking at me. He pulls his hand from mine to reach into his jean pocket for a thick silver band which he hands to me to slide over his finger. He takes my hands in his, gripping them tight.

"And who takes this woman, Dana Maraschino, to be their lawfully wedded wife, for better or for worse, until death do you part?

"I do, for always and forever," Axl states with a determined tone.

He pulls my hands to his and places a sweet kiss on my ring since I was already wearing it.

"You may now kiss your bride." Family and friends yell out their congratulations, but that's all drowned out by the man standing in front of me.

Axl takes my face gently with both of his hands and pulls me to him. As the sunset is glowing through the large windows, he gives me a loving kiss that will last forever in our hearts.

# BONUS SCENE

**Operation "Drug Axl": Failed Attempt Number One...**

"Do you have it?"

"The drugs, Dana?" Kat says, toying with me and enjoying my discomfort.

"Yes, that," I snap.

"Say it and I'll give it to you," Kat challenges me. Vegas holds her hand up over her mouth and a snort escapes since she finds this all too funny.

"Give me the drugs," I whisper to her and I feel heat flooding my cheeks.

"You're too cute, my little cherry pie. Here you go." Kat goes to hand me a tiny bag of powder, flipping it between her fingers toward me.

My teeth rake over my bottom lip as I worry if I can do this. Opening a bottle of coke, I pour the contents inside. Excitement takes over my senses as the coke bubbles up with the laced cocktail I made behind the bar.

I hand it over to Vegas and she shakes her head at me, then we head out into the bar, in search of our victim. Revenge will be mine! Cockily, I follow behind Vegas and Kat.

At the last minute, I change my mind. Feeling more confident, I take the coke from Vegas, wanting to bait and hook my victim all by myself.

She looks at me a little worried, asking me with unspoken words, "Are you sure?" Biting my lip, I nod along like, "Oh yeah, watch me work this asshole."

My hips pick up with a little more sway. I'm ready to execute this plan when I find Axl sitting at a table in the back.

"Hey, babe, I brought you a coke." Setting it down in front of Axl, a sweet smile spreads across my face.

Axl eyes me wearily, then the bottle that's sitting in front of him. "You sharing one of your cokes with me?"

Sweat starts breaking out over my skin like the condensation that's lining my drugged cocktail for my husband. I swallow, trying to find the words to answer.

"O-f...co-urse, baby."

'Mmmhmm," is all he says. He raises the glass bottle to his lips, and I lean in closer to watch with anticipation.

Axl stops midway from taking the first sip and states, "Your heart is too pure to play these games, princess."

Tank walks by and Axl holds the drink out to him. "Here you go, brother."

Tank stops, looks at the offered drink, then at the both of us and thinks better of it. "Pawn, hey, brother, have this coke. I'm headed out."

"Thanks, bro." Pawn takes the drink and guzzles it down. Nervousness laces my blood and I turn to look at Vegas and Kat who are laughing at me hysterically from behind the bar.

"Fuck." Feeling defeated, my eyes find the table. Disappointment at my loss is filling my thoughts.

Axl breaks the silence when he says to me, "First thing you should know is that you never show emotion or interest. Another is to make it seem like you're doing the other person a favor, or they are doing one for you."

Who am I kidding? I am the girls' sidekick and I'm okay with that. I'm part of the crew, I just don't do the heavy lifting. Defeated, I fall back into my seat and let out a long sigh.

Tank pulls a chair out and slides into it next to me. He leans in close and whispers, "What did we just do?"

"Well, I may as well fess up. There was X in that coke bottle."

"Holy shit, I'm not going anywhere. In fact, you better shut down the bar. I'm calling in some dirty bitches, we're going to have a live porn show. Fuck, this night just got that much better!" He fist pumps the air. "Shut down the bar, Dana. I got phone calls to make." Tank runs out the front door with his cell to his ear already. Shit.

"Last call, everybody."

## Operation "Drug Axl": Attempt Number Two...

It's been three long months since my first attempt at drugging Axl. Kat and Vegas have schooled me repeatedly on how to make this day a success for me. We even practiced on James and others without them knowing. Vegas' words run through my mind, "It's just powdered caffeine, but tell your brain that it's ecstasy and you are okay with it. It's what they want. *You*," she points at my chest, "are doing *them* a favor."

Blade was so pissed at all of us when he found out that Pawn had been drugged. We had to tell him from start to finish how I'd been drugged as well. He forbids it from happening again, or major consequences will ensue from his Sandman wrath.

Axl and Tank got all the shit work for two weeks after Blade's discovery, so that at least benefited me. Tank said it was well worth the show, but Axl held a grudge over it for a long time. This is my house, and the girls and I worked out that Blade can't stop me here.

With steady hands over the picnic table, I call over my shoulder to Axl, "Hey, babe? Potato or macaroni salad?"

"Can I have both, please?" he whines at me.

"Oh, sure, sorry I can do that. I should have known it."

Vegas and Kat stand off to the side. Turning my head ever so slightly, they give me a low thumbs up and continue on with their conversation of work at The Black Rose.

I place one hamburger on the plate, with his minimal helpings of salad, wanting him to eat all of it. Taking the small baggy out of my shorts pocket, I pour the powder over the potato salad. I stuff the baggy back into my pocket and begin to mix it in with a fork. Add a little salt and pepper and we are ready to go.

I place the plate down in front of Axl and begin to walk away when he comments, "Dana, your man is hungry as hell, this is all I get?"

"I'm sorry, baby, I forgot how hungry you get after a long run. Eat that and I'll fix you another plate." Bending over, I kiss his forehead.

Axl beams up at me with pride for his woman. His woman who is going to get him back. Men. They just want to feel like the king of your world, and he is. But we have a score to settle. I have not forgotten.

A half an hour later, Axl is pulling at his shirt. "Are you guys hot? It feels like my blood is pumping right out of my body, my heart is beating so hard. Dana, hand me another beer? No, fuck that, give me a whiskey."

I do my king's biding and take him another drink when the music starts to get a little louder and the sun sets. More alcohol goes around, and the laughter is more frequent.

Axl holds onto me as he slurs in my ear, "Princess, I've been hard for over thirty minutes. Take care of it?"

Taking his hand, I walk back into our house and over to our room where I ask him to sit down on the bed. Axl starts pulling his pants down and trips over himself on the way to it. He stumbles but lands ass first on the mattress, then rips his shirt off over his head and eagerly says to me, "Show me my titties, rub my sweet cherry pie, please?"

He pumps his dick while watching me remove my shirt, and I sway my hips back and forth to the music outside. My hands toss the shirt to the floor and I pull the zipper on my shorts down. As I'm taking them off, I keep the beat in my hips going, rocking back and forth, tossing them across the room with my foot.

I work on my bra and panties next. As I remove those, my hands slide up my body. Cupping my tits, I pull on each nipple. Axl groans and asks me, "Rub that pussy for me." His hands move quicker over his hard length.

One hand stays on my tit tugging and twisting my nipple as the other finds my wet pussy. Watching me pumping two fingers in and out, he groans as he climaxes all over his own hand.

He falls back on the bed letting out a sigh. "I haven't come jacking off to a girl in I don't know how long! Fuck, that was quick."

I walk into the bathroom to grab a towel to help clean him up. By the time I make it back into the room, I'm shocked to find my strong, sweet snoring king passed out and naked. Taking care of my Ol' Man, I clean up his mess then make my phone call.

"Plan worked, we are ready for phase two."

"Dana! Wake up! Something's wrong with my dick! And my head hurts! I don't even remember half of what happened last night. Look at it!  Please, princess?"

I should feel bad, I really should. But living with Axl, and really getting to know the man, has shown me that he doesn't feel guilty at all for half the shit he does to me. And I really am looking forward to this. Opening my itchy eyes, I roll over to a panicked Axl.

I pick up the sheet and blanket and look down his body. "It all looks okay. What does it feel like?"

"Like someone shoved a rod through my dick." Axl picks up the covers and looks for himself. He hysterically yells and jumps out of bed. "Why is there a bar running through my dick?" He points at it, like I can't see it from here.

"Because you wouldn't do it consciously and I claimed that dick. It's mine, and I can do what I want with it," I tell him smugly.

On a flat tone, he repeats, "You pierced my dick without telling me? You let a stranger touch my dick? And how, Dana? How did you do this?"

"One word, Axl. Ecstasy."

Axl shakes his head in disbelief before he says, "Well played, well played indeed, cherry pie. Truce now?"

"Aye, truce," I agree

"You crowned my cock with jewels, princess. I really have the king of all dicks in all the land now. When can we use it? I can't wait to call Tank and tell him of my crowning."

# The End

# EPILOGUE

## Axl

"Mom?" I open the front door to the house while holding the infant car seat. I set our little newborn, Maddox, down in the living room. This little guy came as a surprise because the doctors told us we couldn't have any more kids. Our first little angel almost didn't make it to full term, so we were okay with the news then. Little Maddox here was a fighter, not one problem through the whole pregnancy.

Dana walks into our house and slowly lowers herself to the couch. The back door slams open and my little princess, Maddison, comes barreling for me with a happy Charlie right behind her.

"Daddy! Is baby Maddox here?" She squeals when I pick her up and toss her into the air. Kissing my little princess' cheek, I hold her to me. "Yes, baby, you want to hold him with your grandma?"

"Yes," she says as she's holding my face in both of her tiny little hands. "But I'm still your princess, right?" she asks with her tiny worried little green eyes that match my own, and blonde golden hair like her momma's.

"There is only one princess in allllll of the land. She is my favorite because there is no other like her."

Mom giggles from the side as she listens to my fairytale conversations that she's heard over and over again.

"She really is a princess. I know that her grandpa would tell her the exact same things you do. Sometimes your voice sounds just like his," Mom says. "Now, where is my little prince? Hm? It's been a whole twenty-four hours since I held you." Mom moves over to the couch and starts unbuckling little baby Maddox from the car seat.

Maddison wiggles from my arms and goes to sit next to her grandma. She lovingly runs her small hand over his soft head.

"You know, Maddox," she talks quietly as he sleeps in his grandma's arms, "that Grandpa told me to be a big girl and take good care of you and everyone. I told him I would because Daddy said I was the big sister. He agreed and said I was special to him too and he would always love us and take care of us and to give Grandma hugs as many times as I can. And I said I would."

Mom's heartbroken face looks up at me as she fights the tears along with me, when Dana calls Maddison over to her. "Baby girl, *mi corazónsito*, come here and give your momma a hug?" Maddy wiggles down from her spot and jumps into Dana's arms.

"Baby, are you talking about Papa from California?" she asks Maddy as she settles into her lap.

"No, Momma. Grandpa, Daddy's daddy, comes to me in my dreams to play with me and tells me to do things for you all or for myself. He's always in my dreams. I love my grandpa, he's so funny and fun. He said that someday he's going to hold me again."

"Come here, baby." Dana holds little Maddy to her chest and Mom does the same with little Maddox as we all try not to cry. I take my hands and hold them to my eyes when a tiny little tug at my pants alerts me to my princess.

Looking down at her, I see her smiling up at me. I kneel to see what it is she has to say.

"Daddy, that feeling you have here," her tiny little hand pats at my chest, "Is grandpa letting you know he's with you and it's okay. Please don't cry, Daddy."

My seven-year-old baby has so much heart, just like her momma. Holding her to me, I say a silent prayer to Maddox, Mad Max, my best friend, my dad and my old man, a thank you for watching over us, and, mostly, for watching over my babies.

# BONUS EPILOGUE

## Many years later...

## Dana

Axl stands at the window looking through the curtains of the home that we made. He's gained some gray hairs over the years that I just find so sexy. He's also slowed down a little. I think that watching over all of us and his club has worn him out. Although, he still is that funny, tough man I met all those years ago. Every obstacle we've faced in our life, we've learned to embrace each other and has made us, and especially me, stronger.

We never moved from the house we made together all those years ago. We did build upgrades or remodels on it. As we grew, so did our home. Our family life, along with the club's, grew into a powerful bond. Blade and Axl did that.

Vegas grew her brewery, the Battle Born Brewhouse, into a national selling brand. All the brothers and some Ol' Ladies work there. True to her belief in family, she's built an empire with those she loves and shares her dreams with.

Me? I enjoy the flexibility of The Black Rose. Being a partial owner, I manage the financial end, and I don't have to work much behind the bar, if ever, anymore. I got to be home with my kids as much as I wanted all these years.

Our roll of the dice, with three young girls moving to Reno, was a big gamble. But it sure did pay off big, like Vegas always said it would.

Walking over to Axl, I place my arm around his back and his comes around my shoulders, holding me to him.

"Baby, what are you looking at?" I ask kissing his cheek.

"Cortez," is all he says with steeling determination lining his features.

"What's wrong with Cortez?"

"He's taking my Maddy, my little baby princess, out on a date," he grinds out.

"They are seventeen."

"I know that, Dana. I know you remember the shit you girls were doing then at their age too."

"Yeah, I do," I say with a little too much fondness.

Axl's jealous eyes find mine and, after all these years, I love that he's still so possessive of me.

"You are mine, my Maddie is mine too," he claims.

"Yeah, baby, we are all yours," I whisper back since there's no point in telling him any different.

Axl did do a lot of healing before Maddy was born, after his dad passed. When she came into his world though, she lit him up in a way I never could. She healed pieces of him that no one else could have touched.

It also made me understand my father in a way I never could before. '*Mi corazon*' had a whole new meaning for me. Axl is her most favorite person in the world to this day.

Little Maddox isn't so little anymore either. He and Axl have been inseparable since he was little. Axl poured all the love he could into this boy that I think he wishes his own father could have done. Two of the tiniest gifts that grew into a world Axl and I desperately needed.

"Daddy, is Cortez here?" Our beautiful girl comes skipping down the hallway.

"What the hell are you wearing, Maddy?" Axl reprimands.

"It's what auntie V says looks phat on me."

"Fat. Vegas said you're fat?"

"No, Daddy," she giggles, and her cheeks turn red, just like mine used to. I can see Vegas telling her these things for this very reaction, to poke at Axl as much as possible.

"P.H.A.T., pretty hot and tempting," she answers, looking down at the floor. Lord knows I've tried telling her not to repeat *'what auntie V says'* to her dad. This kid though, so sweet and innocent.

"I'm going to kill her, Dana. What the fuck?"

There's a rumble of an engine pulling up into the driveway as Cortez parks his bike and walks over to the front door, then rings the doorbell. Maddy runs over to open the door with a wide smile across her face as she looks over Cortez.

"Hey, Tez." Her cheeks flame a bright red as Cortez looks over her denim short shorts, red tank and riding boots. Her long, golden blonde hair flows down her back.

"You ready to go to the movies?" he eagerly asks.

"Yeah," Maddy answers as she wobbles her toed boot back and forth, her gaze not leaving his.

I'm getting her on birth control. STAT. Not even Axl will stop me.

"Hey, Max!" Axl yells for Maddox in the living room. He's in there playing his video games. "You're going to the movies with Maddy and Cortez."

"I am?" There's a shuffle of movement before an excited ten-year-old boy is front and center, ready to go to the movies. He loves Vegas and Blade's twin boys. They are older and sooo awesome in his eyes. He would do anything that involved them.

"Yeah, in fact, we all are. Come on, kids, jump into the Suburban."

We all collectively groan except for Axl and Max. That same old guy from years ago, this is what I was talking about. Right here.

"Mine," he claims with an evil glim in his eyes. "Come on, Max, you do get your dad." Axl high fives little Max who has no idea what his dad is really up to.

Nothing does last forever, but what I didn't realize is that a lot of good comes with those changes too. The biggest lesson I've learned in life is to keep making new dreams along the way.

Love does last forever.

# AUTHOR'S NOTE

Please understand that when I wrote the parts where the characters drugged Dana and Axl, I truly did not believe in my mind that it was okay. I absolute did not, nor do I condone it. It is only intended to be funny and I would never purposefully intend or harm a living person.

Also, while I was writing Jenn's drug abuse, rape or murder of her mother or any woman, it was hard for me to write that at times. These scenarios are also not okay.

If there is a person out there suffering, I hope they can find the help they need.

# OUT NOW...

**Living for Forever (Battle Born MC Book 3)**
Jenn & James' story

*Continue reading for an excerpt...*

# Prologue

Somebody help me.

There are just times when I feel like giving up. That what I am is just not enough. My thoughts run wild in my mind, reminding me of the things I have failed at. The hate that I feel for myself disgusts me, and I can just imagine what others think of me too.

The cool morning air whips my long hair into my face, the sting unfazed and unnoticed. High up on the old dirt road on the mountain behind the bar, I look down at the people pulling up and walking into the bar or the tattoo shop. Sitting on the hood of my Mustang, I can feel the cold seeping into my jeans and legs. The cold can't touch what already feels hollow inside.

I bring the bottle of vodka to my lips and tip my head back. I close my eyes from the morning rays, and I wash down another pill. Another pill that only helps to numb my thoughts long enough that I don't feel like cutting my own wrists. For now.

I take two large gulps. The burn brings tears to my eyes. Shutting them for a moment, I beg for the relief to come soon.

My phone pings with a message. Setting the bottle down on the car, I see it's another text update from Dana.

**Dana: So, today sucked, I got drugged by our friends and then tattooed last night. I guess I'm an Ol' Lady now. Not the Ol' Lady part, that doesn't suck. The part where I woke up with a headache and then ran out of hot water because the man you live with is a child. That part sucks.**

More tears prick at my eyes as the walls start caving in around me and my reality. I feel the pain slicing through my heart.

I know she wants me to respond, but I can't. I can't let go of what's happened and what I've done. I do miss them so much, but I can't let anyone see how ugly it is inside of me.

Staring at my phone, I start responding...

**Me: I'm leaving today. I am going back home to my aunt and to check on my sister, Ashley. Actually, that's bullshit. I'm running away because it all has come to be too much, and I want to end it all. I hate everything here, and I hate myself. I want to tell you that I love you, but I can't. That's a lie. I hate everything so much that it hurts. What I hate most of all is that I can't even stand to look at you long enough to say it.**

My thumb hovers over the Send button. An ugly demon wants me to push the button. The demon begs me to embrace more pain. But I can't do it. I erase the message and sit a while longer, feeling more hollow as the minutes tick by. I know that it's time to leave. It's time to move on from this place that was once called home, even if for a short period of time.

Anger builds with my self-pity. I'm so angry of losing in this life. Feeling broken when something good starts to build, then it's ripped from my heart.

I'm done. Fuck it all.

Flipping the keys around in my hand, I'm ready. I'm ready to see what kind of hell on this earth I can find.

I grab my bottle of vodka and phone from the hood of my car. I toss them onto the passenger seat and push the keys into the ignition. I feel the engine roaring to life. Turning the steering wheel, I hold on tightly with both hands before my boot hits the gas hard, and the wheels spin, tossing up a cloud of dirt as I peel out and head down the empty dirt road.

I've accepted the ghost that haunts the girl that I once was. There's nothing left in this barren soul.

I am the walking dead.

# ABOUT THE AUTHOR

Scarlett Black is the author of the Battle Born MC Series. Not really knowing where a story will take her is what she loves most about writing. She strives to write about strong women and the men who love them. She believes in love and the miracles that come from it. She enjoys giving her fans a happily ever after worth melting their hearts. These may be books, but they are written with her heart and soul. She is Battle Born. Are you?

**www.authorscarlettblack.com**

Made in the USA
Monee, IL
30 October 2020

46407843R00174